Y0-BCU-959

GILDED
LILY

DELPHINE
DRYDEN

BERKLEY SENSATION, NEW YORK

5164987

THE BERKLEY PUBLISHING GROUP
Published by the Penguin Group
Penguin Group (USA) LLC
375 Hudson Street, New York, New York 10014

USA • Canada • UK • Ireland • Australia • New Zealand • India • South Africa • China

penguin.com

A Penguin Random House Company

GILDED LILY

A Berkley Sensation Book / published by arrangement with the author

Berkley Sensation Books are published by The Berkley Publishing Group.
BERKLEY SENSATION® is a registered trademark of Penguin Group (USA) LLC.
The "B" design is a trademark of Penguin Group (USA) LLC.

For information, address: The Berkley Publishing Group,
375 Hudson Street, New York, New York 10014.

ISBN: 978-0-425-26579-6

PUBLISHING HISTORY
Berkley Sensation mass-market edition / July 2014

PRINTED IN THE UNITED STATES OF AMERICA

10 9 8 7 6 5 4 3 2 1

Cover art by Claudio Marinesco.
Cover design by Rita Frangie.
Interior text design by Kelly Lipovich.

Acknowledgments

All my usual admiration and then some for Kate Seaver and the wonderfully talented folks at Berkley. Y'all have made this series not only possible, but gorgeous, and working with you is a pleasure. Thanks also to my family and friends, for all the love, support, encouragement and understanding. And a very special nod to Dana, Duncan and Mina, for sharing and confirming my innate love for and fascination with cephalopods. Maybe it's genetic!

ONE

~~~⊱✦⊰~~~

ROLLO FURNEVAL WAS in a position to make demands. Sitting on a warehouse full of priceless product, backed up by a steely-eyed contingent of his most heavily armed lads and more importantly no longer answerable to a crazy man an ocean away, Rollo had begun to feel invincible.

"What's it worth to you?" the woman in front of him asked, her voice not quite as steady as she probably would have liked. He made her nervous and was glad of it. It meant that word of his power was spreading.

"Dunno. Haven't heard anything yet, love. My boys, what they told me made no sense at all. Nothing worth paying for." He raked his gaze over her body, then shrugged as if he'd assessed that she too was not worth much.

"Told 'em the truth. Not my fault if nobody believes it."

One of the lads leaned toward her, letting the long barrel of his pistol graze her arm. The woman snatched herself away, shooting a glare at Edwin and his firearm.

"That's enough, Ed. Don't frighten her." He could afford to be magnanimous. The Benevolent Overlord was Rollo's new favorite persona. "Step closer, miss. He won't harm you."

At Rollo's beckoning, the woman—barely older than a girl, really—approached, still eyeing Edwin with suspicion. "It's Missus."

"Of course, Mrs. Hill. I remember. Now tell me what you told my lads, won't you? We'll see if we can sort this out."

"It was three nights ago," she started, her voice regaining some confidence. "My Tom come home from the docks drunk as a lord, but he were still shakin' in his boots. He said he went out that afternoon with Jimby as usual, to check the marker buoys, but something awful happened out on the water. Some . . . monster." She faltered, less eager to share the unbelievable part of the tale.

"Monster? A sea monster?"

"Tom said it came up when Jimby started singing, you know how he does. Did. 'Rule Britannia.' And there they came like snakes, over the side of the boat, and just took Jimby, neat as you please. By the time Tom knew what was what, it had already dragged him under. It was too late."

Whatever had happened, the woman seemed to believe her husband's version of events. Rollo, however, was not so sanguine. "What came over the side? Was it snakes, or a monster, or something else? Or nothing else, Mrs. Hill, but Tom forgetting himself in an argument and doing something he later regretted? He wouldn't be the first to make up a tall tale to cover his own guilt."

"Not snakes, Mr. Furneval. Tentacles."

"Tentacles."

"Big around as your—" She glanced at Rollo's meaty thigh, then shrugged. "Big around as Tom's leg. He said he won't go back on the water for anything."

"And who could blame him, after what he saw? But I can hardly pay him wages for failing to work, can I? And nobody's seen Jimby Evans since that afternoon."

"Because the monster—"

"Snatched him from the boat, yes, so you've said. Or so Tom has said to you."

"It's the truth."

"But it's old news, Mrs. Hill."

"There was something." She bit her lip, brow furrowing. Rollo gave her another look. Pretty enough, he supposed. And she looked clean. Rather wasted on a dispensable unit like Hill. He waited her out until she spoke again. "Something else Tom and Jimby saw, before the . . . before it happened. Something I think they weren't supposed to see."

Awareness prickled under Furneval's hide, all his senses attuned to the change in the woman's demeanor. This was the real news. Something bigger than giant murderous tentacles, which was a remarkable thought. "Tell me."

"They were at the farthest buoy, the one the boys go to with the lantern to signal sometimes. I don't—" She seemed to realize her error and added in near-panic, "Everyone knows around here, sir. It ain't no secret. We can see the light from shore on clear nights. If—"

"Just get on with your story."

After a pause, she continued cautiously. "Well, it weren't night then, but bright day, and the water was calm. That buoy's near a shallows. And they could see it. Tom and Jimby both, Tom said. One of them submersible machines, passing right underneath the boat. Bigger than any they ever seen and painted in colors. And bristling with funny sticks in the front, like thick whiskers. It didn't look like no Navy ship, he said. And that water's supposed to be no-man's-land. Only the Navy can go there, since before the end of the war."

Ah. "I see. Well, that is another matter, as you've obviously surmised. And Tom chose to withhold this information from me?"

Mrs. Hill shrugged. "Ain't seen Tom again. He went back out next day and hasn't been back. Word is, he's at the opium parlor."

Rollo knew for a fact that Tom Hill was no such place. He never allowed his boys to partake of the product; it was grounds for instant dismissal, with prejudice. Prejudice in the form of Edwin or one of his boys in a dark alley with a swift, well-placed knife. This practice—which he liked to think of as his own form of morality clause for his workers—gave him the advantage he'd sought so long. Violating it, Rollo fully believed, had been his former employer Lord Orm's greatest mistake. The Lord of Gold's drug-addled minions had been no help to him in the end.

That had been a glorious day, hearing about Orm's defeat at the hands of two posh steam car drivers at the thrilling conclusion of last year's American Dominions Sky and Steam Rally. Orm, trussed up and hauled away to molder in prison, leaving Rollo and his boys in London with a full warehouse of opium and nobody to account to for it. He'd guarded it jealously from all contenders until the smoke cleared, and emerged as the new leader of Orm's notorious opium cartel. And he would keep it as long as he chose, or his name wasn't Rollo Furneval. Because, while he was no genius like Orm, he was no lunatic like Orm either. He was no Lord of Gold, he was a businessman.

Tom Hill was either dead or long gone, and if it was the latter case Rollo would dispatch somebody to take care of him in short order. Businesslike.

"That's worth something, innit?" the young woman before him ventured. "Giant whiskered submersible in the no-man's-land like that? Tom may not have told you but I did, Mr. Furneval. I came to you and nobody else."

"So you did, Mrs. Hill. You've shared this vital information with me and nobody else, you're quite sure? Not even your mother? None of Tom's associates, perhaps the one who suggested he was at the opium den?"

"No one, sir," she insisted.

"Thank you, my dear lady. That makes things much simpler." While she smiled tentatively at Rollo, he gestured to Edwin, who quietly cocked his pistol and stepped up behind the woman. "No, not with that, you idiot. Think of the noise. Think of the mess. Now, Mrs. Hill, let's see if we can't reunite you with your husband."

Ed had nodded and traded his gun for a long, wicked knife. It slid over Mrs. Hill's slim neck without a sound, and quick-thinking Ed caught the spurt of blood with his other sleeve. Sacrificing a coat, but saving the warehouse office floor from inconvenient stains. After a few startled attempts to gasp, a feeble clutching at Edwin's enormous arm with skinny fingers, Mrs. Hill hung limp against her killer's chest, pinned there by her still-bleeding throat.

With a snap of his fingers and a point, Rollo commanded Edwin's associates to tidy away the body.

"I was fond of that coat," Ed complained. He'd slung it off and let the boys take it to keep the blood from dripping, but he hadn't kept the rest of himself as clean as he must have wished. One cuff was soaked in blood, so his shirt was probably a loss as well.

Rollo shrugged. "I'll give you the direction of my tailor. He's a good man. Doesn't ask unnecessary questions."

With any luck, Mrs. Hill had been telling the truth, and nobody else outside his inner circle knew of Rollo Furneval's secret cargo submersible with its array of experimental hydrophonic "whiskers." And now, nobody else ever would. Just the way he liked things. No fuss, no mess, no untidy loose ends.

All business, that was Rollo Furneval.

Two

❦

THE HAT WAS too large, and it gave her away. Only to somebody looking hard, of course, but Freddie knew the risk was there. Someone looking hard, or someone who knew what they were looking for.

It was practicality, as much as vanity, that made her balk at cutting her hair off. As long as she kept it, she could blend seamlessly back into that other world. The world in which, ostensibly, she belonged. And it was far easier to disguise the hair in this world than to explain its absence in that one. Lately, some daring young ladies had taken to bobbing their hair. But it was not yet the general rage, and Freddie hesitated to draw excess attention to herself by leaping into the vanguard of fashion.

So for now, at least, she remained the plumpish, round-faced lad in the comically oversized hat. Fred Merchant, tinker-makesmith extraordinaire. Quick and curious, clever with his hands and known not to adhere to Marquess of

Queensberry rules when cornered in a fight. Handy chap to know, bad chap to cross, such was the consensus on the streets of London.

Chap whose bosoms have been strapped down far too long for one day. Freddie tucked an almost-escaping auburn curl more firmly back under the outmoded black top hat, mindless of the engine grease on her fingers. She was sweating under the bandages and padding, the many layers of her disguise. The device in front of her was still in pieces, the purposeful array of parts revealing the order of their removal. She loved looking at them like that, their symmetry and sense. She could discern the purpose each component served in the whole, could already see where the flaw was. And she saw, as clearly as if the process were playing before her on a stereopticon, how it would all fit together and work again in the end. Where everything belonged, and how and why. The machine flew back together in her mind, whirring into seamless action.

"Wot, then? Beyond repair, is it, Fred?"

"Never." She spared a scowl for Dan Pinkerton, who always assumed things were beyond repair. "It's an easy fix, I just haven't time to finish today. And you know sod-all about steamers, mate."

That last was reassurance for the client, who had shown some dismay at Dan's assessment.

"You'll not get a farthing until that dog's running again," the butcher warned. "If I'm not making anything off it, you won't neither."

"I'll be back same time tomorrow," Freddie reassured him. "Finish it up in no time." The butcher depended on the mechanical "dog" to run the spit on which he roasted his newest product, ready-to-eat sliced meats. He'd taken a chance by setting it up as a spectacle in his shop window, to draw the attention of customers. The prospect of losing his competitive promotional edge was clearly weighing heavily on him, and it bothered Freddie as well. Her clients among the fishmongers were closing up shop left and right lately, the result of an unusually high rate of fishermen gone missing on the job and a simultaneous decline in the numbers of local fish schools. The rivalry between butcher shops had only heated up as trade shifted to place a higher demand on them in the absence of fish.

"Why not now?" the fat man demanded. "Pressing social engagement?"

Dan snorted into his glove, then tried to cover it with a cough. Freddie just smiled and shrugged. "When the Queen calls, Mister Armintrout."

He looked ready to take offense, then shrugged it off. Freddie was his only real option and they both knew it.

"Give Her Majesty my best."

The laughter carried them outside, where Dan bustled Freddie onto the trap and down the lane in less than his usual time.

"You'll get caught, joking like that," he scolded once they were on the high street, safely ensconced in the noisy flow of traffic. The little trap bounced along the cobbles, tugged along behind the steam "pony" that Dan controlled with deft flicks of the levers in front of him. Most of London's flesh-and-blood horses were inured to the steam engines now, and didn't even shy at the noise and sudden bursts of speed from the surrounding vehicles.

"I'm bound to get caught eventually. I don't think cracking wise will make much difference one way or the other. Bloody hell, it's warm out here for May."

"You're sitting right in the vent path. Told your father we needed a cowling on this thing when it was converted, but would he listen? And you shouldn't be using coarse language, it ain't ladylike."

"Don't be such a prig, Dan. You sound like my old nursemaid."

"Because your old nursemaid was my mum, or have you forgot?"

"How could I? You're the very image of her. Oh, bother. I've ruined these trousers with grease. My last. I don't suppose you could procure another pair for me tonight?"

"You're supposed to be saving your earnings, I thought. I'll get Mum to clean those ones."

"But they're not your size, won't she suspect?"

Dan's laugh rang out above the noise of the street. "You don't think she already knows? She knows everything, miss. She probably knew your scheme before you even thought of it yourself."

Freddie glanced around, a reflex with her now. "Don't call me that now."

"Right. Pardon, Fred old chap. Are we headed for your piece of skirt among the quality, my lad?" He swung wide to get around a slow horse-drawn carriage, then cut through a narrow gap between two cabs and down a quieter side street.

"Who's the coarse one now? Yes, to Lady Sophronia's." Freddie's closest friend and ally aside from Dan himself, Sophronia Wallingford could always be counted on to provide a hot bath and the loan of a maid when Freddie completed one of her little moneymaking ventures and needed to clean up before returning to proper society.

"Ah, the beautiful widow Wallingford." Dan let his voice deepen, and his rough accent managed to make even those few innocent words sound like lewd speculation. Freddie knew he teased to cover his genuine adoration of Sophie, a poignant longing that society would always make it impossible to requite. A footman could love a gentlewoman from afar all he liked, but the emotion could never bring him anything but empty daydreams and misery.

Freddie didn't know why Dan subjected himself to it, but she tried to be sympathetic while at the same time subtly discouraging him. "You wouldn't say that if you'd ever seen her before her maid was through with her in the morning."

She also didn't understand the embarrassed laugh and cough Dan hid in his glove, much like he'd done at old Armintrout's earlier. But that was Dan, he'd always had inscrutable moments as long as she'd known him. All her life, in fact. He was the big brother she'd never had, except that she'd more or less always had him.

A heavier-than-usual patch of traffic and slow-moving pedestrians held them motionless for a few minutes, long enough for Freddie to grow anxious. The nearest walker, a youngish gentleman, had stopped alongside them. He stared in bewilderment from his map to the surrounding scenery, then in dismay at the cobbled road beneath their carriage.

"Haven't they ever heard of asphalt?" she heard him say into the lull, apparently to no one in particular. Clearly the street noise was too much for him. Delicate sensibilities, perhaps. Or he was a tourist; he had a foreign look about his clothes, an accent that hinted at time spent in the American Dominions.

"They've started it north of the river," Dan remarked to him, leaning down sociably from his seat. "But it'll be a cold day for Lucifer before the nobs this far west allow that much change. Not to mention the smell when they lay it down. Nah, here it'll be cobbles and setts until they die, I'd wager."

Unheard-of cheek, especially coming from Dan, who was usually so sober and proper. The tourist was obviously no commoner. But it was safe enough, Freddie supposed. The next moment the steam coach ahead of them lurched forward, and all was noise and motion once again. The puzzled, fresh-faced gentleman was lost in the crowd, left alone with his map to speculate on road surfaces and how to find his way through London. Freddie forgot him the moment he was out of view.

Wallingford House loomed ahead of them for a moment, before Dan diverted the pony down another side street to the mews. They would enter as two rough tinker-makesmiths, then Dan would reemerge in his livery and return with the trap to Rutherford Murcheson's stately Belgravia residence several streets away.

Miss Frédérique Murcheson would return home again only after attending a ball under the watchful eye of her friend and frequent chaperone, the Lady Sophronia Wallingford. With her mother now settled resolutely in France, and her father in London only occasionally for business, Freddie was able to get away with quite a lot—but sometimes even she couldn't weasel her way out of an important social occasion.

After all, when the Queen called . . .

BARNABAS STARED AT the map, then at the street in front of him, wishing for the dozenth time that he'd opted to unpack his dirigible and fly to his employer's home, instead of taking the Metropolitan railway from the air ferry stop in Hillingdon, then walking to his final destination. It had seemed like a foolish waste of time to launch himself instead of taking advantage of the local transportation, but now he eyed the individual airships above with envy. He could have at least taken a taxicab, but he had the ridiculous notion that he knew the town well, and he'd judged the cab not worth the expense for such a short distance.

London was not as thickly populated as New York, but it sprawled for what seemed like endless miles. Ancient, meandering streets were overlaid by the new. What had seemed straightforward on the map was rendered meaningless by the scale, the bustle and the overwhelming noise of steam cars and horse-drawn conveyances vying for space on old, cobbled roads or wood-block paving. The few times he'd come to the city with friends during his Oxford days, it hadn't seemed so daunting. Or so cacophonous.

"Haven't they ever heard of asphalt?"

"They've started it north of the river," a voice commented from the nearest vehicle, a converted steam-drawn pony trap of a type that was all too familiar from the streets of New York. This one looked slightly down-at-heels, and its driver's and passenger's coats were frayed at the cuffs and collars. Tinkers, by the oil stains on their clothing and the assembly of tools in the back of the trap. No expertise with fine clockwork, but they could likely repair an engine or a pump for anyone who couldn't afford a proper makesmith. Barnabas didn't begrudge them their living but wondered how the local guilds viewed these independent competitors.

"Not to mention the smell when they lay it down. Nah, here it'll be cobbles and setts until they die, I'd wager," the driver finished.

The trap disappeared like magic as the traffic suddenly picked up its pace, and Barnabas stared dumbly for far too long at the space the little cart had occupied. There was something odd about the trap's passenger that had diverted his attention from the driver almost instantly. He tried to pin it down but was unable. Something, though. About the eyes and jawline, the fit of the clothing . . .

A prodding hand jolted Barnabas from his bemused stupor, and he lashed out just in time to catch the wrist of his attempted pickpocket.

"Hey! Stop that!"

The boy dropped Barnabas's coin purse back into his pocket and escaped with a sharp twist of his hand against his intended victim's thumb. Obviously not the first time the youth had been in that situation. A cluster of other boys lurked near the next corner, looking too nonchalant.

More alert, Barnabas transferred all his valuables to safer inside pockets, then returned his mind to the task at hand. He knew from his map he was close to Belgravia, and the rough tinker's remark about nobs was confirmation. Rutherford Murcheson's house couldn't be too far off now. He should be able to find it in time to change and dress before the evening's festivities. Whether he would actually find it festive, trying to keep a watchful eye on Murcheson's wayward daughter, remained to be seen. At least it would be a relatively honest evening's work.

Rutherford Murcheson hadn't especially wanted Barnabas for the job of looking after his daughter. Barnabas had suspected as much from their correspondence, and his impression was confirmed by the man's edgy, dismissive demeanor when Barnabas finally arrived at his tasteful home.

"You resemble your brother," the older man said flatly after they'd shaken hands. "Are you going to disappoint me, as he did?"

Barnabas's younger brother Phineas had seemed destined to greatness in his military career before he allegedly succumbed to the lure of opium and fell off the map. But that shouldn't mean anything to Murcheson. "Who was he to you, sir, that you had any expectations of him?"

Murcheson was an industrialist, a manufacturer of

clockwork devices and steam engines. Few knew of his other work, as a spymaster for the Crown. Barnabas himself had only learned this recently, and there was no reason young Lieutenant Phineas Smith-Grenville should have known it at all. But Barnabas had reason to believe there was much more to Phineas's disappearance than his family had been led to believe. Finding out the truth about his brother and restoring honor to his name was still his primary objective, regardless of what assignment Murcheson might make. His last attempt to locate Phineas had resulted only in more shame for the family, as it involved Barnabas performing very badly in the American Dominions Sky and Steam Rally. He'd made it no farther than the first rest stop before succumbing to influenza. His friend Eliza Hardison—now Eliza Pence—claimed to have spotted Phineas in San Francisco during the finishing line ceremony. But a more recent sighting by a former shipmate of Phineas's placed him in London, so here Barnabas was.

"Lieutenant Smith-Grenville was an unreliable operative. You have clearance to know this officially, now. Your younger brother worked for me, as I'm sure you already know from his own mouth, and was meant to be in deep cover to infiltrate a ring of opium smugglers. Instead he fell victim to the poppy himself and disappeared into the western Dominions. Weak character. But my good friends Baron and Baroness Hardison assure me you're made of sterner stuff."

Barnabas was shocked to hear that Phineas had been working for Murcheson as a spy, but it was clear Murcheson thought Phineas had revealed his assignment to his brother. Ultimately, though, it seemed important parts of the story were confirmed, that whatever he'd been doing previously, Phineas had subsequently disappeared into the world of opium addiction. Barnabas covered his startled stammer with a feigned cough, giving him a moment to regain his composure.

"I like to think my actions speak for my character, sir."

"I'd like to think so too, but I've little confidence. Your last major action was taking a spectacular and costly loss in a race your family had invested in. You seem set to waste their time and money. Still, here you are, and I suppose I must make use of you. Incidentally, you'll find a trunk full of your brother's effects in your room. He'd left it in the keeping of his landlady, but it seemed fitting that you should have it. Perhaps you can deliver it to your family when you return to the Dominions, which I suspect will be sooner rather than later. If you actually last a fortnight, I'll see to finding a house for you to let. For now, you'll bunk here. Cheaper that way."

Murcheson's attitude was more than disheartening. The Hardisons had seemed so much more enthusiastic when they recruited Barnabas to their cause. The timing was perfect—his desire to search for Phineas in London, their European colleague's need for a fresh operative there with an upper-class background. They had assured him that just as their own blue-blood heritage had served them well in forming a cover story for espionage, Barnabas's social credentials made him ideal to pose as a young industrial dilettante abroad. A feckless fop of a son, perhaps, foisted off on the Makesmith Baron to train some sense into him. The story could be that the Baron had assigned Barnabas the ridiculously easy but lucrative sinecure of finalizing some negotiations that had obviously been conducted months prior between the Baron himself and Rutherford Murcheson. Then Murcheson could instruct Barnabas as he saw fit. And compensate him, a necessity as Barnabas's father had refused to fund any further searching for Phineas following the rally debacle.

Barnabas had pointed out to his spymaster instructors—who included Charlotte, Lady Hardison, and her father Viscount Darmont, much to his surprise—that he knew people in London. He couldn't appear *too* feckless. He was his father's heir, after all, current disagreement notwithstanding. Nor could he play the fop when he'd been notoriously uninterested in things sartorial at Oxford.

"Ineffectual, then?" Charlotte had suggested. She'd been holding her daughter Penelope, gently bouncing and rocking her as she walked about the room. She seemed disinclined ever to give the infant over to her nursemaid's keeping.

"Can't I just be myself?"

They all looked at him as if he'd gone mad. Then Charlotte tilted her head, running her gaze up and down Barnabas as if seeing him in a new light. "It might work. No, let's consider this," she insisted when her colleagues raised their voices to object. "Who *is* Lord Barnabas Smith-Grenville? Look at him. He's cheerful, generally well liked. He's quite earnest but doesn't completely lack a sense of humor. Well enough connected but hardly from a powerful family. Not a fashion plate or a Greek god, by any stretch. Meaning no offense, Barnabas."

"None taken, madam." But he found himself adjusting the shoulders of his coat and trying to recall when he'd last had his hair cut.

"None of those things are bad, none of them are particularly good. There's nothing on the surface that's—"

"Remarkable," the Viscount finished for his daughter, earning a glare from her. "I see it now. Or rather I don't, and neither will anybody else. He doesn't need a show to divert attention, because nobody's attention will be drawn to him in the first place."

"I'm not sure I'd go so far as to—" Barnabas attempted.

"Women will not swoon, captains of industry will not bow down, that sort of thing," the Viscount continued. "Just a perfectly nice chap, nothing more. Penny a pound."

"Precisely," Charlotte agreed, favoring Barnabas with a smile. "It's perfect."

"My boy, don't look so downtrodden," her father explained, leaning in and beaming at Barnabas. "We're not insulting you. On the contrary, we're paying you the highest compliment. In this business, unremarkable is the best thing you can possibly be."

Charlotte nodded. "Nobody will ever suspect you of derring-do, not in a million years. Which makes you the perfect spy."

But evidently the perfect spy was only fit for a job of personal busywork, more suited to an underling or footman in Barnabas's opinion. Spying on the boss's daughter, using his social graces to charm her into a false sense of security. He was to spend all his waking hours monitoring her. When he found out Frédérique Murcheson was his first assignment, Barnabas felt like he'd been had.

Murcheson claimed she was a security breach in the making and needed a tail. But now it seemed Murcheson didn't even trust him with following an errant twenty-one-year-old girl. All because Phineas had let himself become addicted to opium. What was more, if Barnabas was to be on constant call to watch the girl, he would have difficulty spending time in the docklands trying to find a lead on Phin's location.

"I'm not my brother, Mr. Murcheson." Barnabas fell into the plummy, snooty tones of his upbringing. He was no misbehaving lieutenant, he was the eldest son and heir of an earl. Not a particularly important or powerful earl, true. But he still outranked a commoner in trade, at least in terms of social standing, and he had no compunction about reminding this man of that fact by his demeanor. "I was invited into Lady Hardison and Lord Darmont's confidence because they believed me capable of working well for the Crown. If you're not of the same opinion, I can simply—"

"Stop there, lad. Enough huffiness. You do the public school patter quite well, I'll give you that. If you want my good opinion, prove yourself. Everywhere my daughter goes, everyone she speaks to, you will know and report to me. But she mustn't suspect you. You must play the part of the fervent, well-intentioned suitor, do you understand? No matter how difficult you find that, once you meet Frédérique."

"Understood." What more could he say? It was clear any further reassurances from Barnabas would fall on uncaring ears. There was nothing left but to prove himself by outwitting and fooling this young woman into believing he was smitten enough to hound her every move, which ought to be simple enough though potentially a trifle unnerving for the lady. But perhaps not; wasn't forming such an attachment the primary concern of most young ladies during the social season, after all? Even the heiresses whose blood wasn't remotely blue. Except that this heiress was sounding less and less like the typical model.

"I suppose you ought to go attire yourself appropriately," Murcheson sniffed. "It is a birthday ball for a prince, after all."

Barnabas went, accompanied by a creeping sense of dread. What the hell had he gotten himself into?

THREE

GASLIGHTS. CANDLES. GLOSSY silks and polished silver. Everything sparkled and glowed in the ballroom, as befitted a royal birthday ball. The Queen's appearance had been blessedly brief, but her youngest son seemed bent on dancing the night away with as many besotted ladies as possible. At twenty-eight, it was high time he made a choice and settled down with one of them, Freddie thought. With three healthy brothers and two boisterous nephews, he was far enough down in the line of succession that he could suit himself when it came to a bride.

She had plenty of time to think these matters over from the sidelines of the ballroom floor, where she habitually sat alone for the duration of these events.

Things hadn't always been this way, of course. Freddie had started her first Season as the incomparable, a half-French mystery girl with a hint of her mother's legendary looks and a delightful fortune to add to her allure. Her easy manner and wit had charmed potential suitors at the beginning. But as the weeks wore on and Freddie continued to be herself, all but the gold diggers slipped away. She'd considered an offer from one of them, a young man who didn't seem so bad compared to some of the others. But after he was seen leaving a tryst with Honoria Weatherfield during a house party, Freddie rejected him publicly and loudly at the next event in town. She had turned down another three proposals over the course of that summer and the next.

She hadn't had an offer since. During the current Season—which was admittedly just beginning—she hadn't even been asked to dance. She'd become the quintessence of wallflowers, shunned even by the other set-asides. None of which was the real problem.

No, the real problem was that sitting on the edge of the ballroom not talking to anyone was boring. Freddie loathed being bored. So naturally, as she always did, she looked for entertainment of her own. Tonight, however, that option seemed to have been quashed by her father and his meddling. He'd apparently found her a new suitor, some business associate from the Dominions who was to be staying with them in London for a time. After a brief introduction the young man had attached himself to her like a barnacle while her father vacated himself to the punch bowl.

Freddie suppressed a snicker at her unintentional mental wordplay. *Barnabas, the barnacle.* Lord Barnabas Smith-Grenville seemed glued to her side for the evening, indeed. Fortunately for her, he didn't look like a creature from the ocean's depths. He didn't look like much of anything. He was a man of averages, she thought. Average looks, average manner, average taste in clothes. Bland and pleasant as pudding.

This lack of interesting features on his part made her instantly suspicious. He was *too* unremarkable, as though he'd been artificially compiled from a list of criteria for young, attractive, eligible gentlemen. All of which led her to believe that this unremarkable man was no mere friend of her father's but one of his employees. He obviously was who he said he was—his father's title was one she knew, and he'd been greeted by a few others in the room in passing, men he appeared to know from school days—but Freddie suspected he was something else as well. Not one of her father's legitimate business associates, as they'd claimed, but somebody from that *other* line of work. The one she was desperate to learn more about.

"How do you know my father, again?" she finally asked, deciding that the straightforward approach was the best counter to subterfuge. The suspiciously bland man had a ready answer, however, and gave no sign of lying.

"Through Baron Hardison in the Dominions. My people are there for the most part, but as I went to school in England and have some connections here, Lord Hardison thought I'd make a good business liaison between him and your father. They've dealt together on a number of projects."

"It surprises me that Your Lordship would take such an interest in trade."

"My father is the Lordship. I have not yet inherited the title, so you may address me as simply 'my lord.'"

She glanced at his face and saw the tail end of a smirk as it vanished and was replaced with an expression of smooth courtesy. Just because she could—and because she wanted to misdirect at least a little of her anger at her father toward this convenient stranger—Freddie dropped into the rough accent of her tinker role. "You're taking the mickey out o' me, my lord."

That got his attention for a moment, earning her a startled

blink. "A bit, yes. You were doing it first, though, calling me Lordship. You know I'm no one in particular."

"No one in particular. I'll try to remember that. Although as you're not very memorable, perhaps I'll forget you altogether once you're gone."

Lord Smith-Grenville almost smiled. It was there in the corners of his eyes, at the edges of his mouth, followed by tension across his fine brow as he formulated a careful response. "Ah, but I won't be gone. I'm quite smitten with you, Miss Murcheson. And as I've your father's tacit approval to court you, you won't be rid of me so easily. It will take far more than a few backhanded jabs to dislodge me now."

He hadn't been convincing *at all*. Freddie stifled a groan, foreseeing a very long Season indeed. She would have to find some subtle means of revenge against her father for saddling her with this pudding man. For saddling her with this series of watchmen. For putting these unnecessary obstacles in the way of the unconventional life she'd rather be living. "You're smitten? You don't even know me, sir."

"And if I did come to know you?" He turned his shoulders, ignoring the dancers and facing her more directly, placing one hand over his heart in a horrifyingly trite way. "Imagine how enchanted I'd be then, Miss Murcheson. You'd have me in your thrall."

"Disappointing. Very disappointing, my lord. You're trying far too hard." Somebody should have taught him that the ability to fake earnestness was the one critical skill for those who sought to be underhanded. Freddie felt exhausted, deep in her soul, and something like defeated. *This* was what she warranted? She was out of patience for playing her father's game against yet another unworthy pawn. She'd had enough. "I've heard that speech or something like it so many times before. And I've heard it better, frankly. Tell me straight, has my father tasked you with me? You wouldn't be the first. He always thinks I don't know when he sets employees to watch me, but I always do."

He cocked his head, appraising her seriously for the first time. "You shouldn't know about that."

"But aren't you one of his spies?" There. She'd said it. Let the cards fall where they might.

The young lord coughed into his hand, glancing around them almost frantically. No one was close enough to overhear. "What? No! Don't say that word!"

She was right. She'd been right all along. He really was hiring men to follow her in the guise of suitors. "What, then? Agents? Operatives? At least tell me he's working for the Crown and not the other side, I've yet to reassure myself on that count."

"Good God, no wonder he wants you monitored! Yes, for the Crown. But you aren't supposed to know any of this!"

"Thank you." And she meant it. It was a relief, to know at last what she'd only been able to speculate about. She felt an odd wash of gratitude toward Lord Barnabas Smith-Grenville.

"You're welcome. I . . . oh, dear heavens, I think I've just committed treason."

Freddie shrugged, amused at his polite expression of horror and his terrible espionage skills. "Your secret is safe with me, sir. I'm sure you've no reason to believe that, but it is. We can be honest with one another. I like you, Lord Smith-Grenville. You're much more amusing than the usual types my father foists on me. They're always so dour." Perhaps the Season wouldn't be so bad, after all, if she could spend it tweaking Smith-Grenville's tail to make him squeak. And if he was this bad a spy on first meeting, he should be easy enough to shake when she wanted to go somewhere without the benefit of an escort. Had they trained the man at all?

"Your father only has your safety in mind, you know."

She shook her head. "He has his own safety in mind. If he were concerned for me, he would pay enough attention to find out what I do with my time himself. He's just worried somebody will try to use me to get to him. And while we're being honest with one another, I'll be honest enough to tell you that I don't trust you. You're his man, ergo you're not a man I can trust. And you're a truly terrible spy, which also doesn't speak well for you."

"It's my first assignment," Barnabas admitted, clearly disappointed in himself. "I had all sorts of things prepared to say if anybody suspected, or if I was tortured. I never expected anyone to just ask me directly, in the course of polite conversation. Least of all you. I thought this would be the simplest job possible. Damn. I'm going to hang for this, and it's only my first day."

"Oh, cheer up. You're not going to hang. I told you, I always know. Although it was more clever of Father than usual to try somebody from the peerage, and with decent conversation for once. If you'd affected ignorance I'd have probably believed you, and just assumed you were a gold digger. You're a very unlikely spy."

"That was the idea. You really won't tell him you've found me out already?"

"No," she reassured him. "Easier to let him go on thinking we've simply hit it off. Are you going to ask for bribes?"

He drew himself up, puffing like a pigeon. "I should certainly think *not*."

Freddie nodded and smiled. "Excellent, then. We shall pretend to court, you'll report to my father that I'm innocent as a lamb without a suspicion in the world, I won't tattle on you, and otherwise I'll continue to do exactly as I like. Agreed?"

Barnabas hesitated. "I can't agree to that, Miss Murcheson. I'm ordered to know your whereabouts at all times, I'm afraid."

"Catch me if you can, my lord."

He sighed. "This is not turning out at all as I'd imagined."

They stared out at the dancers, each lost in their own thoughts for a moment, before Barnabas gathered himself and offered his arm.

"Would you care to dance?"

Freddie eyed his arm but didn't take it. "Oh, you shouldn't dance with me. It'll stain you indelibly."

"Are you socially unfit in some way?"

"Quite ruined, I'm afraid. Not in *that* way, mind you," Freddie reassured him, though she wasn't sure why it suddenly mattered to her. Lord Barnabas Smith-Grenville's opinion of her, good or otherwise, was irrelevant. "But I'm hopelessly odd, you see. I used to do quite well on the marriage mart. There were proposals and so forth, and though I never accepted, that only heightened my allure. Then at the end of last Season I made a critical mistake and let boredom overcome me at one of these things. I don't do well with boredom."

"You fell asleep?"

"I was caught in the host's study, fondling his big inclinometer."

Barnabas coughed into his hand, a charming blush spreading up his cheeks. Or rather, she observed, a red mottling spread there. It was objectively unattractive, regardless of how she might view it subjectively. A grown man blushing like a schoolboy shouldn't charm one.

"I . . . I'm afraid I don't see."

"A mariner's astrolabe. And I wasn't so much fondling it as reassembling it."

"Ah. Which suggests that at some point prior you had—"

"Disassembled it, yes. Because it was broken. It had a clever display function, a set of powered number wheels to show the latitude and longitude findings, with translucent glass number panels so they could be backlit for use in the dark. On a submersible, say. But the connections on those things are fiddly and tend to jostle loose when the inclinometer is running. I found the thing on his desk with a note to his man of business attached, saying, 'Bin this rubbish and refuse the bill.' But it wasn't rubbish; I could clearly see the problem was just a question of tightening a few things up. My real mistake was deciding to replace the copper wire to the bulb fixture with silver. Too time-consuming."

He seemed to consider this for several moments, then asked a question she wasn't expecting. "You happened to have silver wire about your person at a ball? Just in case you ran across a piece of broken equipment , or . . . ?"

Freddie reached up, touching the blossom-strewn curl that draped down upon her shoulder. "I happened to have silver wire in my hair. It spiraled from the crown of my head down around the loose curls, and between the strands were crystal flowers. It was lovely. Until I cut it out, of course, to use in the inclinometer."

"Of course. I see."

"Now you see."

His lips tightened in what she supposed might be sympathy but was likely either disapproval or another suppressed smirk. "One mistake, and you paid for it with your reputation. Clearly not fit to marry, the sort of girl who takes her hair down and strips a man's inclinometer to its parts the minute her chaperone's back is turned."

She didn't know him well enough to know whether to laugh, but she found herself wanting to see *him* laugh. Or scowl, or do anything other than smile blandly and look polite. "Yes. Well. At least I wasn't spotted in the mechanic's stables, flat on my back on a crawler, sliding under a carriage to investigate a faulty steam pump."

"In a ball gown? As if you could. Preposterous!"

"No, I mean at least I wasn't caught, the time I did that. The gown was ruined beyond repair, of course. I went straight to my carriage and home afterward and everybody just assumed I'd left the ball early with a headache. As I said, I'm not good with boredom. But I am usually quite good at not being found out."

The emotions she'd been looking for on Smith-Grenville's face appeared like magic, a series of impressions that flicked from sudden insight through "surely not" to politely horrified certainty. His gaze traveled down to her midsection, below the level where men's eyes normally paused, then back up to her face. And just before he spoke, she remembered where and when she'd seen his unmemorable face. Only that afternoon, in fact, on a crowded street in a part of London that a young woman of quality shouldn't know existed.

"You're that tourist."

"You're that *tinker.*"

FOUR

THEY WERE BLACKMAILING each other. Freddie tried to frame the dilemma in some other way but could find no other means to describe it. She had seen through Lord Smith-Grenville's cover instantly and could ruin his reputation with her father with a word. But Smith-Grenville knew of Freddie's secret identity as a seemingly male makesmith-tinker. He could rat her out at any time too.

Ratting Smith-Grenville out, however, would mean the end of his assignment, and who knows what her father would do if she tipped her hand and revealed she knew he was assigning operatives to watch her? Besides, the young lord was not entirely unpleasant company. Neither was he terribly hard on the eye, though not particularly compelling either. She could certainly suffer worse companions, and indeed she had suffered worse.

If she'd been able, she'd have quitted her father's household altogether. She made decent money with her tinkering, and while she couldn't have afforded anything like her current lifestyle, she probably could have survived. She might be destitute by the standards of her current set, but she'd be well-off compared to most of London. But at the cost of losing all contact with society, her few real friends, possibly her family as well. And there was the complication of her gender; if she struck out on her own, would she live as herself, or as Fred Merchant? She was so weary of pretense already; Freddie couldn't imagine an entire life spent as her alter ego.

So she would keep the mild pudding-man awhile longer, and meanwhile she would continue making her rounds whenever possible. Practicing the trade that society would deny her. As soon as she acquired another pair of trousers.

The London house was still candlelit instead of gas, and dim at night. Freddie had been raised there and knew all its secrets: the floorboards that tended to creak, the hinges that required oil. The likely timing of servants in the front hall and on the back stair. Tonight, an unexpected maid in the vestibule had sent a sneaking Freddie down a hallway to hide in her favorite discovery, a sort of priest's hole in the wall between the front parlor and her father's study.

What it had originally been used for, she couldn't begin to guess. But the narrow chamber was accessible from either room and the hallway, and the entries were cleverly concealed in the paneling. Only a chance draft had tipped her off, a brief and unexpected draw of air on an otherwise stagnant candle flame as she passed by one night in her early childhood.

That night, her father's study had been empty. Tonight, as she waited for the maid to finish her late tasks and clear the way, Freddie found herself privy to a conversation between Rutherford Murcheson and one of his associates. One of those nonindustrial associates, from the sound of it.

"We can't deploy further units until the testing is complete on the prototype," the other man was saying as she carefully eased the panel closed behind her. "If you had given us a larger test vessel than the lily, we could be—"

"I don't need excuses, Hampton. I'm mothballing the lily; it's not sufficient for our needs. Tell Nealy I need a working unit on a full-sized armed submersible. *Now*. We can no longer assume the enemy is lagging behind. They must have something, some advantage, to have evaded our patrols for so long. And with this latest report from Ruckham's team, we've lost the luxury of time to catch them by conventional means." Her father sounded more anxious than demanding, which was unusual for him. Freddie wondered what a lily had to do with testing an armed submersible.

"Quakes have always been a concern for—"

"Not like the one they're predicting. But they need more data, and with the sabotage, Ruckham is no longer even able to provide us accurate, timely warnings for these minor tremors. The glass octopus is all but useless in several quadrants, and I'm running short of men to run perimeter checks even to repair the legs that are still functional. I couldn't man a constant guard on them all, even if having men posted in those areas didn't defeat the purpose of the station in the first place. We want to avoid alerting people to our presence, not draw our enemies a map."

Glass octopus? Freddie tried to make sense of it but couldn't understand half of what her father was saying. Only that it sounded as though a significant earthquake was coming, and there might or might not be any warning for it.

"Can we be certain it isn't just luck, or good old-fashioned legwork, that's helping them avoid capture? Has your implant reported back?"

"Ess Gee is no longer operating in that capacity," Murcheson grumbled. "He was a disappointment from the beginning, to be honest. Far from bold, and positively squeamish when it came to wet work. But attempting to establish a new implant at this juncture would be . . . impractical."

Ess Gee. S-G? Smith-Grenville? A disappointment even to his employer. Freddie had to stifle a "ha!" of satisfied suspicion. *I knew he wasn't to be trusted!*

Lilies and octopi, submersibles and perimeters. It was all confusing but managed to be worrisome anyway. Thoughts of her client that afternoon nagged at her, along with a prickling sensation as she recalled the growing tension near the docks about missing fishing boats, and the strange changes in the local fish population. Could her father's men be frightening the fish away? Or perhaps this glass octopus was some new, predatory creature that devoured more than its share of cod and flounder.

"Nealy isn't going to listen to me on this, sir. Nor can I give you any assurances, not about changing the deployment timetable. I haven't the authority—"

"Blast! Why does he send you to me, then, Hampton? What is the point of all this? I should have never left Le Havre." He slammed a drawer closed or something similar, from the sound of it. "I'll come back with you. There's only one tram operational this side, yes?"

"Yes, sir. The Admiral won't like it, sir."

"The Admiral doesn't have to like it. Meet me in Tilbury in two hours, Hampton."

"Aye, sir."

The study door opened and closed, and footsteps rang down the hall and dwindled away. More slamming and knocking noises emanated from the study, as Murcheson vented his frustrations on his furniture.

Taking a risk, Freddie cracked the paneling door open and peered into the hallway, finding it empty. Quickly she darted from her hiding spot and past the half-open study door, and just as quickly sped down through the garden and carriage house, then out into the mews behind the house. Resting against the carriage block, she paused to catch her breath and consider what she'd heard. None of it made any more sense after careful consideration than it had on first hearing, but her plans for the night evolved.

She would meet with Dan and obtain trousers as they'd arranged. And then she would make her way to Tilbury to find out exactly what her father and Smith-Grenville were up to.

BARNABAS WAS TERRIBLE at lurking. He stood on the pavement opposite the window he'd identified as Freddie's, which overlooked the side of the imposing corner house. He could see only that one side and the back of the mansion, which meant he was in trouble if she left via the front door. His money was on a back terrace window or through the carriage house, however. Murcheson had forbidden him from hanging about the stairs in the house itself, which Barnabas had thought the most logical approach.

He had already been greeted cheerfully by two neighborhood residents returning from a late dinner, and several passing servants, none of whom seemed to find him suspicious in the least. This, despite his dark attire and what he thought must be a fierce expression. He was trying hard to concentrate on the seriousness of his mission and how critical it was that he keep young Miss Murcheson from placing herself in harm's way. This was the only way he'd found to keep from despairing that he'd come all the way to London merely to keep a headstrong young woman from causing his employer any undue convenience or distress.

Or a young man, he reminded himself. He might be looking for a portly lad in a patched coat and overlarge hat.

It was a woman who appeared at the carriage block, however. Miss Murcheson wore a simple brown dress and a ghastly pink plaid shawl that clashed rather violently with her fiery hair. She carried a biggish satchel.

"For Crown and country," he reminded himself in a whisper, as she glanced up the mews and then over to the park.

When she spotted him, her finger went to her lip immediately. Shushing. As if he might be foolish enough to call out and draw attention to the fact that she was attempting to escape.

Barnabas lifted a hand in silent acknowledgment as she moved off the step and toward him.

"At least you're smart enough not to start with the front door," she complimented him when she was close enough to speak low and be heard.

"Isn't everyone?"

"No. It's rather sad, really. Some of them seem more keen to underestimate me than they are to keep their positions. 'How can I possibly keep track of a woman with enough sense to sneak out the back door instead of marching out the front? How could anyone predict the actions of such a wild creature?' And that sort of thing."

He wanted to resent this woman. He'd started out with the assumption that he would feel tremendous disdain for the object of his assignment. It was all so ignominious, after all, and she was just a foolish young thing who couldn't be trusted to keep herself safe. His attempt to place his ill will about the situation at her feet had not survived their first meeting, however. Then, as now, he found her too compelling to dislike even a little. Her face was so expressive, so animated when she spoke that he found himself losing track of what she said because he was fascinated with watching her say it.

"I'll do my best not to underestimate you," he vowed. "But I'm afraid I must insist you return home, Miss Murcheson."

She didn't even blink but simply replied, "No." Then she turned and started briskly down the walk toward the high street.

"But—" Barnabas hesitated, then scurried to catch up to her. "But I caught you, fair and square. You have to go back."

Freddie snorted, not bothering to look at him. "Or what?"

"Or . . . but I caught you."

"That hardly creates any obligation on my part. This isn't a schoolyard, sir."

"It's dangerous for you to be out alone." That much was true, at least. Young ladies didn't belong out on the street at night, and that was that.

"Are you staying behind?"

"What? No, I have to go with you. Except—"

"Then I won't be alone."

"Except you shouldn't be going anywhere."

She strode toward a steam-pony trap, one he recognized from earlier that day. It seemed an age ago.

"Miss." The hulking driver in coarse workman's clothes tipped his cap at Freddie and shot Barnabas a skeptical look. "And a good evening to you, sir."

"Lord Barnabas Smith-Grenville," Freddie piped up, settling herself on the seat next to the man and gesturing for Barnabas to climb into the open bed of the vehicle. He did so reluctantly, pushing equipment aside and hoping against hope that his suit would survive the incident free of oil stains. "Lord Smith-Grenville, this is Daniel Pinkerton."

"A pleasure, Mr. Pinkerton." The courtesy was automatic, if surreal given the circumstances.

"Likewise, m'lord. You're sure about this, Fred?"

"Absolutely. You said your mother knows anyway. I mean to thank her for all she's done. I'm not going to the butcher's yard afterward, however," Freddie continued as Dan kicked the pony into gear and started down the road. "I have a more urgent errand. You needn't join me, though. Lord Smith-Grenville will be coming along, it seems."

"What are you up to, Freddie?" It was clear from Pinkerton's tone that he was no stranger to Miss Murcheson's wayward tendencies. "Is this one of your 'missions'? I'm not about to let you stroll into God only knows what, with only—meaning no offense, m'lord—some unknown toff to watch your back."

"No offense taken, I'm sure," Barnabas muttered. The dingy vehicle was poorly sprung, and he felt each cobble beneath the wheels as a separate insult to his tailbone. The pain was almost welcome, as it distracted him from the obvious insanity of going off with Miss Murcheson and this unknown scoundrel.

Freddie sighed, clearly exasperated. "Dan, you're not coming with me because I don't want you implicated if I'm caught. Lord Smith-Grenville is already implicated. Besides, he's a trained espionage agent of the Crown."

"He is?" Pinkerton risked a glance over his shoulder at Barnabas, the spy. "Him? Really?"

Barnabas nodded unhappily. "They're probably going to hang me," he volunteered.

"Wound up in it already, eh? She does that." Pinkerton

nodded, turning his attention back to the road. They were heading away from Belgravia, and without a map or compass Barnabas was already lost. "She does that. Say, don't I know you from somewhere, m'lord? Begging your pardon."

"We spoke this afternoon. On the street, as I was making my way to see Mr. Murcheson."

"Ah! Of course! The fellow with opinions about the roads."

"The same."

"They'll be worse from here on out."

Pinkerton spoke only the truth. By the time he pulled up in a narrow side street beside a distinctly tilted house, Barnabas had come to wish they were back on the simple cobbles.

"Daniel's mother lives here," Freddie explained as she and Dan alighted. She wrestled her satchel down with her. "She has a pair of trousers for me, and then I can change. Wait here, I'll only be a few minutes."

Before he could protest, she'd disappeared into the ramshackle structure, Dan close behind her.

Ineffectual. That was what Charlotte Hardison had suggested as his cover. He'd asked to play himself instead, but here he was, as ineffectual as he could possibly be. Dragged along by events instead of affecting them.

Barnabas knew they'd had his best interests at heart. His friends had been concerned for him, wanted him to find some new purpose in life after the loss of the Sky and Steam Rally had brought him low. He'd been moping, petulant and melancholy about his loss and failing to find Phineas; he'd be the first to admit that. And the Hardisons thought well enough of him to take him into their confidence and recommend him to the agency and to Murcheson. Another aristocrat volunteering for the cause, to serve as an unlikely spy where others could not. It had sounded exciting, like an adventure.

But instead of France and airships and races against time and the elements to save lives, as Charlotte had evidently experienced during her tenure with the agency, Barnabas got London and tagging God knew where after a girl of no strategic importance. And he had revealed himself as a spy after a moment's conversation, because he was an idiot, so now he was stuck in this ridiculous position on the back of a pony cart in a grimy street where he'd probably be knifed for his pocket watch before Miss Murcheson and Pinkerton returned. As if he'd needed a pedigree to wind up here, in a place like this.

Examining the array of possibilities in the trap's bed, Barnabas hefted a large monkey wrench in one hand. It was well worn and sported a few rust spots, but the weight of it comforted him. He might be accosted, but at least he'd give his assailant a solid conk on the noggin to remember him by.

He didn't know what he was doing anymore. None of this was getting him any closer to finding Phineas. He hadn't even made it to the dock where Phin had been spotted, much less spent time showing his portrait around and questioning people. He considered the new information Murcheson had unwittingly revealed. Perhaps his family was right, and Phineas was truly gone forever. He should return to the estate in New York and get on with the wrenchingly tedious business of learning to take over for his father one day. Make them happy and proud again, as he used to in his school days.

In those days, Phin had been his shadow, ever at his heel but scarcely noticed. A thin, quiet boy who observed everything and came to his own private conclusions about it all. Barnabas, the responsible elder brother, looked after Phin and saw that he came to no trouble. He'd been charged with that at the start of each school term, and he'd taken the duty to heart although it had hardly been difficult to undertake. His brother wasn't the kind of boy to find trouble, and it rarely found him. Still, even after Phin finished his studies at Oxford and took a commission in the Royal Navy—to the surprise of them all—Barnabas had never forgotten his duty.

He'd failed, though, long before Phineas disappeared from his post. Something had happened, while Barnabas's back was turned. After years as a steady, deliberate presence in his life, Phineas had turned moody and angry. He'd stopped confiding in Barnabas, and their easy relationship had vanished. Letters went unanswered, expected visits were canceled. The last time he'd seen his brother, they'd barely spoken. Phineas was on leave in London, Barnabas on a visit to friends in the city, but their plans to meet materialized only once for a brief and awkwardly silent meal at his hotel.

"This was the latest in a long string of very bad ideas," Phin had told him as they sipped port afterward. "I'm sorry for it." He'd shaken hands and left abruptly.

And then, finally, nothing.

Their mother insisted that Phineas must have been under the wicked influence of opium even then. Barnabas knew better. He'd seen opium addicts before, and although Phin had looked unhappy he'd shown no signs of impairment or deterioration. In fact, except for his expression, he seemed as fit and well as Barnabas had ever seen him. Not a man who required looking out for anymore. So instead of pressing him to explain what was wrong, Barnabas had let him leave unchallenged.

But that expression . . . the pain in his brother's eyes continued to haunt Barnabas at night, and he'd vowed not to rest until he either rescued Phineas or confirmed that further searching was hopeless. No matter what Murcheson said,

Barnabas felt there was more to Phineas's story than the little he already knew. It couldn't be over yet; his brother couldn't truly be gone.

Looking about him at the grimy, gloomy buildings, Barnabas wondered if hopelessness had somehow arrived when he wasn't looking. But it was late, and he was exhausted; he'd already had a very long day of travel, socializing and spying. Things would almost certainly look better on the morrow. Assuming, of course, that he survived whatever caper Miss Murcheson tried to pull him into tonight.

FIVE

꩜

"MY HERO," FREDDIE murmured when she returned to the pony trap to find Lord Barnabas Smith-Grenville recumbent and gently snoring among the tools of her trade. He cradled a monkey wrench in his arms like a child cuddling a favorite blanket.

Despite the shadow of stubble on his cheeks and chin, Lord Smith-Grenville looked years younger in his sleep, quite boyish, in fact. And Freddie noticed one thing remarkable about his face, at last. Even in the guttering light of the small lantern she carried, she could see that the man's eyelashes were dark and absurdly long against his cheekbones. His rather fine, high cheekbones, which the chiaroscuro lighting also revealed.

"He's prettier sleepin'," Dan noted, cementing her observation. "No good to you, though."

She stayed his hand when he would have reached for Lord Smith-Grenville to shake him awake. "He's had an eventful day.

And travel can be very wearing. I'll let him sleep until we're outside Tilbury. It will do him good. You can come along to protect me on the drive, if it will make you happy," she relented.

"Not happy, no. Less concerned."

"As long as you limit your involvement to driving and watching the cart once we get there."

"Aye. Let's be off, then. Hour there, hour back, and whatever time you spend on your wild-goose chase. It'll be nearly dawn by the time we get you safe home, at this rate. Lucky tomorrow's my holiday."

He topped off the boiler and stoked the coals quickly, then joined Freddie on the bench and departed for Tilbury. If he allowed the trap to jerk somewhat more than usual at the start, it still failed to wake up Barnabas.

As they wended their way into the docklands, Freddie pulled her pistol into her hand, eyes scanning the side streets diligently. Comfortable as she now felt in this territory during the day, nighttime was another matter. Only a fool would drop her guard. She was nearly as tired as Barnabas, in truth, but her anger and curiosity lent her stamina.

In the two years since she'd started her tinkering business, she'd come to appreciate the folk who inhabited the rougher parts of town. They were good people who worked hard, for the most part, and many of them seemed smarter and kinder than their so-called superiors in the upper classes. But naïve, even the canniest of them. They lived in blissful ignorance of the machinations taking place in the chambers of Whitehall and the quiet studies of country estates. They didn't know they were pawns, and when they suspected it and tried to remedy the situation, things usually went badly for them as a consequence.

"It isn't right, you know," she told Dan. "He doesn't care

if people are losing their livelihoods. He doesn't see. Even when it's right in front of his face."

"You know I can't say aught," Dan reminded her. And he wouldn't either. His job was already at constant risk because of his helping her, but he drew the line at disparaging the man who paid his wages. Whatever his private opinion of Murcheson, he kept it to himself.

"You needn't. But this time Father's gone too far. Playing about with some nonsense in the channel, scaring away the fish and fishermen alike. And for what? We aren't even at war with the French anymore. Mother's been able to return home for the first time in so many years. Father's business has grown a staggering amount since he expanded into Europa. But he doesn't own the channel. He can't just go playing God." It was bad enough when her father's heavy-handedness affected her alone. She couldn't bear the thought of it making life a misery for a population already so downtrodden.

"Tilbury dock ahead. We need to get off the main road, miss."

"Fred."

"Aye, Fred. We don't want to be the ones spotted, we're trying to do the spotting. So which way?"

"You remember Jameson, the tobacconist? Cut down the road past his shop and pull up at the end near the fishing guild hall. We'll be able to see the entrance to my father's warehouse from there. I'll wake Lord Smith-Grenville."

She leaned over the back of the bench and prodded the top of Barnabas's head. His bowler had slipped off while he slept. His hair was soft, barely springing back against her fingers as she tapped.

"Wake up, my lord. We're in Tilbury."

"Who—huh?" He came to and jerked to a sitting

position, facing the back of the trap, wrench held in front of him like a shield. "Where?"

"Up here." She waved her fingertips at him when he turned around, wild-eyed. "You fell asleep. Long day?"

"I—yes, I suppose. I apologize. Is this your wrench?" He held it out to her politely, and Freddie had to restrain a grin.

"Yes, but it seemed to bring you some comfort as you slumbered. By all means keep it if you like. Are you otherwise armed?"

She showed him the impressive pistol she carried, and after blinking for a moment he reached beneath his jacket and withdrew a slightly smaller firearm of his own. "I forgot I had it."

Dan muttered something under his breath that sounded very much like, "Bloody hell." Freddie nudged his boot with her own.

"At least you've remembered now."

Barnabas nodded. "And now that we're here, what is the plan, Miss Murcheson?"

"Fred, please. When I'm dressed like this, it's Fred. The plan is to wait on that corner there," she explained, pointing, "until we see my father arrive and meet his colleague. Then to follow them without being seen, and find out what they're up to."

"But Miss—Fred, if it's a matter of state secrets, I can hardly condone . . . oh, blast."

"So my father is privy to state secrets. Thank you for clarifying that. Do you know why he's meeting this man Hampton here?" She ran her fingertips over the barrel of her weapon, caressing the wood.

He eyed the pistol as he felt around him, then replaced his hat on his head. "Your father hasn't confided in me regarding his schedule. You clearly know more than I do about his intentions. Shooting me won't get you anywhere."

She clamped down on the impulse to apologize for the

implied threat, reminding herself that this harmless-seeming young noble was an admitted spy and her father's man. It was entirely possible his accidental sincerity and naïveté were an elaborate front to gain her confidence. In fact, that was a more plausible explanation than the face value of Lord Smith-Grenville.

Freddie checked her pocket watch. "He's due to arrive any minute now. Come with me, take the rear, and do try to tread lightly and keep to the shadows. Mr. Pinkerton will guard the trap." She hopped down to the street, automatically adjusting her balance to account for all the heavy padding but still less hampered than she would be in a skirt. Dan's mum had found her a new pair of braces to go with the trousers, replacing the old, worn pair she'd liberated from her father's wardrobe and cut down to size. She felt even more comfortable and mobile than usual. "Dan, if we aren't back in two hours, feel free to come looking."

"One hour."

"One and a half. Coming, Lord Smith-Grenville?"

"Do I have a choice?"

A sudden rage threatened her vision for a moment, a flicker of red in the dark. Did he have a choice? Lord Barnabas Smith-Grenville, a first son of the peerage, an agent of the Crown, a titled young gentleman in the prime of his life?

"You've nothing but choices, my lord," she managed against the angry tightening of her throat. "A world of them."

She turned and made for the corner, not bothering to look behind to see if he would choose to follow.

BARNABAS HEFTED THE pistol in his hand, taking confidence from its weight and the memory of his successful last turn at the firing range behind Hardison House.

As Miss Murcheson had predicted, her father and another man had rendezvoused in front of the warehouse, then disappeared down a side alley without speaking a single word to one another. Both men were on foot. The streets were empty, as befit the ungodly hour. The church bell up the road had tolled three as Freddie and Barnabas slipped across the pavement to steal down the alley after their quarry.

It was clear Miss Murcheson had a knack for this sort of thing. Although most of the narrow passage was lit only by the moon and stars, she never faltered. Her movements were swift and sure as a cat's in the dark, and when she pulled Barnabas with her behind the cover of a row of barrels, he noted that the spot afforded a perfect view of the door through which Murcheson and his colleague entered one of the warehouse's outbuildings. A moment later, the painted-over window by the entrance flickered with a tracework of warm light. A muffled rattle of metal on metal wafted to them on the damp breeze. The glow brightened, then slipped from view as if a lantern shade had been pulled down over it.

Then silence again, and darkness, punctuated only by Miss Murcheson huffing out a puzzled, "Hmph."

"What?" he whispered.

"It reminds me of something. I'm trying to think what it could be."

"I see. Are we stopping here, then?"

"Of course not." She stepped from behind the barrels and strode toward the door, no longer bothering with stealth. He caught up to her as she peered into the window. The glass was dark, the cracks invisible now that they were no longer backlit.

"I have a pocket torch," he offered, hoping it might forestall the inevitable break-in. He pulled the slender rod from his breast pocket and slid his fingers down its length until he found the tiny latch that held the crank lever flat. With a flick of one fingertip, he loosed it and used it to slide the mechanism free. The crank needed only a few brisk turns before the rod's tip began to shine.

"Very clever," Miss Murcheson granted, though she didn't sound as though she meant it. Her father was Rutherford Murcheson, after all; Barnabas suspected the young lady saw a dozen more fascinating technological marvels than this on a slow day.

"I shouldn't be helping you. But as I'm doomed to hang anyway . . ." He pressed the torch to one corner of a windowpane, sliding it along the seam between glass and wood, looking for the gap in the paint that the earlier flash of light had revealed. There was nothing, then a flicker he nearly missed.

"Go back a bit," she urged. "There. Just there."

In the feeble glow, they could see the network of paint cracks again. Freddie peered through the largest one into the room beyond, then gasped and backed away.

"What?"

"I've seen this before."

"It's your father's warehouse, isn't it?" Barnabas pressed his eye to the gap and observed what appeared to be an all-but-empty storage chamber. "I don't know why you'd have spent time looking into the closets, but—"

"No, no. I've seen this, but not here. There's a room exactly like this one in my father's factory in Le Havre."

Giving the torch crank another spin, Barnabas shrugged. "I'd venture to say there's a room like this in almost any factory or warehouse in the world, Miss Murcheson."

"No. I mean exactly alike. The same paneling. The same few crates in the corner, mouse-eaten papers on the floor. The closet in Le Havre has a broken chair and this appears to have a stepladder with a broken step, that's the only difference. I used to hide in there when I'd go to visit Father, just to see if anyone would notice I was missing. Nobody ever looked for me there; it was as if they didn't know the room existed."

He looked again. "It's a wholly unremarkable storage room. Perhaps they weren't looking very hard?" He regretted that the moment he'd said it, but she didn't seem to have paid him any mind.

"The same room," she insisted. "In two busy establishments, in two different countries. The same storage room with nearly nothing stored in it. Why are they empty? And where are Father and Mr. Hampton?"

Blast. "The light. This must just be a pass-through to something else. They must have opened a door. I don't see one, but it's the only explanation. I mean they had to have gone somewhere."

She was already working at the lock with a hairpin, cursing softly. Her absurdly large hat obscured her profile from his view, and she sounded more tinker than lady. For a moment, her disguise worked on him, causing him to doubt his own sanity. The illusion broke when she spoke to him directly. "Shine that over here, please, sir."

Even after he obliged, it took Freddie several minutes and two broken hairpins before she finally turned the knob with an air of supreme satisfaction.

"That lock wasn't put there to protect a few empty crates and a broken ladder, Lord Smith-Grenville."

Clearly not. But the longer she'd worked on it, the more anxious Barnabas had become about what it might be protecting. Nothing that would help his case, he suspected.

"The light shone straight through the window. I think it came from that wall, but I don't see any door."

The wall opposite the door was faded gray paneling,

unpainted, undistinguished. But where the light of the pocket torch slipped over the wood, Barnabas detected a spot that looked out of place. A seam where one needn't be, and a patch where the touch of many hands might have worn down the rough wood. He pressed his palm to the wall, and after a moment the grinding clank of chains announced his success.

"Oh, well done, my lord. Very well done indeed."

The light flickered on from behind the dull paneling, and a moment later the wall itself slid to one side with a whir of gears. An ordinary lift cage greeted them, unassuming brass and wood with an accordion door and a lantern that appeared to be electric. Beyond the framework, bare wooden walls were visible.

Barnabas didn't want to take that lift. He wanted to be anywhere else. But Fred was already pushing the latch up, sliding the door open. She entered the cage and looked back at him, and then she smiled as though embarking on a delightful adventure and inviting him along for the ride. It was the grin of a mischievous tinker lad with nothing to lose . . . or that of a society maiden who excelled at playing such a dangerous role.

A world of choices, she'd ascribed to him. He saw few choices at the moment, and none of them good. But he found he couldn't look at that smile and not follow it. The ridiculous hat, the padded tummy, the hands covered in grime to mask the dainty and well-manicured fingers, none of that mattered. Miss Freddie Murcheson was grinning at him and beckoning, and he must follow. So he did, and let her shut the lift door behind him.

SIX

FOR A MOMENT, Freddie doubted herself. That moment fell when the lift sank into the earth and she saw the bare rock walls beyond the fragile brass framework in which she and Lord Smith-Grenville stood. The light flickered a few times as they descended, and more than once she felt her mind flirt with panic when she thought they might be plunged into subterranean darkness.

But clever Smith-Grenville kept his pocket torch out, occasionally spinning it back into brightness as they clattered downward. If the lift motor was electric, the torch wouldn't help much, but at least they would be buried alive with enough light to see by. Or they would discover something new, something she hadn't been meant to find. A familiar rush of energy seized her, the impending thrill of exploring the forbidden.

She risked a longish look at her companion when he seemed distracted by the passing geological display, and wondered at her first assessment of him. Although he looked somewhat ghastly in the harsh light, she could also see every minute action of his face's musculature, each subtle change in expression in that visage she'd thought so calm and bland. Perhaps it was exhaustion, not just lighting, that laid Smith-Grenville so bare now, but whatever the reason Freddie liked the outcome. The subtle hint of curiosity and fear in the fine lines beside his eyes, the puzzled tension of the corner of his mouth. Even in profile she could see the almost-furrow of his brows, as the lightbulb sputtered and he gave his torch another crank.

He wouldn't hang. She was almost certain of that. Even if her father did find out what a horrible spy Smith-Grenville made. Still, perhaps it had been harsh of her to drag him along for this evening's work. She had no idea what she was doing, which was all very well and good for her, but hardly fair to someone who was practically an innocent bystander. Usually she worked alone.

"Can I help you, Miss Murcheson?"

"Sorry?"

He met her gaze, and a long moment ensued during which Freddie could feel herself blush, and Smith-Grenville's face went through an array of minute expressions she couldn't quite read.

"You were, um . . . you were staring. A bit. Or so it seemed to me. Do I have something on my face?"

Your lovely soul. "No, nothing. I apologize. I didn't mean to stare." But she kept doing it. He was the first to look away.

"We seem to have arrived."

The lift settled into place with a grumbling thump, and Barnabas slid the door open and practically threw himself out of the tight space.

Following more cautiously, Freddie saw a large chamber that was clearly a work in progress. Hewn from the bedrock, the lift vestibule was twice the height of a large man and as long and wide as her bedchamber in the manor house outside Le Havre. The floor was polished native stone, and the corners were full of the detritus of construction. Tools, finely milled wood planks, lengths of copper tubing, and what appeared to be a partially assembled lift cage of much more elegant make than the simple model they'd traveled in. Glass panels with a frosted pattern at the edges, held in place by a hardwood frame with elegant brass fittings. When it was completed it would rival the lift in any fine hotel.

At the far end of the room an archway led to a broad corridor with two pairs of narrow grooves carved into the floor along each side. The pile of lanterns and wiring at its entrance suggested it was as yet unlit, and this turned out to be the case. Barnabas fired his torch again and they set off into the darkness.

"It looks like a track for some sort of vehicle," he ventured after they'd walked for several minutes in silence. His whisper echoed harshly against the stone walls. "There's a metal rail in there."

"I wish we could find whatever it is that runs on the track," Freddie whispered back. "I suspect it would make this distance in a fraction of the time we're taking to walk it." They couldn't walk all night.

"Your father and the other one must have used it. Oh, what's this?"

On the right-hand track sat what appeared to be a handcar—or rather, on closer examination, a velocipede. The simple metal framework sported two seats and a complicated system of treadles and gears that led, to Freddie's great delight, to a rudimentary Stirling engine.

"Bring the torch closer! Oh, this is brilliant. Look, the treadles create a charge to heat the element that powers the engine, then the engine maintains the speed after you shift this gear. This will take us as far as we care to go. All we need to do is provide the momentum."

"You believe you can operate that after a cursory glance?" He sounded less disbelieving than amazed, to his credit.

She nodded. "It's what I do. Climb on."

It wasn't as smooth as described, of course. Building momentum from a dead stop was a good deal of work. Then finding the switch to start the heating process once they were in motion took Freddie a few extra moments, during which they had to hurtle into pitch blackness because she was using the torch to examine the controls on the engine casing. She had to stop pedaling in order to crank the engine itself when the element seemed sufficiently hot, the attached indicator needle creeping into the comforting green zone on the dial. Barnabas had to work all the harder in those moments, complaining bitterly as he did so. Then the first time she attempted to engage the gear shift, the velocipede shuddered so badly she thought it might come apart, and she had to ease back and reconsider, all the while pumping madly at the treadles until she thought her legs or lungs would surely give out. The second time, however, she coordinated a brief pause in their pedaling. The gear clunked into place and engaged, and suddenly they were whirring down the track along the torch's narrow beam, faster than could possibly be safe.

Barnabas laughed aloud as he resumed pedaling in a slow, easy motion. The velocity was in the engine's hands now, the treadles merely providing its sustaining heat and helping maintain momentum.

"I could go like this all night," he claimed.

"We should agree on a time. Especially as we've no idea how fast we're really going."

He checked his pocket chronometer, a lovely gold piece that gleamed even in the weak light of the torch. "Twenty minutes?"

"Forty-five. I don't suppose you have a compass as well? I didn't think to bring one."

"Thirty minutes," he countered. "We've been some time down here already, and I suspect Mr. Pinkerton won't give the full hour and a half before he investigates. We need to allow ourselves time for the round-trip and the lift ride back up. And no, I don't have a compass."

"Fair enough. Oh . . . shine the light forward again? Not on the tunnel," she corrected, "on the bar in front of us. We're both idiots." Leaning forward, she pulled a lever and the tracks before them were flooded with light from the velocipede's headlamp.

"Of course it has one. And of course we only find it after I've been turning the crank on this silly thing until my hand is ready to come off at the wrist."

"That thing isn't silly. It's gotten us this far. And your wrist will recover, I'm sure. Oh, seeing farther ahead doesn't make it any less unnerving, does it?"

"Not one bit."

They tried not to dwell on what would happen if there were an unexpected obstacle up ahead, an unfinished track or construction debris in the way. Freddie couldn't see a way to adjust the speed, so they continued their dizzying, heart-stopping pace for the full half hour. When she finally shifted down to begin the braking process, it was almost a relief to feel the strain on her legs return, the sensation that the beast below them was once again under their control.

With the brake engaged, they slowed to a halt, and as soon as the engine stopped, the headlamp flicked out as well. Fortunately, Freddie had already noted an important feature of the tracks. At regular intervals, there were panels with levers on the tunnel wall, and they'd stopped close to one. A closer look with Barnabas's pocket torch confirmed her hypothesis.

"It's a turnaround. See there?" Training the light on the track, she followed along until she found a curved set pulling away from the straight track and leading back to the other side. She attempted to pull the lever, but to no avail. She put the torch between her teeth, using both hands to haul down on the thing. Finally, when she was literally dangling from it, she sighed and flashed the light toward a smirking Barnabas. "That's unchivalrous of you."

As she was speaking around the torch, it sounded more like "At'th udsiwawous oh you,' but he seemed to understand her quite well.

Shielding his eyes from the glare, he grinned back, unrepentant. "You're highly entertaining to watch."

She removed the torch from her mouth. "Would you just help, please?"

Together they managed to activate the switch, and they used pedal power to ease the cart around to the facing track before restoring the switch to its original position.

"I don't suppose this means we can go straight back?" he asked, without much hope.

"Of course not. Keep the torch fired up, my lord. Now we explore."

The tunnel where they'd stopped looked much like it had all along, a featureless dark corridor of stone and a gridwork of comfortingly solid-appearing beams of some hardwood. Unlike the polished, shining wood in the vestibule, the beams here were yet to be finished. A few bore painted markings, possibly instructions of some sort for the workers. Other than that, however, there was not much to distinguish one section from another.

"Do you suppose they'll bury them all when they're finished, like the slaves who built the pyramids at Giza?" she mused, as they ventured deeper along the corridor.

"What, the builders? I think they'll just pay them a good deal of money to keep quiet."

"That would certainly be the more civilized thing to do. Wait, what was that?"

He swung to face her, nearly blinding her with the torch, his hand shaking. "What was what?"

"My *eyes*."

"Oh, I apologize. Better?" He flicked it away, and Freddie blinked until the stars cleared from her vision. She pointed to where the light now fell on the wall, which finally looked different here from one beamed-off section to the next. On one side of the beam was stone. On the other, the torch revealed a section of riveted metal sheeting. As her vision resolved further, she made out a row of three round glasses in brass frames, at roughly eye level. It took a moment for her to realize they were portholes.

"That there. Oh! We must be nearly to the mouth of the estuary by now, almost to the channel itself, if we're headed in the direction I think we are. Turn out the torch. The moon is up and it's nearly full; perhaps we'll be able to see into the water."

"I doubt it."

He closed the device anyway, and they waited for their eyes to adjust to the gloom. The darkness was disorienting, and Freddie nearly lost her balance when she stepped closer to the faintly visible circle of the nearest porthole. It seemed to brighten as she watched, her eyes making out more of the dimly illuminated underwater scene.

"It just moved," Barnabas whispered.

"What just moved?"

"Everything."

As if in confirmation, everything moved again, a disturbing sideways jolt underfoot.

At the same time, something flashed outside the porthole, and they jerked their heads in unison toward the unexpected light. Barnabas leaped to press his nose to the glass, and Freddie heard him say a word no gentleman should, as the world shifted again and the metal panels groaned. Flying to the next porthole, she gasped as a huge, dark shape in the water resolved into an approaching submersible. It shone a light on the seabed below and in front of it, nearly blinding them when the sub turned and the light blazed into the window for a moment.

Close, far too close and too fast, the sub loomed toward them, then passed mere inches overhead, just as a klaxon began sounding in some distant part of the tunnel.

"We need to move!" shouted Barnabas, grabbing her hand and jerking her back down the corridor in the direction they'd just come from. "It's an earthquake!"

She scrambled to keep up with him, wishing she'd been more enthusiastic about sport in school. "I thought it was a submersible!"

"Are you joking?"

To her dismay he let go of her hand and let her lag behind. He was only procuring the torch, however. As soon as he'd cranked it back into glimmering life, he turned and caught her hand up, pulling her along as the ground shivered beneath them once again. They made it to the velocipede and likely set a record for starting it up and bringing it to full speed, racing down the track in the direction they'd come. Freddie lost count of the times one or the other exclaimed as they went how clever they'd been, to turn the cart around before exploring. She knew it was a lie, every time. It had been luck, nothing to do with cleverness. But she would take it, either way.

The journey was an exercise in the relativity of time. The speed of the velocipede was constant, so they knew it was a half hour out and a half hour back in. But it had seemed like hours as they traveled the distance the first time, into the unknown darkness. On the way back, with their hearts racing from fear, the trip seemed the work of mere moments. They came to a jerky halt as soon as the vestibule was in sight, abandoning the velocipede and heading for the exit at a dead run.

"We've left the cart on the wrong track, and far too close to the entrance!" Freddie realized with horror. "Somebody will know it's been used!"

"I'm not going back to turn it around. You can do what you like, but you'll never get that lever down alone."

Neither of them stopped running, in any case.

Barnabas hit the lift first and tugged the door open, then slammed it decisively behind Freddie once she was safely in. The device jerked upward as soon as the door was secured. Overhead the bulb guttered madly, but the motor operated smoothly, to Freddie's vast relief.

"It was an earthquake," Barnabas repeated, sinking down to the floor and resting his arms on his knees as he caught his breath.

"I know. We had two in Le Havre when I was living there." The space was cramped, but she slumped down beside him, sides heaving. Now that they were relatively safe, she felt foolish for having run. Surely the tunnel had been built to withstand a few minor tremors.

"But you said—"

"I *was* joking."

"Oh." He blinked, then smiled hesitantly. "That was quite

good, actually." The smile faded almost immediately and was replaced with a grim look that made Freddie even uneasier.

"Thank you. Are you all right, Lord Smith-Grenville? You look—" *Serious. Adult. Not as though you're having a bit of a lark.* "Concerned about something."

He nodded, his lips tightening even more. Now that she was learning what to look for, Freddie saw all sorts of emotions on Smith-Grenville's face.

"Did you notice anything unusual about that submersible?"

"Other than the fact it nearly plowed into the porthole and killed us?" But she was already thinking back, trying to remember the details. There had been something, she was sure of it. She cursed herself again for bolting.

Barnabas shrugged. "That too. I meant the bristles all over the front of it."

That was it! "I know what those are, I think! Or at least I know something about them. I overheard my father talking about some prototype of a device for catching smugglers. And something about a lily. There was a flower painted on that sub; I saw it when the thing banked, right before it swooped over the tunnel. A big yellow flower. The sub must be called the *Lily*. Though I can't think why; it doesn't look even vaguely floral. And Father seemed to think it was too small, but that one looked enormous to me. Perhaps the water made it look bigger?"

"That was no military vessel," Barnabas corrected her. "And it wasn't a lily painted on the side. It was a poppy. A golden poppy."

He'd grown paler still, and without thinking she reached over to touch his hand. He took her fingers in his, and a queer feeling sifted from her chest down to the bottom of her stomach. "Why is the poppy so important?"

"It's the emblem of an opium smuggler. Baron Orm, but he called himself the Lord of Gold. He's in prison in the Dominions, and in theory his operations were shattered. Obviously not, however."

The lift creaked to a halt, but Freddie remained where she was, her heart beating as fast as it had when the earthquake began. "I read about him in the newspapers. You're not telling me everything, are you?"

Barnabas lifted his gaze to hers, frowning with his mouth but smiling with his eyes. "I've always had an excellent poker face, Miss Murcheson. I can't tell if you're unusually perceptive or just more persistent than most in trying to see past it."

She matched his somber moue. "Unusually perceptive, of course."

He snorted, then got to his feet, offering her a hand up. "So I might as well go on and tell you everything to save time, I suppose? I don't want there to be a submersible owned by opium smugglers. Particularly not that opium smuggler. Because I fear that somebody I know may be involved."

They exited the lift together, and Barnabas cracked the door to the alley to scout for passersby.

"Who is it? Who's involved?"

He put a finger to his lips and held the door open to let her pass first. As she brushed by him, he murmured his answer.

"My brother, Phineas."

Seven

He had slept, which helped immensely. But Barnabas still felt a touch of the surreal as he guided the curricle around the park the next afternoon. Miss Murcheson sat behind him, prim and lovely in a pale green frock that managed to be entirely modest yet show off her curves to great advantage. He wasn't sure if he preferred the fashionable ensemble to her workman's attire. He did know, however, that he had never courted anyone remotely in Frédérique Murcheson's category. Here, in this setting and in these garments, she was the paradigm of fashionable, demure loveliness. He found himself convinced, even though he knew full well it was a sham. She had a charmed glow about her, something indescribable and irresistible.

Barnabas eased the pair of matched grays past a halted landau and matched the deliberately sedate flow of traffic along the broad avenue. He enjoyed the responsiveness of the animals, the quiet surrounding them. Steam vehicles were not permitted in Hyde Park, a stricture most of the current generation railed against. Barnabas liked that the horses knew where they were going without constant monitoring. This team had come with his cover story, apparently. They'd been waiting for him this morning along with the keys to a reasonably fashionable steam car for longer excursions. Everything a young man-about-town might need.

"Father has spared no expense in outfitting my latest suitor, I see," was Miss Murcheson's comment once they were moving along again and past the risk of being overheard.

"He's certainly made me plausible," Barnabas agreed. "If I last, he said he'd arrange a house for me, as well. As my family no longer maintains a London residence, I have to admit it's welcome. Saves me the time of finding a place to let and a decent livery. And this probably does a great deal to restore your status on the marriage mart. Having a well-bestowed chap such as myself so eager to ignore his business obligations and drive out with you instead." He spoke with a cheer that was not entirely false. It was far from an unpleasant task to take this drive, and throwing himself into the role of ardent suitor was still the best way to go about it.

"He said, humbly," she retorted. "I have no desire to restore my status on the marriage mart. But more importantly, you fell asleep again on the way home last night and never told me the rest of your brother's story."

He glanced around automatically, paranoid about the proximity of the surrounding carriages. Nobody was close, and aside from a few curious glances at the new lordling from the Dominions, nobody seemed to be paying them any attention. Most of the talk he'd caught centered on last night's earthquake, which the members of the *ton* seemed to consider a bit of a thrill. The morning paper reported three dockworkers dead from a building collapse. Barnabas suspected the rank and file were less than thrilled by the quake, and he wondered how any of them would respond if they knew a much larger quake had been predicted to occur soon. Or so Miss Murcheson claimed to have overheard. Such news might cause a panic, even among the jaded aristocracy.

"I shouldn't have told you what I did about Phineas. I was exhausted and delusional."

"I saw the poppy on that submersible too. It was no delusion."

"Yes. But perhaps it was simply an old mark, or a coincidence. It can't be Orm. When I left the Dominions he was still incarcerated. Isolated. No communication with the outside world, not so much as a carrier pigeon."

She pulled a fan from somewhere about her person and snapped it open, waving it prettily in front of her face as she thought. "You thought of this man Orm and your brother instantly. One should always trust one's first instincts. And what about the whiskers?"

"What whiskers?"

"On the submersible. If that wasn't some sort of sensor array, my name's not Fred Merchant."

"Your name *isn't* Fred Merchant."

"You know exactly what I mean. The point is, there was some sort of nonstandard equipment, and that was no military vessel. You knew that instantly, and I must concur. What's more, I've consulted a map my father had handy—"

"He had it handy? Just lying about in a parlor, I suppose?"

"Don't interrupt, please. I have my ways. If we were where I estimate we were, that part of the channel is supposed to be off-limits to all but the military. There's a narrow passage for commercial vessels into the estuary, but most of it was never opened up after the war ended. Not so much as a fisherman squeaks by. The military doesn't like to cede ground or water once it controls it. But if that was a civilian sub we saw, and it had some sort of underwater sensor attached, perhaps a proximity detector . . . well, it could be using that to sneak past the Navy patrols."

"That would definitely give the smugglers an advantage," he admitted. It would allow one smuggler the drop on not only the authorities but any competition as well. And if the criminal in question were indeed smuggling opium, he might gain the upper hand even against the British East India Company's monopoly.

It was bizarre, discussing matters of such great secrecy there in the sunlight, in the midst of so many peers. These were topics for clandestine whispers in the darkness, not open discussion in carriages in broad daylight. Miss Murcheson's lace-bedecked parasol did not provide nearly enough cover for all they had to say. She looked extremely fetching beneath it, however. But then she always looked fetching, even dressed as a plump male tinker with grease smears on her face.

"If Father suspected a civilian, a smuggler, had already developed the equipment his men were still trying to build, that would explain his determination to speed up testing. To use something larger than whatever the *Lily* is. And he hasn't returned home. I think he is in France. I believe we still have some sort of military installation in Le Havre. No, listen," she insisted, when he started to protest that the terms of the treaty with France prohibited such a thing, "that storeroom in his factory there. Exactly the same, my lord. What if it leads to another tunnel? Another underwater passage? What do the tunnels lead to?"

"A faster way to get across?" he suggested. "People have talked for years about building a tunnel under the channel. If the Navy started working on such a thing during the war, they're hardly likely to have abandoned it just because of the treaty. As you pointed out, they don't like to cede territory."

"But this side's tunnel looked new. They were still building it. There was fresh sawdust. A new lift cage. Lighting still to be rigged. I saw the Le Havre entrance—"

"If that's what it was."

"I saw it years ago. When his factory was only a few years old. He used to take me there all the time when we first moved to France; it was only a year or so later that my mother started to forbid it. The tunnel wouldn't have led to nowhere, would it? There's a *destination* down there somewhere. That's why they're still keeping people out."

"But the channel is hundreds of feet deep. What would be worth the inconvenience and danger of keeping it under that much water?"

"Something that's underwater anyway," Freddie posited. "Some sort of mining operation, or specialized research facilities. Or a docking station for submersibles with special hydrophonic sensors that the Navy doesn't want anyone to know exist."

"This is giving me a headache." He steered toward the shadiest side of the drive, slowing the horses. "I should just tell your father what we saw."

Freddie snapped her fan shut and glared at him. "You wouldn't dare."

"I'm done for anyway, Miss Murcheson. I've failed in this assignment from the start. Now look there, everyone passing also sees you staring daggers at me, and you know how fast these things travel. Before too long word will get back to your father that I'm not even an adequate suitor."

In a twinkling, her expression and posture altered, everything about her intimating a coquettish willingness to be courted. She even tapped his shoulder with her fan, and giggled.

It was all quite devastating. "Oh, Lord Smith-Grenville, you're a delightful suitor! Never doubt it for a moment!"

"Thank you." He attempted to match her demeanor, but the girl's skills were far beyond his own. Once again, he could only coast along in her wake, anxiety warring with admiration.

"Now, tell me about your brother. Do you really think he's an opium smuggler?" She flipped the fan open again and batted her eyelashes as she asked this. It was completely egregious, but Barnabas was still utterly charmed. Miss Murcheson's eyelashes were longer and thicker than he'd realized before, and the dress brought out the green in her eyes.

"Oh. That. Honestly, I don't know what to think. Phineas was a naval officer serving in Europa until a few years ago. Then he went missing, and all the evidence suggested he'd succumbed to an opium addiction."

"How horrible!"

"I never believed it. His commanding officers told us, but it seemed so out of character for Phineas. I looked for him everywhere, even in Le Havre and Paris. My friend Matthew Pence tried to enlist your father's aid in the search, in fact. But by that time all the people who'd seen him said he'd gone west to the Lord of Gold."

"That myth? I suppose it turned out to be true, though. All those poor people on that farm . . ."

Baron Orm had kept thousands of workers addicted and enslaved on his vast opium farm in the western foothills of the Sierra Nevada. More than half of them had died, unidentified, when their source of the drug had been incarcerated. Only a few had been healthy and lucid enough to come through withdrawals with their faculties somewhat intact. Of those, a mere handful were able to testify as to the conditions at the farm that Orm had called El Dorado.

Phineas hadn't been among that handful. He hadn't been

among the wretches doomed to live out their half-witted lives in sanitariums. Nor had his body been found among the legions of dead.

"My friend Mrs. Eliza Pence, who won the Sky and Steam Rally, swears she saw Phineas at the finish line ceremony. He was one of Orm's men. Not an opium slave, but a hired mercenary. A pirate."

"Oh, dear."

"She ascribed him higher motives than I can. Assumed he was there for some good reason, and that he didn't come forth to help her because he saw there was no need. But I can't be so sanguine about it. Phineas always did have a hidden side. Why would he hide it if it wasn't dark?"

Freddie sighed, toying with the edges of her fan. "He might have assumed nobody would accept it. Even if it wasn't a dark side. We all have our reasons."

Barnabas navigated a corner before responding. Their turn around the park was finished. "I can't equate your desire to thumb your nose at your father by working on shopkeepers' equipment to my brother's decision to abandon his family and commission—and evidently his clandestine job as a secret agent—to throw his lot in with a band of criminals. If he did, which I find I still have trouble believing."

To her credit, Miss Murcheson maintained the sweetly flirtatious smile she'd worn since he pointed out that people were watching them and gauging the course of their supposed relationship. "My feelings about Father have nothing to do with my work, Lord Smith-Grenville. I would do it all in the open if I could, but I do it in secret anyway because I must. Machines speak to me. I hear them, I see them, I know them and I can no more resist their call than you can resist looking for your prodigal brother. These are our passions. Even though you tell yourself you've given up on his character, you still look. And you still won't tell my father about the submersible we saw, until you're sure you won't be incriminating Phineas in the process."

She was right. He was a fool, but he wouldn't go to Murcheson. "Probably I just don't want to incriminate myself."

"That too. It occurs to me . . . I heard Father say something about 'S-G.' He seemed to be talking about an agent, someone he was disappointed with. I assumed at the time he was talking about you, but now I'm not so sure. What if Mrs. Pence was correct, and Phineas was working for the Crown when she saw him in San Francisco? Still working for my father? He'd be an S-G too."

His jaw dropped. "I *knew* it. I *knew* your father wasn't telling me everything he knew about Phineas. Good God, this could change everything!"

"Perhaps. By the way, what's wet work?"

Barnabas's gut clenched, hearing the ominous term fall from such tender lips. "Wet work? Your father said that Phineas . . . ?"

She shook her head, artistically arranged curls bobbing around her smooth shoulders. "He said that S-G was squeamish about it. Father sounded rather disappointed. It sounds like something a scullery maid would do, so I didn't quite understand. Is it a type of work you're supposed to be doing? Or something to do with working on submersibles? If not, it's still entirely possible Father meant you, you know."

"Good heavens, no. That's not in my brief. Wet work is—" He lowered his voice to a whisper. "It's killing people. I don't kill people. I'm the one who forgets he's carrying a pistol, remember?"

"Wet. Oh, I see. It's meant to be a clever euphemism for bloodletting. That's appalling. Like something schoolboys would say."

"We were all schoolboys once," Barnabas pointed out. "Well, *you* weren't, obviously. But the men who thought up these names for things were. Your father wasn't talking about me. I suppose you have only my word on that, but I was brought on to gather and relay information, not kill anyone. So he must have been talking about Phineas. How many S-Gs can there be? And why would he lie to me, after telling me as much as he already had? Perhaps it's just another cover story! What else did he say?"

"It's difficult to recall everything. I had no context for it, you understand. But something about it being impractical to replace him. And lying is second nature for Father. He might well have done it as a reflex."

Eliza had been right, Barnabas was sure of it. The more he considered it, the more he thought the opium addiction *must* be a cover. When Eliza saw Phineas he had been embedded in Orm's employ, and for whatever reason he was still under cover. Was he still pretending to work for Orm, or Orm's successor? Was he indeed in London, or were the sightings Barnabas had heard about in error? Wishful thinking on the part of some well-meaning friends? Barnabas wanted to go to Murcheson that instant, to demand the truth. But revealing what he knew would mean revealing how he'd learned it, and everything else in that chain of implication. He was trapped by ridiculous circumstance.

"I have a thought, my lord; would you like to hear it?"

"I don't suppose I have a choice."

"Again, sir, you have all sorts of choices. I'm choosing to take you into my confidence. You might find it more convenient to allow this, rather than attempting to follow me blind later this evening. But the decision is entirely yours."

He wanted to take his frustration out on something or

somebody, but there was no appropriate outlet for that here. "Fine. Out with it."

"Manners, please!"

"I do beg your pardon, Miss Murcheson. Kindly proceed to enlighten me regarding your thoughts."

She gestured toward the road, allowing him to negotiate a merger with the general traffic before speaking. "We saw something that might interest my father greatly. A submersible, possibly a smuggler, carrying secret technology only the military should possess. And you think you may know who's behind it, except that the obvious suspect is in prison on another continent. So."

"So?"

"I don't want to thumb my nose at my father per se, but I wouldn't mind seeming more valuable in his eyes. It might afford me more freedom to do what I like, if I can bring back something of use to him. Information. A name, perhaps. And you might be forgiven many transgressions if you helped deliver that name."

He fingered the reins, contemplating the notion. Cushion the inevitable blow of his failure by achieving some intervening success to trump it? The idea was probably insane. Miss Murcheson was probably insane. But really, at this point Barnabas had little left to lose.

"I find your thought not entirely without merit."

"Excellent. Do you know, my lord, I think I'm beginning to enjoy our courtship."

Despite himself, despite everything, he smiled. "I do what I can, Miss Murcheson. I do what I can."

ANOTHER BOAT HAD been lost in the night, and half a dozen men along with it. They'd been at the signal buoy again, edging on no-man's-land at the estuary mouth, and the rumor on the docks confirmed Rollo's worst fears. Mrs. Hill, God rest her soul, had been telling the truth. A late-returning trawler had spotted the monster pulling the boat down, glowing tentacles as long as the masthead Robson was tall, and now every ship in the port was buzzing with talk of the giant killer squid. Some were even trying to link the squid to the earthquake, heaping nightmare upon nightmare.

Rollo had slept through the quake, so he wasn't sure he believed in it. Even the deaths didn't make it real to him. They weren't his men, and buildings collapsed all the time. But he believed in some creature with unholy tentacles and a vicious temper when it came to flashing lights. That was the key, he'd decided. The underwater lamps they'd been testing to signal to the submersibles must have attracted the hellish squid, and it had lashed out at the nearest moving object. Tom Hill had escaped the beast—although he hadn't escaped Edwin, who found him in an opium den a few days later and dispatched him with a minimum of fuss—but the larger boat hadn't. The squid was escalating its hostilities.

"Or it were a different one," his pet cartologist Robson suggested, as they breakfasted on buns and studied a map of the channel. "Bigger and meaner. Maybe Tom's squid 'as a vengeful mother. A kraken, like."

Maybe so. Robson had spent years serving on merchant ships before coming to work for Rollo, and he'd seen many strange things in his travels. He'd never seen a kraken, though, he'd had to admit.

Rollo stared at the pattern of pins on the map and absently fingered the enameled gold poppy on his lapel. His new talisman, all the way from the California Dominion, courtesy of a lad who had worked for the Lord of Gold himself but managed to escape the authorities' sweep of Orm's employees. An airship pilot, or so he claimed, who also knew his way around a submersible. A useful type, this lad Finn. Young, to know all he did, and suspiciously posh in accent and manner. He reminded Rollo of himself at that age, and Rollo suspected they shared a certain type of history—the history of grasping bastard brothers who hadn't quite come to terms with the limitations of birth on the wrong side of the aristocratic blanket. But he'd have been wrong to accept those limitations himself, so perhaps this Finn was too. After all, who ran things now that Baron Orm was moldering in jail? Belowstairs maid Alice Furneval's boy, not the son of the late dowager baroness. Rollo, the lad who'd been lucky to receive acknowledgment from his sire, and grudging time with his half brother's tutor.

His brother had always shown an interest in botany and horticulture, and he'd adopted the poppy as his motif even as a young man. Finn could have brought no surer proof that he came from Orm's employ. The boy reported that before his arrest, the Lord of Gold had a different golden poppy ornament for every day of the week, each with its hidden cache of snuff and its even more cleverly hidden blade. This particular one had been for Tuesdays, apparently. But Rollo had worn it every day since acquiring it from Finn two months prior. It was a source of strength, a symbol of his ascendancy.

The map in front of him had changed dramatically over the course of those same two months, donning an array of color-coded pins and lines that stood for all sorts of hard-won knowledge. The givens, such as the boundaries of the military's blockade and the position of various ports within and without that zone, were marked in white. But now there were green flags standing for the "safe" routes the military allowed approved traders like the British East India Company, and a network of blue to indicate the various regular submersible patrols they'd ferreted out with the help of the new hydrophone array. Orange flags with times penned on, showing the windows of opportunity for travel to avoid those patrols.

This afternoon, however, Robson was focused on the red pins, and Rollo nodded as the man added a new point of interest. "Our lad Billy Walthrop confirmed it this morning. The Navy's seismograph failed 'em again. His cousin in Le Havre sent him a message with reports from three different clients. All officers. The alarm in Atlantis Station didn't trip until the quake had already started. They had to shuffle the crew out on subs, no time for the tunnel. Which means none of the sensors to the west of the base are functioning anymore."

"Or so we surmise," Rollo countered. "We're basing our deductions on the word of an expatriate whore with a side business in illicitly gotten opium, after all."

"Aye. But Billy says she's a good girl, for all that."

"I've told you before, we need a new source. I don't like relying on a whore; they're not dependable. My mother was a whore, after all, and she sold me to my father when I was still in swaddling clothes. I know whereof I speak."

Robson frowned at him. "I thought she were a scullery maid?"

Grinding his teeth, Rollo pointed toward the newest red pin. "Flashing lights, Robson. We've been assuming for months that the Royal Navy's fancy geological equipment has suffered sabotage from one of our competitors. Or from the French. But their seismic sensors use some sort of flashing light signal, correct? I think I know who their saboteur is."

"Oh, aye?"

"Aye, as you say. Aye indeed. The squid, Robson."

After a moment of incomprehension, the light dawned

on Robson's broad face. "It's going for the lights! It's probably yanked them all clean out o' the bedrock."

"They've been doing all that good work, and we've certainly reaped the benefit. Sooner or later the Navy will have to abandon the station or risk being flooded if a big enough quake occurs and they've no advance warning. No station means more difficulty refueling and deploying their damn submersibles. They'll have to rethink their entire blockade strategy."

"Beggin' your pardon, sir, you don't seem best pleased about it."

Rollo flicked at one gilded petal of the lapel poppy, triggering a minute tray to slide out with a handy pinch of snuff. "I would be, if the damn sea monster hadn't taken two of my own boats by now. I can't risk the creature going for any of my submersibles, can I?" He took the snuff with a slightly indelicate snort. "They'd flood the whole channel with opium, for one thing. I've two large shipments ready to send, and a batch of the new Afghani product to receive next week. Enough to worry about with the Navy and the British East India Company's investigators looking out for the stuff. I don't need to add dangerous boat-eating squid into the equation. If I have to choose between the sabotage continuing and my shipments continuing, I choose the shipments."

"What, then, sir?"

Tensing his upper lip against the urge to sneeze, Rollo gestured toward the array of red pins that fanned out on the map over the western inlet to the channel. "The hydrophonic array has proven successful against the military's submersibles. It has let us avoid our hunters. Now it's time we put it to use on other prey."

EIGHT

❧

TWO DAYS HAD passed since their very proper-seeming turn through the park. Freddie didn't like to admit she'd enjoyed the time spent with Barnabas, especially given the circumstances driving them together. But she had no trouble acknowledging her amusement now, in this new setting she'd dragged him to. Her own adopted turf, where she was comfortable but poor Smith-Grenville was decidedly not.

"Don't know about the new lad," Mr. Armintrout whispered as she tightened the final nuts on his steam dog and prepared to fire it up. "Seems a bit at sea. Old to be starting at this too."

She bit back a smile and cut her eyes toward Barnabas, who was attempting a casual crouch on the other side of the dog's wheel enclosure. Even in coarse-woven trousers and a miserably patched jacket, hunkered over a pile of machinery with a grease smear on his cheek, Smith-Grenville managed to look like he belonged in a drawing room. Or any place populated by gentle folk, which definitely didn't include butchers, fish-mongers, or the like. His posture alone gave him away as a product of public schools, she thought. But to anyone who didn't know, he just seemed supremely uncomfortable.

"Just nervous, I expect. He'll learn. How's business been, Mr. A?"

"Can't complain. No thanks to you. You're a hard man to get hold of, Fred Merchant."

"I wouldn't want to make it too easy for my adoring public to find me. All right, would you care to do the honors?" She pointed to the flint trigger on the coal hopper.

Armintrout gave the lever a practiced jerk, raining sparks down on the coal and kindling until the wood caught fire. Within a few minutes, the water in the dog's belly was heating nicely and it began its endless journey on the spit wheel.

Scattered applause filtered into the shop from the crowd assembled outside the window. Small boys and layabouts, mostly, who'd strolled by and stayed to see the steam dog go back into action because they had no place else to be. Freddie spotted a few familiar faces as well, potentially useful faces. Armintrout's shop was close enough to the docklands, and his clientele was rough enough, that he knew all sorts of people and facts. Getting him to discuss them was another matter, of course.

"'Ow much, then?" he demanded when she straightened to admire the restored dog's smooth action. "Mind you, I had to wait those two days more with no word."

"I came back," Freddie reminded him. She slotted her equipment neatly back into her broad tool belt. "It's working now, better than ever. Drawing a pretty crowd too."

"Aye. I suppose. What cost to me, though?"

Deflecting his enquiry, she scanned the faces beyond the window. The onlookers were beginning to disperse, only a few of the younger boys remaining with their faces pressed to the glass to watch the spectacle and slaver over the slowly roasting haunch on the spit. "You strike me as a man of knowledge and discretion, Mr. Armintrout."

The butcher wiped his hands on his bloody apron, cocking his head at her. "I might be."

"For the right price?"

Armintrout glanced from Freddie to Barnabas, then out the window. "Not here." He stalked off to the shop's back door, jerking his head for her to follow. "And not him. Just you."

"No problem at all. Barney will just tidy up while we talk. Won't you, Barney?"

She smirked at Smith-Grenville's glare and followed the portly butcher into the back room of the shop, where the floor was stained red and the stench greeted her like a malevolent entity. "I need something other than meat, as you may have surmised." She might well never eat meat again, in fact, after encountering it in this state. In the shop's front half, neatly trussed clean carcasses hung in tidy rows for display. Here, where the meat was not yet dressed, the less palatable part of the business was all too clearly visible.

"Surmised?" The big man lifted his eyebrows. "'Ow you do talk, Fred. Should I *surmise* you want a good or a service?"

The partially butchered carcass of a pig occupied a bloodstained table in the center of the room, an invitation to flies from miles around. The smell turned Fred's stomach, and she regretted letting Armintrout dictate the location of their discussion. Too late to turn away now, though. The butcher had been in trade here for nearly forty years, and if anyone was selling anything near the docks he knew about it.

"A good. A very bad good, and it isn't for me, I assure you."

"For a friend. I see."

"A friend of a friend. I don't want to buy, I just want to know who's selling."

"You still 'aven't told me what." Although they were alone in the room, he'd dropped his voice.

Fred did him one better and mouthed the word so there would be no risk of eavesdropping. "Opium. Not in a den. The actual supplier."

"No," he said too quickly. "No, I don't know nothing about that."

"Emblem of a golden poppy."

"I most definitely don't know about *him*. You don't want to either, Fred. Not if you value that neck o' yours." Armintrout moved to a workbench in one corner of the gory meat parlor and began sharpening a cleaver, working the grindstone's pedal with his foot. Not as a threat, Freddie gathered, but simply for something to do because he was anxious. She'd struck a nerve.

"I could disassemble the dog. Or worse yet, leave it like I found it."

"Aye, you could do that. Shop did well enough before it, it'll do well enough without, I expect."

Armintrout's apprentice, a boy half Freddie's size and probably less than half her age, scurried into the room and stopped upon seeing his employer in deep discussion with the tinker. The butcher nodded toward a side of beef hanging on a hook, and the lad retrieved it and staggered away with it to leave them alone again. The meat had appeared to outweigh the apprentice, and Freddie had no idea how the youngster managed. But he was one of the lucky ones, she knew, with the prospect of gainful future employment and a roof over his head. How many fishmongers' apprentices and children were starving on the street today because her father had inadvertently robbed them of their livelihood? How many might be killed if there was a terrible earthquake and the person who might have warned them failed to do so?

"Or I could maintain the device free of charge for the rest of its useful life. That must be worth something."

He turned, lifted the cleaver and brought it down with a crack on a handy gobbet of what appeared to be organ meat, testing the edge. The blade sank into the scarred wood of the table, embedding bits of gore even deeper in the surface. "If you ain't buying, why do you need to know?"

"I told you. For a friend of a friend. Somebody who may be in trouble." It wasn't exactly a lie. If Phineas Smith-Grenville was involved with the illegal opium trade, whether as a spy or not, he was potentially in a great deal of trouble. And Lord Smith-Grenville might not be quite a friend, but explaining the actual relationship even to herself seemed impossible.

Armintrout sighed over his knife and bits of meat, his wide shoulders slumping. "Free service on anything in the shop that breaks and you know how to fix."

"Fine. Give me something. A name, a location."

"I will. But know who you're dealing with, Fred. My cousin Tom turned up missing a week or so ago. They found him in an opium den, strangled. His wife had gone looking for him and she never came back. Not all of her, at least. Neighbor heard some cats fighting in the 'ouse, had a look and found the lady's head sitting on the kitchen table. No body. Just the head. Cats were having their supper."

Freddie suffered a wave of nausea that had nothing to do with the gruesome setting. "How is that relevant to my question?"

"*Relevant.* Another one o' them words, Fred. With those words, and those questions, I wonder 'oo you are sometimes, I really do."

"I'm nobody."

"You sound too much like somebody. All right, my cousin, he called himself a fisherman. He worked on boats, but he weren't no fisherman. Worked for this fellow Rollo Furneval." He rattled off a street direction to one of the most distant and least savory docks outside London, far down the estuary, nearly to the channel itself. "It's on a deep-water dock, fronts on the free zone where the big ships come through, so I sometimes go there to pick up specialty items. On ice from Europa, costs the earth, so I haven't had cause to go lately 'cause nobody can afford to buy that stuff now. It's always half empty down there these days. But I doubt anything's changed much aside from that. You won't miss the warehouses. All behind a fence, and the biggest has a giant yellow flower painted on the side, with extra gold leaf 'round the edges to make it stand out. But that place is guarded like the crown jewels were in it. Nobody gets in. Not even cargo ships. Only occasional steam cars."

"But it's a warehouse," Freddie protested. "There must be goods going back and forth."

Armintrout shrugged. "Said too much already. Get your nobody apprentice and go, Fred. I'll get word to you through Dan Pinkerton the next time I need you. Don't ask for me otherwise."

BARNABAS HATED THE surroundings but found the risk entirely acceptable for the reward of getting to follow around Freddie Murcheson while she was wearing trousers. Although her tinker's costume was designed to obscure her female figure, not flatter it, most of the obfuscation was accomplished by extra padding in the front, under the waistcoat. She hadn't thought to mask the rear view. He knew he should be shocked at himself for looking in the first place, much less appreciating what he saw, but his character was evidently lacking.

"You might want to look in the back and make sure I've put all the tools away properly," he suggested quite shamelessly once Freddie had joined him on the seat of the idling pony trap. As he'd known she would, she twisted and leaned over the seat, giving him an excellent perspective on the curve of her hip and buttock as her jacket rode up.

"It all looks fine," she confirmed. "You're a terrible apprentice, however."

"I'm too old to be an apprentice," he reminded her. It had been his primary objection to the day's cover story to begin with. It had allowed them to venture forth without waiting for Dan Pinkerton to be off duty, however, so he'd donned the costume and done his best. "And you're no master. What did you learn from the butcher?"

Barnabas had been all in favor of heading straight to an opium den and questioning whoever seemed in charge. He didn't know much, but he knew that Murcheson had lied to him and he must now reevaluate all he had heard and discover the facts for himself. At the very least, if the part about the opium had been true in any way, he might be able to find out if Phineas had frequented any of the local dens. Or he might rule it out.

Freddie had been the one to point out that they didn't care about the opium dens or what happened along the chain of suppliers. Finding the operation that bore Orm's logo was still the best lead to Phineas, as well as to the saboteurs. What they needed to learn was where a smuggling operation with cargos requiring large submersibles might be headquartered. And they didn't want to tip their hand while finding this out.

All that might be true, but Barnabas wasn't sure he trusted the butcher any more than he trusted some random drug trafficker.

"A name. Rollo Furneval. And a possible location."

"You sound dubious." He didn't think it seemed right, Freddie being the anxious one.

Freddie eased the cart into motion. "It sounds as though the location might not help us much. Armintrout said it's a warehouse but it doesn't seem to be used as a staging area for cargo. Which makes one wonder what it *is* used for, but as we're specifically looking for evidence to tie this man Furneval to either the illegal opium trade or the submersible sensor array or both, it doesn't sound like the warehouse will help us much."

"Are you driving back into Belgravia? Dressed like this?"

She chuckled. "Of course. We're paying a visit to my friend Lady Sophronia in Wilton Crescent. She helps me get tidied up when I've someplace to be in the evenings and I've spent my days gathering grease."

"Lady Sophronia? Not Sophronia Wallingford?" The name flew out of his past with the force of a body blow from a cricket bat. He hadn't heard it in three years.

"Yes. You know her?"

Did he know her? Not half as well as he'd once thought. Depending on whom one asked, Sophie Howard Wallingford was a martyr or a gold digger, a devoted wife or a heartless deceiver. And apparently a friend in need to Fred Merchant when he wanted to transform back into Frédérique Murcheson in time to appear properly groomed for the soiree her father was throwing that evening. Assuming, of course, that Rutherford Murcheson returned from his undersea journey in time to host his own party. As of that morning, he'd still been mysteriously absent from the house.

"Phineas knows her. Knew her. Before she married Wallingford."

His tone must have given something away, because she pursed her lips in obvious disapproval. Of him, of Sophie, of Phineas, he couldn't be sure.

"I see. Did Phineas have any money?"

"Well, I suppose one must give Lady Sophie credit for being honest about her motivations, if her friend knows that's the important question to ask. No, of course he hadn't any money. Not to speak of. Nothing like Wallingford has, naturally."

She shot a frown his way. "Nothing like Wallingford *had*, you mean."

Barnabas wanted to crow a bit, but something in Freddie's eyes stayed him. "He lost his money? A tragedy, to be sure."

"Lost it? I suppose you could say so. He left it all to Sophie. Alas, he has no use for it where he is now."

"What, dead?"

"Yes. Over a year ago, just after their second anniversary. The time's flown. I asked whether Phineas had money because if he hadn't, I wondered at his being allowed to know Sophie at all back then, if he was just a young naval officer with nothing much else to recommend him. Her parents controlled her every move until she married Wallingford, kept her locked up until it was time to parade her in front of eligible bachelors. Wallingford essentially bought her freedom for her. He was the only one who could meet their price. Their debts were quite heavy."

"I suppose that's one perspective." She'd let herself be bought, if Phineas had the right of it. Actively marketed herself to the highest bidder. "She never seemed particularly unhappy with her circumstances."

The glare Freddie leveled at him could have razed buildings. "Of course she didn't *seem* so. What good would that have done her? I take it your brother was a would-be suitor. Consider that his view of things may have been skewed."

About that, Miss Murcheson was absolutely correct. Phineas hadn't been a mere would-be suitor, he had been deeply in love with Lady Sophie Howard. Whatever the facts, Phineas had taken her rejection three years earlier all too much to heart. He'd turned to the oblivious solace of opium to forget and disappeared shortly thereafter. Or perhaps not; perhaps that was only what he'd let people think as part of his cover story. What Murcheson had told people so they'd be less likely to come looking for him. Barnabas didn't know what to believe anymore.

"Your parents have you on the marriage mart, at least ostensibly, and yet you seem to have managed a good deal of freedom." He gestured at her costume, at the steam pony before them and the street beyond.

"My parents don't keep me locked up. Did you think I was speaking figuratively about Sophie? I wasn't. There were literal locks involved. I was the one who taught her how to pick them."

"But how . . . that's ridiculous. That's something from a novel. Things like that don't happen anymore."

Now her look wasn't so much angry as disgusted, and far too weary for such a young woman. "If you believe that, you're a fool, my lord. A fool who's very lucky to have been born a man. And firstborn son to a peer, at that. You know nothing of how the world works for the rest of us. Just as I've no real idea how bad things are for these poor people my father seems bent on putting out of work. All I can do is imagine, and be grateful I don't have to know firsthand."

He pondered that all the way into Belgravia, where the late-afternoon traffic dwindled to a polite minimum. He didn't like the lingering, angry tightness around the corners of Miss

Murcheson's lush mouth. Nor did he care for the silence, which was all the louder because she was usually so voluble.

The grooms at Wallingford House were clearly familiar with Freddie. Scarcely had she brought the trap to a halt before two strapping lads whisked it away into a stall, flinging an oilcloth over it. Another stood ready with a brush, to knock any tinkering-related debris from Freddie and Barnabas's coats and shoes before they proceeded into the house proper. Brisk, efficient, respectful . . . and apparently paid to be blind and deaf about their lady's unorthodox visitor.

Freddie—it was growing difficult to think of her as Miss Murcheson, after calling her Fred all day—led the way up the back stairs to a broad corridor, and thence to a daintily appointed salon that appeared washed in every shade of pale green. It was as though they'd stepped into a fresh spring morning.

Its only denizen, however, wore a somber gray afternoon dress and a frown.

"Freddie, darling, you're late. I was beginning to worry. And who have you brought with you—*oh*."

"Lady Sophronia." Barnabas bowed curtly, never taking his eyes off the woman. She hadn't changed, other than the exchange of a girlish frock and curls for postmourning attire and a simple chignon. "A pleasure to see you again."

Upon her seeing an unexpected face, her visage had cleared into a smooth mask of beautiful affability, an illusion as practiced as any parlor trick. "Lord Smith-Grenville. I'll assume you meant that ironically. Freddie, what is going on?"

Freddie was still frowning, a state of affairs that Barnabas found he categorically disliked. He wanted her to be smiling always.

"Lord Smith-Grenville came to London looking for his brother. Just now he told me that you knew Phineas

Smith-Grenville as well. I believe there are misconceptions to be aired between you."

Sophie Wallingford would be an excellent poker player, Barnabas decided, if she ever chose to do such a thing. Far better than he. Her expression never altered, her clear brown eyes and heart-shaped face remained as gently welcoming as anyone might wish for. "We're cutting things a bit fine, so we'll have to air them succinctly. But all right, if you must."

He didn't know that he must do anything. "Another time, perhaps?"

"Now will suffice. No time like the present, my lord. Freddie, do hurry up to my rooms. Angelica is preparing a bath for you. And none too soon, I might add. You're even a bit more pungent than usual."

"We were at a butcher's. I'll go up. Lord Smith-Grenville, I'll speak with you this evening. I have an idea."

"Oh, dear," he blurted before he could stop himself.

She smiled, a flash of sunlight on an inexplicably dark day. No matter what, it was better than the frown. "Don't worry. We won't even need to leave my house to implement it."

Biting back another *Oh, dear*, Barnabas nodded and watched her out the door before turning to Sophie. The agent, perhaps, of his brother's destruction.

"You look well," she offered.

"As do you." She always had, he recalled. Always beautiful, always composed. Serene to a fault. Phineas had said once that loving Sophie felt like a moth loving a warmly lit window. Burning himself on the flame would have been almost a relief, if only he could have gotten close enough. Barnabas preferred his beauty less chilly, more accessible. If he were going to immolate himself, he'd rather get straight to it. Freddie was a merry bonfire of a girl.

"If you come seeking news, I'm afraid I can't help you.

I haven't seen or heard from your brother since . . . well, it's been three years. I'd heard he resigned his commission and returned home to the Dominions."

"Was thrown out under a cloud of opium smoke, you mean. Don't pretend you hadn't heard the rumors. He did return to the Dominions, apparently, but not home. He was in California, I believe, at least until recently. But one of my brother's former colleagues here swears he spotted Phineas back in London a few months ago on the West India docks. Father was skeptical, but it's all I have to go by."

"Your father is no longer bankrolling your search efforts? Is this why you're Freddie's latest shadow, or is there some other connection between you and Murcheson?"

In for a penny, in for a pound. "I'm the latest in what I gather is a long line of shadows. I can't tell if she thinks I'm the worst or the best one yet."

The placid Madonna before him smiled, a hint of wickedness showing around her eyes. "You're certainly more honest than the others. And she never invited any of them along on her adventures as Fred the tinker. She always had to dodge them to get out and work. Freddie tells me your relationship is one of mutual extortion."

"More or less. Sometimes," he confessed, "I wonder if I'm not still back in the Dominions, delirious with fever from influenza, and simply hallucinating this entire episode in my life." If it was a hallucination, would he consider it a good or bad one? Hard to say.

Sophie's smile faded. "You're not the only one to wonder that. It's time you returned to the Murchesons' house to prepare for the evening's entertainment, Lord Smith-Grenville."

He wasn't quite ready to leave, however. "Do you have any insight for me as to why Phineas might have gone into such a sudden decline, Lady Sophronia?"

"Are you asking me if he suffered from unrequited love, my lord?"

Barnabas was stunned at her being so blunt, but he decided he could follow her lead, especially as he knew the answer already. "Yes."

She inhaled, the tiniest whisper of breath, then sighed equally quietly before answering. "I was never anything but truthful with your brother, sir. He would have pursued me. I was not in a position to accept his suit, and I told him so. We . . . didn't part happily, when last we saw one another."

Subtle as she was, he could see it all there on her face, now that he knew what he was looking at. The same pain he'd seen in Phineas's eyes. The years had eased it, perhaps, but not eliminated it. That pain and her words implied more than a passing relationship between this lady and his brother, but he'd already asked and she had told more than propriety allowed. He wouldn't press for the salacious details.

"I see."

"Will there be anything else?" She was already moving toward the bellpull, summoning somebody to see him out.

What else could there be? "No. I've taken enough of your time, my lady. Thank you for speaking with me. I'm aware it was a topic of some sensitivity."

"I wish I could have eased your mind."

"I wish you could have eased his," he countered before he could censor himself.

She laughed, but the sound was more pain than joy. "Oh, I wish that too. So much."

"I apologize, I didn't mean to—"

"That's not necessary." The door opened to admit a footman, and Sophie schooled her face back to its customary pleasant blankness. "Jacob will see you out now, Lord Smith-Grenville."

Nine

❧❧❧

FREDDIE'S GOWN WAS a buttery-pale yellow silk with white lace trim, and she hated it. Her mother had insisted on including it in her wardrobe, claiming that it helped Freddie appear mild and innocent, and that she might one day find it useful to give off such an impression. The lace itched where it edged her décolletage and under her arms. The bodice was designed to conceal, rather than exploit, her bosom. All in all it was an insipid ensemble, for all it was beautifully made. She wondered, as she always did, whether it might not be improved or done away with by timely "accidental" exposure to a measure of ratafia.

It was a strategy worth considering. Spilling a drink on herself might also excuse her absence from the "entertainment" portion of the evening, a musical interlude featuring a popular soprano and her accompanist. Although Freddie's mother remained in France this Season, her renowned exotic Continental tastes still dictated the Murcheson household's social mores. Father was always inviting singers of border-line dubious repute, violinists and the like, world-famous chess players, and an assortment of other examples of untrammeled culture. A visiting poet had once composed an ode—ex tempore, or so he claimed—to Freddie's hair. She gave him full marks for effort, but had deducted points for egregious overuse of the word *titian*. Which did not, as she'd felt compelled to point out, rhyme with *frisson*. He'd never been back.

Tonight's soprano was giving her a headache. And to her surprise, she found she missed the company of Lord Smith-Grenville. She'd thought up one or two pointed remarks about the performance she thought he might appreciate. He was seated all the way across the salon and at the back, however, and might as well be miles away.

She'd seen him in rumpled, rough clothing all afternoon, things he'd borrowed from Dan. They hung on him loosely, adding to his disheveled appearance. Tonight, he was back in his own exceedingly well-cut, proper clothing and sport-ing a fresh shave. Upon greeting him earlier she had discov-ered that he smelled very nice as well. Freddie wasn't sure which version she liked better, but properly clad Smith-Grenville looked more comfortable in his skin than poor Barney the aging apprentice.

The soprano trilled out something Italian and lyrical, and Freddie risked a glance over her shoulder. Smith-Grenville was no longer in his chair. He was standing behind the rows of seats, in the small crowd of duly appreciative-looking gentlemen near the back of the room. A few more steps and he'd be next to the door. He'd evidently decided to take a slow, subtle approach to leaving the room without arousing suspicion.

Seated up front as she was, Freddie had no hope of slipping

out unnoticed during the performance. But during the performance was her only chance to sneak into her father's study unobserved. As host, Murcheson would be compelled to stay for the duration. She could sneak in through the priest's hole, have a good look around, and be out before anyone was the wiser. Though it would be safer still if somebody—Smith-Grenville, for example—could stand lookout for her.

She'd finished the small crystal cup of ratafia in her hand without realizing it. There was nothing left to spill.

Damn.

What would her mother do in a situation like this? Mignonette Murcheson always seemed to get away with whatever she liked, socially. Freddie had spent most of her life wishing she'd inherited even a fraction of her mother's skill at navigating the web of relationships and rules that governed their lives. She would have been able, no doubt, to come up with a reason to leave discreetly that was compelling, but not so compelling as to rouse anyone's suspicion.

Lady DeVere's cologne wafted over her, rosy and redolent, tickling her nose and adding to the soprano-induced headache. Freddie groaned inwardly as she felt a sneeze coming on.

A sneeze! Of course!

She didn't do anything so vulgar as actually *a-choo*. A delicate almost-touch of her gloved finger to her upper lip. A not-quite-sniffle, and a less than ladylike fumbling for a handkerchief. None to be found, how unfortunate. Then a slightly louder sniff, drawing the attention of Lady DeVere.

Smiling apologetically, Freddie breathed deeply of the cologne and let the sneeze have its way with her until it finally broke forth, stifled but painfully obvious nonetheless. Her father leaned forward from his front-and-center seat and shot her a glare. Trying to look suitably mortified, she departed the room in a flurry of yellow silk, under the disgruntled eye of the soprano. She hoped Barnabas correctly interpreted the subtle wink she threw him on the way out the door, but as she was trying to muffle another sneeze at the moment he might have mistaken her gesture for an involuntary one.

The hall was blissfully free of guests, and only the pair of upstairs maids were in evidence when Freddie ventured from the room.

"Janet, have you a handkerchief?"

"Of course, miss." The older of the two young women produced a tidy, starched square of linen, dropping a pretty curtsy as she presented it. "Will there be anything else? If you're feeling ill I could fetch Mrs. Hudson."

The housekeeper was the last person Freddie cared to see. "No, thank you. Lady DeVere's scent just gave me the sniffles, I'm afraid. I'll listen from out here for a bit."

"Yes, miss."

The two disappeared silently, leaving Freddie alone. They'd been listening at the door, obviously, and she felt bad to spoil their treat. She might not enjoy the music herself, but she didn't begrudge anyone else's pleasure from it. Still, better to have them gone. She plied the handkerchief, waiting a few moments to be sure the coast was clear before slipping down the hall to the front parlor. It was lit only by the few remaining embers in the fireplace, and she fumbled at the paneling before finding the catch and easing herself into the priest's hole.

Only afterward did it occur to her she might have just as well used the study door. That was apparently what Smith-Grenville had done while Freddie was working her way along the dimly lit parlor wall. She spied him by her father's desk when she cracked the study wall panel open, and had to keep herself from giggling at the notion of tiptoeing up behind and surprising him. It would have been too easy. In fact she could scarcely avoid it.

"Lord Smith-Grenville," she whispered. He jumped and spun to face her, which was most gratifying.

"What the—what are you—how? Good *Lord*, Fred, don't sneak up on a fellow like that!"

She should have corrected him for calling her Fred, but she was too busy trying not to giggle at his startled reaction to bother. "You should have seen your face!"

"I thought the jig was up." He straightened his cravat and tried to look dignified again.

"I believe it's an aria, and no, she's still singing it." The sound was muffled, but still audible, even this far away and through two closed doors.

"Oh, very droll. Yes, the noise should provide us ample cover, at least." He returned to his examination of the papers on Mr. Murcheson's desk.

"How did you know I would be here?"

"I didn't. But you mentioned earlier you had a plan that didn't involve leaving the house. When I came out of the salon to inquire after your health, or pitch my woo, or whatever it is a real suitor would likely do in such a case, you weren't there. I considered what I knew of you and this seemed the most likely place to look. Now tell me what exactly we're looking *for*, so we can find it and get back before we're noticed."

He'd said *we*. Freddie smiled, inordinately pleased at the unexpected sense of camaraderie. "I can't say exactly, but anything related to an undersea station would be a good start. Plans, or some sort of correspondence. Our window of opportunity to search is as least as long as that woman continues singing."

She moved to the large portrait of her mother, commissioned by Murcheson shortly after their marriage. It always hung on his study wall in his primary residence and had been the first item unpacked when they moved back to London to marry Freddie off. A swag of dark green velvet arched over it, with ornately beaded tassels hanging down on either side.

"It's a good likeness," Barnabas commented. "A bit impersonal, perhaps. I prefer you smiling."

"Not of me," she corrected him. "My mother. I'm told I look just like her, but personally I've never seen it. Oh, where is that catch—ah!" With a push on the concealed latch, the counterweighted tassels dropped slowly to the mantel as the painting rolled up the wall with a faint rattling of chains and gears. A small wall safe was revealed. By the time Freddie was halfway through the combination, Barnabas had abandoned his halfhearted search of the desk and was standing behind her.

"How do you know the combination?"

"I had it from the chap who installed the safe. I was seven or so, and the fool had it written on a scrap of paper. He knew I was watching him, but he must have assumed I was too young to know its importance."

"I can't believe he left something like that lying about."

"He didn't," Freddie confessed. "I nicked it from his coat pocket. I was a very naughty little girl. Here we are."

She turned the lever, opened the safe, and stared at the contents for several moments memorizing where everything was. Collecting herself too and trying not to crow at the fact that the combination had actually worked. She'd never dared try it before.

"Are we waiting for something good or bad to happen, here?" Barnabas asked over her shoulder.

Freddie turned, startled to find his face only inches from hers. She could feel his breath against her cheek, her lips, a ghost of warmth and a hint of the flavor his mouth might have if she leaned forward and kissed him.

Not that she would do such a thing. Of course not, it would be ridiculous. Absurd. Preposterous.

Even if she *had* dreamed about him the night before. Which she wasn't entirely convinced she had, because she couldn't quite make out the face in her dream. It had been dark. But the rest of him had seemed achingly familiar. In the dream they had been on more than friendly terms.

He was staring at her expectantly.

"Um. Sorry?"

"The safe," he reminded her. "Are we going to see what's inside?"

"Oh. Of course. I wanted to make sure I knew what it looked like first, so I could put everything back just as it was."

There wasn't much. A canvas pouch containing a thick stack of notes in varying denominations, and a handful of sovereigns. A velvet box that held a diamond necklace and some other fine pieces that had belonged to Freddie's grandmother—her mother had feuded with her late mother-in-law, so had never worn her jewelry. A few loose documents related to her father's personal finances and the household. And a slim leather portfolio, which Freddie opened to find—

"Pay dirt," Barnabas whispered near her ear. "Can we go now?"

"What's pay dirt?"

"It's what miners say when they've struck a vein of something good."

"Oh. We can't go now. We can't take anything with us, we have to look at it here."

On top of the stack of papers lay a diagram, a carefully inked depiction on foolscap of what appeared to be a submersible. Someone had penciled in a sketch of "whiskers" on the vessel's nose, clearly an array of hydrophonic sensors like the ones Freddie and Barnabas had seen on the smuggler's sub. The drawing's scale, though, suggested that this was quite a small submersible. A mere dozen or so sensor stalks were sketched in, as opposed to the multitude on the larger vessel.

"No wonder he wanted a larger trial vehicle," she murmured, running a finger along the bracket that indicated the submersible's length. "This is nothing compared to the one we saw. Oh look, the name's on the side. The *Gilded Lily*. That makes sense. It does resemble a lily flower before it's fully opened up, I suppose."

The tiny sub was roughly bullet-shaped in front, but the flared tail evoked petals, and the propellers could probably be taken for stamens if viewed from a certain angle. Extending the analogy, the tendril-like sensors on its nose resembled roots. The name was apt enough. And if she recalled her father's words correctly, the sub's sensor array was operational, if underscaled. What a shame he apparently planned to scrap it.

"We need to hurry," Barnabas reminded her.

She ignored him and rifled through the other papers in the stack, spending some time studying a diagram of what appeared to be the sub's main control panel. There were several submersible schematics, and a hasty sketch of what looked like the tunnel entrance they'd seen, but a frustrating lack of correspondence or other useful text. "It would be so much more convenient if there were a neatly labeled file. 'Top Secret Plans,' or something like that. 'Steps to Take When Spying on the French or Smugglers, with Helpful Appendices.'"

"I think I hear somebody coming."

"Nonsense. The soprano is still at it."

She heard the voices in the hall just as Barnabas insisted, "I definitely hear somebody coming."

BARNABAS ADMIRED FREDDIE'S quick thinking. He'd forgotten all about the hidden cupboard behind the paneling, but once she'd shoved the portfolio back into the safe, closed it, and hit the switch to lower the painting back into place, she whisked him into the cupboard and had the wall sealed behind them within seconds. The space was far too small for two people, particularly when one of them was wearing a voluminous dress. And it seemed like the type of place that would have numerous spiders lurking in it. It was too dark to see anything, but he could feel Freddie's body brushing against his, the tip of her shoulder pressing into his arm, the springy push of her skirt against his legs. She seemed to be standing at an odd angle, and after a moment he realized she had her ear pressed to the wall. When he followed suit, he was close enough to hear her breathing. Her scent wafted up to him, the clean, delicate aroma of some flower he couldn't identify.

It was hard to believe this sweet-smelling creature in the darkness had, mere hours before, been arm-deep in the oily innards of a mechanical spit dog. Or, moments ago, broken into a safe to peruse documents that were almost certainly state secrets.

He should be turning her in to her father. Instead he wanted nothing more than to tag along and see what fantastic scheme she'd concoct and enact next. She was better than a penny dreadful. And something in the sound of her silk and lace skirt rustling in the darkness aroused him.

This attitude on his part was, he realized, hardly conducive to a continued career in the service of the Crown. Not that he was sure he wanted one, anyway, given how horribly things were going with Murcheson. He wasn't sure he could live in a world of constant lies.

In the study, multiple male voices were raised in discussion of racing, with somebody in favor of one popular horse to win an upcoming event, and a vocal opposition speaking the praises of another. Somebody's groom had dropped hints of a temperamental knee and a secretive visit from the animal surgeon, apparently. Another's rider had assured him these rumors were balderdash, deliberately spread to throw off the odds. The clink of glassware suggested that the talk was a thin excuse for escaping the soprano and partaking of liquid refreshment.

Freddie brushed closer still, tipping her head up to whisper in his ear. "None of them sound like Father. If we both try to leave through the parlor door we might get caught. Probably safer to stay put and hope they decamp soon so we can leave as we came in."

He inclined his head to return the whisper. "This is all a world of madness, but as you're clearly mad too I suppose you're in your element. I'll defer to your lunatic judgment."

"Don't pretend you're not enjoying yourself."

He was enjoying himself rather too much. She was so very close, and it was such a small space.

"You're a very exciting girl, Miss Murcheson."

A soft puff of air crossed his cheek and ear, perhaps a laugh. It set every inch of his neck tingling.

"Men usually say things like that only when they intend to become a good influence on me."

"I think you're far beyond my influence. And besides, I don't fancy my women in trousers." This was a blatant lie but seemed an appropriate assertion to make. He really wasn't *supposed* to fancy anything in trousers, was he?

"I'm in a skirt right now. And you take things too seriously for a man so young, Lord Smith-Grenville."

"Call me Barnabas." He should have invited her to call him Smith-Grenville. He'd skipped a step. Too late to take it back now, though. He wanted to hear her say his name.

"I will in a minute."

Her vision in the dark must have been better than his. She found his lips with no trouble at all and pressed a lingering kiss there. He was so shocked he almost didn't respond at first, but just when it seemed she might pull away he recovered himself and kissed her back.

It was clear from the start that one kiss would never be enough; they would need to do more of this and do it often. It was also clear that neither of them had any idea what they were doing. A great deal of awkward nose-bumping and tooth-knocking transpired before Freddie shifted her head to one side and Barnabas countered just so, and—bliss, heaven, a paradise of velvet lips in a sensual tussle in which no contender could ever possibly lose. Freddie sighed into his mouth, and Barnabas realized he would never be able to hide his erection when they left this magical cupboard. He was reacting to her like a schoolboy, a green lad, a . . . *oh, sweet heavens, is that her tongue?*

Yes, it was.

He met her move for move, catching up to her pace, exploring her mouth as if he might never have another chance. Warm and soft, and almost painfully intimate. He realized, when he ran the tip of his tongue along their edges, that her teeth were perfection. Strange it had taken knowing them this way for him to become aware of that simple fact. Teeth, tongue, lips, all of her, perfection. Kissing her felt like coming home at last, but finding that home was some wonderful new place straight out of his most secret dreams.

He would have happily spent all day at it, but Miss Murcheson pulled back woefully soon.

"Barnabas," she whispered, to his delight.

"Freddie . . . I hope I may call you Freddie?"

"Of course you may, don't be ridiculous. Only when we're alone, though. This is extremely ill-advised, you do know that?" She actually sounded flustered for the first time since he'd met her, though that might have been a side effect of the whispering.

"Oh, yes. Possibly the worst idea in the history of romantic encounters." Her father would probably change his mind about that hanging if he found out, and have Barnabas drawn and quartered instead, for one thing. He needed to distance himself, no mistake. "When can we do it again?"

"I don't know. I think they're gone, by the way."

"Who?"

She pushed against his shoulder, a gentle reprimand for his lack of attention. He caught her hand and held it there. "The men in the study. I believe they were primarily interested in raiding my father's private stock of liquor while he was detained by his duties as host."

"That's shocking." He brought her hand to his mouth, feeling his way kiss by kiss across her silk-clad knuckles, then turning it over to press his lips to her palm. "Absolutely shocking."

"Barnabas, we need to leave now," she reminded him. "We can't be caught canoodling in the wall."

"Canoodling?" He wasn't sure he'd ever heard anyone actually say the word aloud. "A Smith-Grenville does not *canoodle*, madam."

"I'll keep that in mind for next time. Now go. And be thinking of a good plan."

He'd missed something, obviously. It was possible his brain was not functioning optimally. "A plan to kiss you again?"

"No. Well, if you like. But I meant a plan to help me steal the *Gilded Lily* from Father's secret underwater base, so I can use it to track down the smugglers. As I said the other day in the park, if I prove to him that I can do this—especially succeeding where he's failed—maybe he'll finally accept that I can take care of myself, and then I can stop all this sneaking about. No more monitors, no more double life. I can finally just *live*."

She framed his face with her hands and deposited another all-too-swift kiss on his startled lips, then slipped out of the cupboard on the parlor side.

He took longer than he should have to compose himself before exiting through the study. The aria was over, and the guests were beginning to depart the salon. Murcheson spotted him leaving the room and pinned him with a glare from down the corridor.

Barnabas tried to think of something, any plausible reason to have been in Murcheson's study. Anything other than perusing the man's confidential documents and making love to his daughter in the secret closet. His mind was a lamentable blank, however. All he knew was fear as the man bore down on him.

"Have those bastards been at my private stores again? Happens every time I invite this many people and get caught up with the other guests. Don't let them rope you in again. Anything to report, Smith-Grenville?"

He didn't look very interested in the answer. His eyes were already cutting to the side, to the next conversation he planned to hold. Cold relief swamped Barnabas from head to toe. "No, sir. Just the odd jaunt to Wallingford House. I believe Lady Sophie is a wonderful steadying influence on Miss Murcheson."

"Hmm. She steadied poor Thomas Wallingford right into an early grave. Still, Frédérique seems to have learned some manners from the woman. She's seen no one else? No suspicious strangers lurking about?"

Down the hall, Freddie caught his eye, her face full of dismay. Her lips and cheeks were decidedly pinker than they had been earlier in the evening, he was sure of it. Barnabas forced himself to look away. "No, sir. It's all been quite uneventful."

"Good. Let me know if anything changes. Well, carry on, Smith-Grenville. Carry on."

"Yes, sir."

Murcheson strode off. Barnabas ignored Freddie's effort to gain his attention again and made his way down the hallway and to the stairs, pressing his fingers to one temple as though suffering a headache.

Once in his room, he closed the door firmly behind him, leaning back against it as though trying to hold back everything on the other side.

He had kissed a woman. Very much the wrong woman. He had lied to her father, his employer, a man who could throw him in prison or have him hanged for treason. He had given Freddie every reason to believe he would go on lying, and kissing her. *Canoodling.*

What's more, he was no longer certain he wanted to work for Murcheson at all. But leaving the agency's employ would mean leaving Freddie as well, a prospect he looked upon with dread.

What the hell was he doing with his life? He could be at home in the New York Dominion, living a life of ease and privilege, learning to take over the affairs of the family estate like he must one day do. But his father was still hale and hearty, his brother was still missing, and . . . he *wanted* something. Something he could taste on Miss Freddie Murcheson's sweetly inappropriate lips. She tasted like adventure. Barnabas realized that Freddie, with her ostensibly circumscribed life as an unmarried girl, had managed more adventure in her twenty-one years than he had as a wealthy bachelor only a few years shy of thirty. He found her completely baffling and absolutely delightful in equal measure. Lately, perhaps, the balance was tipping in favor of delight.

Barnabas's restless mind propelled him across the room, to stop in front of the trunk Murcheson had sent up to him. Phineas's things, which he hadn't had time to look through. Phineas had left the key with his landlady—was he that trusting, or had he censored the contents of the trunk that carefully?—and it was tied to one of the handles with a bit of twine.

A sartorial passion for tool-concealing clockwork lapel flowers had spread to Europa, and Barnabas wore one that night. It was an enameled rosebud, with leaves that twisted in various ways to reveal several useful attachments. He used the smallest blade to cut the key loose and opened the trunk after a moment of trepidation at what he might find. Opium paraphernalia, or damning correspondence. The remnants of a life wasted, the pieces Phineas hadn't even bothered to take with him.

The top of the trunk was covered by an inset tray, and it contained exactly the sort of keepsakes one might expect from a young man. A few school medals tucked into a woolen mitten, a small tin of smooth rocks that Barnabas recognized from the stream they'd played in every day as children. Skipping stones. There were also half a dozen books, one of which Barnabas recognized as his own; Phineas had borrowed it and evidently never remembered to return it. It might well have been meant as a message of some sort, but if so he wasn't sure of the meaning.

"*The Sorrows of Young Werther*. Really, Phin, who would have thought you had a melodramatic side?"

In a carved wooden box, he found a stack of paper. Tickets, theatre programs, invitations, a handful of visiting cards. A few letters.

"Lady Sophronia Howard," he read, from the outside of one envelope. It had been addressed to her but either never delivered, or returned with the seal unbroken. Barnabas replaced it in the box, unread.

Lifting the tray away, he stared into the depths of the trunk and thought instantly of Freddie. Or rather, of Fred.

Phineas had left behind his uniforms, rank insignia, even his spit-polished shoes. Everything one might need if one wanted to walk right into a secret undersea naval base.

Ten

SHE WOULD HAVE rather gone in her gown than in a night rail. That would have drawn suspicion, however. Freddie had needed a maid to help get the elaborate gown off, and the maid had already laid out the nightclothes. So she felt more exposed, yet also less constrained than usual as she crept up the stairs from one floor of the silent house to the next. The one where Barnabas was staying.

This was all very unlike her. She had to wonder if part of the attraction was the sheer convenience of this man who couldn't tattle on her, with whom she was bound in a mutual embrace of lies. It made him curiously safe. Then again, there had been nothing safe about the way she'd tingled all the way down to her toes when they finally managed to get the kissing straightened out. The bit with the tongues had been an especially pleasant surprise, an accident on her part that had turned out astonishingly well. And Barnabas was definitely forbidden fruit, which had an allure all its own.

He might not want to let her into the room, of course. He was an honorable thing, and probably had a lot of notions of propriety and appropriateness impeding his judgment. All the ideas that Freddie's string of governesses had tried so hard to drum into her as a child. But if she led with something innocent, like a discussion of ways to steal the *Gilded Lily* and what they might do with it once they'd secured it, she could surely talk her way into the room. And once the door was closed, anything might happen.

She scratched for entrance, servantlike, and heard some rustling and knocking before Barnabas opened the door. He was still in his trousers and shirtsleeves, no ascot, collar open. Not formal, not rough—nascent undress. This was definitely the version of his wardrobe she liked best. Freddie was seized with a sudden, inexplicable urge to lick the long, vulnerable column of Barnabas's throat. She had to remind herself she'd planned to start with business.

"What the devil are you doing here?" he half-whispered, half-screeched, obviously panicked to find her on his threshold. Without another word he gripped her arm and jerked her into the room, checking the corridor before closing and bolting the door. "You can't be here, Freddie."

"You just locked me in," she pointed out. "I wanted to talk about our plan."

Barnabas looked shifty. "Plan?"

"To steal the submersible," she said slowly, as if to a dimwit. "Here we can talk without having to whisper. Nobody else is housed nearby at the moment. This floor doesn't see a lot of use since my mother elected to remain in France. We don't have nearly as many houseguests as we used to."

"Ah, yes. She's French herself, I take it?"

She nodded. Sometimes Freddie felt as though her mother were France itself. "Yes, and very proud to be so. She supported the Égalité government during the war long before they overpowered the post-royalist faction, and her family were among the many exiles in London. But I've always gotten the distinct impression she hated all things English other than my father. We moved to Le Havre for Father's business shortly after the treaty was signed, and she's never been back here."

"Not even for your first Season?"

"Especially not then. It was Father who insisted on my coming out in London. He placed me under the care and tutelage of my aunt Lydia, who promptly foisted me off on my dear friend Sophie. Sophie had spent a year with our family in Le Havre before her own debut, in lieu of finishing school, and she and I got along together quite well."

"You taught her to pick locks?"

"Indeed I did. And I added a great deal to her French vocabulary. Things I doubt she would have picked up had she gone to one of the fine Swiss institutions for producing young women of quality. But I didn't come here to discuss Sophie's education."

"The submersible. You can't really mean to steal it?"

He glanced behind him again, at a trunk sitting open near the foot of his bed, then back at Freddie. He really was the worst at subterfuge. He might as well have erected a marquee over the trunk, directing her attention to it.

"Borrow it, rather. Since it's obvious Father's people aren't getting good use from it anyway. I fully intend to return it without getting caught. Somehow. What's in that trunk?"

"Nothing."

She could see some books, a swath of dark fabric, some sort of wooden box. Nothing spectacular on first look, but if there was nothing interesting in it, why was he being so secretive?

"People only say 'nothing' when they mean it's something but they don't want to say what."

"I believe I had this same conversation with my brother more than once. When we were schoolboys."

"Touché."

"You shouldn't go nosing into other people's things, you know."

"I already said *touché*. No need to belabor the point. Nobody likes a scold, Barnabas."

"I shall endeavor to be less didactic, Freddie."

They'd said each other's *names*. For a moment they could only stare at one another, smiling, mired in the treacle pull of calf love. Freddie felt that odd little pull in her tummy, the stirring of things below there, and a delicious sense of daring that seemed entirely at odds with the man she'd so recently thought of as bland and puddinglike. Here in his room late at night, with her in her night things and him with his collar hanging open, he seemed anything but bland. He was raw and real and just as on edge as she was, by the look of things. She had no idea what to do or say next.

"This," he gestured, breaking eye contact first, "is my brother Phineas's trunk. He left it behind when he disappeared into the wilds of the Dominions. There's nothing much of interest in it. Just keepsakes, that sort of thing."

Freddie stepped past him and stared down at the contents. "That looks like—"

"His uniforms, yes. He left those as well."

"But if we had Navy uniforms, we could simply walk into—"

"No, we couldn't, because they would catch us and hang us. Which is why I didn't particularly want you to see them."

Freddie held up various pieces of the uniform gear, noting some older, slightly more worn garments in addition to those that looked more recent and possibly larger. Phineas had grown after receiving his commission, it appeared. It was serendipity. Her mind was already spinning out the scenario. "Mrs. Pinkerton can tailor one of these down for me. My hair will never fit under this hat, though. Were you and Phineas roughly the same size?"

"Roughly. Miss Murcheson—Freddie, we really cannot do this. It would be madness. Not just because of the consequences if we're apprehended, I mean the entire project itself. There will be guards, passwords. I'm not even sure which of these uniforms one would wear in an undersea station. Some of them are for workdays, some for dress, and then there's the question of which medals and other bits to use. It's quite complicated."

"I'm sure a trip to the library would answer those questions. As for the rest, the tunnel entrance wasn't guarded. Not the one on this side, at least. It doesn't even look ready for general use yet. How stringently will they be guarding a secret entrance they don't expect anyone to be using yet?"

"We can't go in the middle of the night again. What about the workmen?" His voice cracked under the strain. She hastened to reassure him.

"They'll see two officers who clearly know about the lift and the secret tunnel, so they'll assume we're authorized to use them. They're workmen, not guards. If we look like we belong there, they'll never question us. It isn't their job." It was a truth she'd learned on the streets of London, and it seemed to apply in all walks of life. "The trick is not to pay them any notice. And if one of us is carrying some sort of file or paperwork, that would help too. People always look more purposeful when they're carrying pieces of paper."

He frowned, considering that for a moment. "You're right. Why is that, do you suppose?"

"I haven't a clue. Here, put this jacket on."

Barnabas took it from her with clear reluctance, shrugging it on. Freddie's breath caught when he settled the jacket into place on his shoulders, fastened a few of the brass crown-and-anchor buttons on the double breast, and looked up at her for approval. There really was something about a man in uniform, she decided.

"It seems to fit well enough. You also look quite dashing."

"Thank you. I wonder if impersonating an officer of the Royal Navy is a hanging offense. One to add to my list. Is it a worse offense, the higher the rank?" He frowned and examined the stripes on the jacket's cuffs, fingering the gold braid. "That's odd."

"What's odd?" She swung another of the jackets into place, one of the smaller-looking ones. It was still several magnitudes too large. Mrs. Pinkerton would have her work cut out for her.

Barnabas plucked at one of her jacket sleeves, holding her arm up to compare to his own. "See the difference? Yours has two stripes, for a lieutenant. Mine has that third one in the middle. I think that means a lieutenant commander."

"Well done, Phineas." She tried not to notice that he'd stopped holding the jacket cuff and was now holding her wrist. She wasn't a particularly small woman, nor was he especially large for a man, but his fingers overlapped easily.

"Yes, I suppose." She heard the frown in his voice before she raised her eyes to see it on his face. "But he never told us about the promotion. It must have happened right before . . ."

On impulse, she lifted her free hand to his cheek, smoothing her thumb over the worry line next to his mouth. "We'll find out what happened to him."

"So optimistic."

When he smiled, she could feel the muscles in his face

move under her fingers, a strangely intimate connection. He had shaved before the evening's event and his skin was still smooth. She knew she should take her hand away, but it simply wasn't happening. In an effort to seem less like she was fondling him, she moved her fingers to his forehead and adopted an expression of concern.

"Earlier you looked a bit overcome, and you disappeared before I had a chance to inquire as to your health. Are you well?"

"Do I feel feverish?" His smile had changed, warmed somehow, sparking his eyes with unexpected devilry.

"Not particularly."

He lifted her hand away and brought it down to his lips, kissing bare skin where he'd previously been thwarted by silk. She'd had her hand kissed before, many times. Why was this so very different?

"I ought to. I'm burning with passion."

"*Ugh.* Terrible!" She tried to pull her hand away but he kept it firmly in his, grinning wildly as she started to laugh despite herself.

She'd come to his room with some level of seduction in mind and been distracted by talking and uniforms and plotting. The plotting had led to humor and hand-kissing, however. Now it seemed the most natural thing in the world to lean toward him, tugging gently on their joined hands, and rise up on her toes to kiss his smiling mouth.

They'd sorted some things out in the closet earlier. This time, things went more smoothly from the start. So smoothly, in fact, that in no time at all her arms were wrapped around Barnabas's neck, and his hands were venturing down toward her bottom, and she couldn't even remember taking the naval jacket off but she must have, because there it was, flung over the open trunk.

His lips and tongue felt too perfect against hers. She couldn't stop kissing him, possibly ever. She was drugged on it, intoxicated, as hopelessly enthralled as any opium addict. And his body, and the way hers fit so neatly against it. How had she done without that for so long? How could she ever leave this room again?

"God. Freddie, we really can't do this."

But he *would* keep talking.

"Shh. Kiss me again."

He did, sweet and soft at first, a feathery sweep of his lips over hers. Then, after a pause, he dove in and did some things with his tongue that made her knees go trembly and the rest of her tingly. And hands . . . he stopped pretending he wasn't trying to fondle her posterior, and simply reached down and did the thing properly. Cupping, and squeezing, and pulling her closer. She could feel his erection, hard against her belly, a source of trepidation and interest. When she squirmed, his grip tightened and his kisses grew more insistent, demanding. He shifted from her mouth to her neck, burning her skin with his breath until she melted under the heat.

"We need to stop," he mumbled, sounding less than convincing.

His exposed throat drew her again, as it had earlier. Freddie turned her head and flicked her tongue against the divot between his collarbones, then licked a path up to his ear. By the time she arrived at his earlobe, Barnabas was groaning, his head thrown back, eyes closed.

"We should lie down," she suggested, nipping his ear.

"That is the last thing we should do. Oh, hell." He wrapped his arms around her waist, lifted her and staggered to the bed. They climbed up together, ending in a messy tangle of limbs and night rail with Freddie on top.

She had officially ventured beyond her previous

experience around the time of the bottom-fondling, so she was now operating purely on instinct and guesswork. Shoving her voluminous skirts out of the way, she straddled his hips and sat up to assess things.

"Perhaps it's a bit like riding a horse?" When she moved experimentally, Barnabas bucked, not unhorselike, beneath her. Except it was somehow absolutely nothing like a horse, and it made her light-headed with wanting more.

"Your legs . . ." He ran his hands from her knees to her thighs until his fingers disappeared beneath layers of cotton voile and lace. And then he kept going. "You're not wearing drawers."

"You've gone past my legs," she gasped, at the feel of his hands on the bare skin of her hips. He gripped and pulled her down as he rose again, and Freddie felt a blush begin to spread from her face down to her chest. Overheated, overcome, she tugged at the ribbon that closed the neck of her night rail, and unbuttoned the top button so she could breathe more comfortably.

He arched his hips into hers again. "Like riding a horse."

"This is nothing at all like riding a horse and you know it." Was that her voice, low and breathless? She could hardly recognize it, hardly recognize herself in this wanton creature she'd become. But she liked that woman. She could *be* that woman. Fearless, taking what she wanted. Once she learned what that was, at least. She moved her hips, scraping her most sensitive flesh against the fine wool of his trousers and bearing down just so, seeking the spot that needed the pressure most and groaning in appreciation when she found it.

Barnabas freed one of his hands and unhooked more of her buttons, until a draft ran down the center of her chest. Then his fingers disappeared again, finding her breast beneath the ridiculous nightclothes. It was good, almost too good to bear, when he brushed close to her nipple and squeezed. Freddie stopped moving for a moment and he gripped tighter on her hip, reminding her of their tempo.

When he finally stopped teasing around its periphery and plucked at her nipple, her body experienced a confusing rush of too-much-to-sort-out, all the sensations overwhelming her. Then the heat between her legs and the tingling ache of her breast met somewhere in the middle and Freddie exploded, whimpering helplessly as the pleasure took over. Hot, wet, then wetter still as Barnabas cried out and froze beneath her, gasping.

She collapsed to his chest, nose buried in his neck, embarrassed now that the moment was over to know that he'd seen her lose herself like that. Barnabas's arms encircled her, holding her tight, as their breathing slowly settled back to something approaching normal.

Somehow this hadn't been quite what she expected. Though she was no longer sure what she had been expecting, nor was she sure what to call what had just happened. Finally, the silence grew too thick and she took it on herself to break it.

"What did we just do?" she mumbled into the warm, salty skin of his throat.

Barnabas kissed her forehead. The gesture was so sweet that tears sprang to Freddie's eyes. "I'm not sure, but I'm fairly certain I've ruined you. It seemed quite ruinous. Delightfully so."

"If anything, I ruined you. But nobody saw us. Ruining requires a witness, I think."

"You think? Aren't young ladies supposed to know these things?"

"My mother is French," she reminded him. "Different set of rules."

When he laughed, she loved the way his body moved

under hers, solid and reassuring. She snuggled closer as he spoke. "I'm certain her rules still wouldn't allow for . . . that, whatever that was."

"But it wasn't . . . the thing itself? The primary activity that—"

"I know what thing you meant, and no. It most certainly was not."

"Are you sure? Have you ever done . . . that?"

"Gentlemen don't speak of these things. But I am quite sure."

"So you have."

"I—yes, if you must know. A few times."

She lifted up, bracing herself on her arms so she could see him. His face was flushed, hair at his forehead slightly damp as if he'd just run a race. He looked quite happy and peaceful, and more than a little sleepy.

"I should go back to my room."

"You should have stayed in your room to begin with," he chided her gently. But he was stroking her thighs again, up and down in slow, easy passes, not as if he minded at all that she'd behaved in such a shocking manner. "And you should go back soon, it's true."

Irrationally, she wanted him to beg or command her to stay, express an inability to survive the rest of the night without her and the consequences be damned. She definitely hadn't come with that sort of thinking in mind, and suspected it was a product of the same strange emotional weight that seemed to accompany this . . . whatever they'd just done.

Now that their bodies were cooling off, things were growing sticky and unpleasant between them. Peeling herself away, Freddie slipped off the bed, settling her night rail down around her and smoothing it out as best she could with her hands.

"I didn't mean you had to go right this second," he protested, following her off the bed. He dropped his braces from his shoulders as he did so, tugging his shirttails out to let them hang. Covering up the evidence, Freddie realized, because his trousers were probably a mess.

"Too many long afternoons and late nights recently. We both need our rest." She reached into the trunk and pulled out the uniform pieces she thought were most promising, bundling them in her arms and holding them in front of her like a shield as she faced him again.

"You really mean to go through with this, Freddie? Walking right into that station—assuming it's there to begin with—and leaving in a submersible?"

"With or without you," she confirmed.

He grimaced, then pried the wad of clothing from her and tucked it firmly under one arm, pulling her closer with the other. "With me. God help me."

He kissed her forehead again—sweet, why was that so inexpressibly sweet?—then her nose, then finally her lips. The heat wasn't spent, and they both left the kiss reluctantly.

Barnabas escorted her to the door, checked the hallway, and pressed the bundle back into her arms before pressing a final swift kiss to her mouth.

"Tomorrow, we'll plot. Tonight, we sleep."

She nodded, not trusting herself to speak without her voice breaking.

"Good night, Freddie."

A whisper wouldn't give her away. "Good night, Barnabas."

She had planned to make it back to her room before letting herself cry. But as soon as his door was closed, the tears began to fall.

Eleven

"You're mad, miss."

Dan had said it before, but this time he seemed to mean it literally. There was not a touch of admiration in his voice, and Freddie heard more than a little fear.

She fingered the tips of her newly bobbed hair as she settled into the barouche for the short drive home. The curls sprang back against her touch, surprisingly strong and resilient. Sophie had *tsk*ed and her maid Angelica had wept as she cut it, but even she had to admit the end result was charming and at the very vanguard of fashion.

"You don't like my new hairstyle?"

"What? Oh, I see. You've gone and whacked your hair off. No, I'm not one for bobbed hair on women. I wasn't talking about that and you know it." He chucked to the horses, who started a lazy, ambling trot down the tree-lined street. Freddie leaned forward to avoid shouting their conversation. The pony trap was so much more convenient for talking, as they could sit beside one another, but the barouche was required for a proper daylight visit to Lady Sophronia's. At least the horses were quieter than a steam engine, and the route from the front of the house was infinitely more scenic.

"Do you mean the uniform?"

"You can't have any good use for it. And you've gone and dragged my mum into this. Trousers are one thing, an officer's uniform is another. She can't explain that away if somebody sees her with it. And you're putting Lady Sophie at risk to boot. I don't like it, Fred, not one bit."

The big man didn't like her doing much of what she did, but he'd always come around to her side before. He was fiercely protective of his family, however, and she hadn't considered the possibility that his mother might be at greater risk because of the uniform. While she'd been having her hair cropped, Dan had been delivering the garments to his mother. The threat must have occurred to him then.

"I'm sorry, I didn't think. Retrieve the uniform tonight, please, with my apologies to your mother. I can find somebody else to cut it down."

"Oh, your pet fop knows a good tailor, does he? You'll waltz yourself straight up to Savile Row to have it done?"

While Freddie thought Barnabas had probably patronized at least one good tailor on Savile Row in his lifetime, she also suspected Dan's anger had little to do with tailoring.

"I would hardly call Lord Smith-Grenville a fop. His taste in garments is utterly bland and conventional." She might have said the same about the man himself a few days ago. Now, she blushed to recall their encounter of the night before, the delicious madness and the unaccountable melancholy that had followed. She still had no good explanation for that and was almost glad she'd been able to avoid having to see him today by arranging this open visit to Sophie's. Hard as it had been to leave his room last night, she was confused at her hesitation to confront him now. It wasn't as if she were ashamed, and heaven knew he hadn't seemed unduly upset by the evening's occurrences.

"He's a limp-wristed milksop and you're not safe with him."

"What on earth do you mean?" Why would Dan think she wasn't safe with Barnabas? Had he somehow spotted her sneaking about the house last night?

"I let you out of my sight with him for a quarter of an hour, and a bloomin' earthquake happens. Now you're up to some new foolishness with these Navy costumes, which means it's back to the docks unless I miss my guess. What will it be this time, a typhoon?"

Oh.

"Typhoons do not occur in the English Channel. Dan, you're being quite unreasonable, and more than a little unfair. Smith-Grenville didn't *cause* the earthquake. And he didn't even want to accompany me. He *has* to stay with me. My father hired him, after all."

Was that it, the source of her strange uneasiness regarding Smith-Grenville? She couldn't still think of him as her father's man, not after last night. And yet . . . money and power were strong motivators. Strong enough to make her father destroy the livelihoods of countless fisher folk, apparently without a backward glance. Was Barnabas so different?

"Your father hired him to look after you and report if you seemed to be getting into trouble. He hasn't done that, has he?"

"Well, no. Not that it's any fault of his own. I'm the one to blame, if anything. You know I always find my father's men out."

After a moment of silence, Dan ventured, "But this one's different. Isn't that right, miss?"

They turned onto Freddie's street, which meant their talk was nearly over. She wasn't sure if it was perfect or terrible timing. "Oh, big brother Dan. Is that what has you so worried? My virtue?"

Dan snorted. "You can do as you like with *that*. What you and me have done, tinkering and all, that's been a lark. What you're doing with this lord, this ain't no lark. And I don't mean anything to do with that virtue. There's talk, bad talk down around the docklands. Folk have been hurt. Folk have been . . . murdered, miss. No nice way to put it. You don't want to go messing in this business. Especially not when you have your mind on other things. Love makes you blind."

"*Love?* Who said anything about love? Don't be ridiculous." *Pfft. Love.*

Dan shook his head, drawing to a halt at the carriage block. He leaped down as a boy took the reins, and beat the footman to the barouche's door to hand Freddie out. His neatly gloved hand dwarfed hers. In his midnight blue livery, he looked enormous, and Freddie wondered if that was part of his hesitation at allowing Barnabas to take his place as her escort and bodyguard. Dan relied on his physical strength so much he would naturally be leery of other competencies.

"Safe home, miss." He tipped his hat, reminding Freddie of her need for a new disguise hat now that she no longer needed the gigantic top hat to stuff her hair into. A cap, perhaps. It would be so light and easy to wear.

"Thank you, Daniel."

He kept her hand a moment longer, giving her a stern look before he made a quick bow to excuse his lingering. "Makes you blind, miss," he murmured.

"I shall keep that in consideration, Daniel."

She was inside the house before realizing she didn't know the final outcome of the uniform issue. With any luck, Mrs. Pinkerton would make the changes quickly and have it back to her with nobody the wiser, relieving Freddie's and Dan's minds.

For decades before the long war devastated their economy, the French had set the standard for large-scale nautical construction. Ironically, many of the ships in the British fleet had been commissioned from French shipyards. The flagship of the Lord of Gold's submersible fleet hailed from that earlier, glorious time, and it was Rollo Furneval's favorite spot for imagining he was the Lord Admiral of his own sinister, clandestine navy.

"Steady as she goes, Mr. O'Brien. Keep an even keel, Mr. Finn."

"Aye aye, cap'n," Finn replied. It always sounded so automatic from Finn, all that jackspeak. As if he'd been a real sailor at some point in his life. Rollo had no idea what any of it meant, but that hardly mattered because this wasn't the Navy and the chaps he employed could bloody well pilot the submersible with or without him.

"Ballast . . . ho. We need to get deeper, O'Brien; stay close to the channel floor."

O'Brien grunted and turned a valve on the baffling collection of pipes in front of him. Something creaked out a ticking groan, and Rollo's ears tightened as the slender sixteen-man craft dove.

All about him was brass and curved beams of wood, most of it in need of a polish. He'd had one of the lads maintain the commanding officer's chair in the cockpit, however, and the glowing gold of the brass rivets and fittings gleamed from the dark teak frame. His undersea throne. They were running dark this trip, even the work lights covered with red cloths to limit glare from the portholes, all in hopes they could avoid attracting the squid's attention. In the dim, ruddy light, his throne looked like the helm of hell. Smelled a bit like it too, Rollo noted with a grimace. Too many fearful bodies in too small a space.

"There's something off the port bow." Mordecai Nesdin, the hydrophone operator, fiddled with his spectacles in the jerky, fitful way he always did when excited, then blurted out a bearing. It must have made sense to Finn, who pulled on some levers and adjusted a few dials. The sub turned, its sonic sensor array drifting more slowly to sway before the cockpit window like tendrils.

Or tentacles. Like seeking like, perhaps. Mordecai paddled from one foot to the other, holding his glasses in place as he watched his instruments. "Large. And moving. No, there are . . . Roland, Roland! There are more than one! One, two, three—"

"Don't call me Roland. You know that, Mord. What the hell do you mean there are more than one?" He had known Mordecai since they were both boys. Mord, the tutor's simple-yet-sometimes-brilliant son, and he the evil genius who could always turn Mord's talents to his own uses.

"Rollo, Rollo, Rollo! Things out there! Seven, eight, nine, teneleventwelvethirteen twenty-nine, there are twenty-nine *things* out there, Rollo."

"Fuck."

The real Navy would have somebody sane to do the counting, somebody entirely unlike sad Mordecai with his fidgeting and his undeniable genius with machinery. Somebody who wouldn't engage in self-polluting practices over said machinery more than once, requiring intervention from Rollo to prevent the devices from being lubricated in untoward ways and Mordecai from having his bits ground to bits.

"Count them again, Mord."

"Twenty-nine!" His childhood friend crowed out the number in delight. "It's a prime, Roland!"

He knew how Mordecai felt about prime numbers and declined to comment on that. "Let's come to a halt here, lads."

Finn and the others moved their controls smoothly, proving their worth. The submersible slowed, halted, and Rollo approached the cockpit window to survey the aquatic landscape beyond with his own eyes. Sometimes he simply trusted those more than all the fancy instruments in the world.

He saw . . . seaweed. Rocks, crusted with barnacles or something like that. Murk, and more murk, and—there, darting across the vista as quick as lightning, a shape that went from dark and speckled to a flashing ghostly pale, and a wash of inky black that dissipated quickly in the current but accomplished its purpose quite well. By the time Rollo could see again, the creature that had left the ink was gone.

"What the bloody hell—"

"Cuttlefish?" whispered Mordecai, fingering his bottom lip with one hand and his spectacles earpiece with the other. Then he held up his hands before his face, counting to ten. "Octopus? No, no. Cuttlefish?"

If it could be learned from a book, if it had a classification of some kind, Mordecai knew it. Rollo turned his attention to the savant, rounding the captain's seat and crossing the narrow cockpit to his side. "What d'you suppose it is, Mord? Where's it fit?"

"Too big," Mordecai replied. "Cuttlefish are little, little

fish. Not fish. Cephalopods. Phylum: Mollusca. Order: Cephalopoda. But . . . decapodiform? Eight legs, two tentacles, that's ten. And it was camouflaged in the coral before it moved. Then pulsing. I saw it change. Direct observation. So it *must* be a cuttlefish. But a giant one. Something new."

"What's a cuttlefish?"

Mord turned his head and aimed a scornful glare at Rollo. "A squid, like. Only a squid with eight legs and also two arm sort of things. And can do . . . camouflage. Even more than a squid. And can flash, like light on the surface of the water."

"Camouflage? What's that, then? Sounds French."

"Blowing smoke. Hiding. Disguises. Disguises . . . guises . . ."

Mord lowered himself to a crouch and started to rock. Once he was rocking, Rollo knew, there was no point asking him further questions unless you wanted to trigger an explosion.

"And there are twenty-nine of those bastards out there." He glanced at the notes Mordecai had taken as he listened to his device, interpreting the pings and echoes into a picture made from sound. He'd ended with crude X shapes but at the start he'd created a shockingly accurate picture of something. If it wasn't an octopus or a sea monster, Rollo didn't know what it was. Some unholy combination of the two. "Tentacles. Tom Hill wasn't lying about that."

"Sir?"

He looked up to see Finn watching him, awaiting orders. The rest had lost interest, it seemed. O'Brien was picking his nose with a contemplative air, and the other two lads were arm wrestling on one of the control consoles. Useless, the lot of them. Except for poor Mordecai, and perhaps young Finn.

"Take us home, Finn."

The young man nodded and roused his companions, and together they twirled valves and flipped switches and brought the submersible about with a sickening lurch, pointing it toward what Rollo could only assume was the direction of the home port.

"No torpedoes fired today, Mr. Furneval?" O'Brien asked, as they slipped through the chilly waters of the channel toward their berth. "What about the big squid, then?"

"Not today," Rollo confirmed, taking his seat again and lacing his fingers together as he considered his options. "We'll have to wait until we can assemble the fleet, I think. We're going to need more submersibles."

FORTUNE SMILED UPON Freddie when she learned that Sophie was planning a small house party for the following weekend. This was rare for the widow Wallingford, who usually preferred to avoid inviting speculation about her love life. House parties were notorious opportunities for liaisons, and people would surely gossip about whomever she chose to invite. As she told Freddie, however, she couldn't bring herself to care.

"It's simply too hot in town already," she'd complained. "It's not yet June, but it's dusty and horrible and the flies are in full force. Some fresh air will do us all good."

Freddie didn't want fresh air. She wanted the close, intense atmosphere of an undersea catacomb, or the no doubt stale and stifling environment of a tiny submersible vessel.

"The country does sound delightful. But do you think you could spare me?"

"Spare you? I suppose so. Or would you rather I invite Lord Smith-Grenville along too? I'd planned to, you know."

The older woman refreshed her own cup of tea and smiled at her in a knowing way, which Freddie felt in no position to rebuke. "Do say you'll come. My favorite mare has foaled, and by all reports the baby is absolutely darling. Well worth the trip."

"I'd like to go. Or rather . . ." She was venturing into novel and dangerous territory. Sophie was her oldest, dearest friend, but Freddie was well aware that her antics had long pushed at the limits of Sophie's comfort. Though Sophie wasn't above a little subversion, she might well balk at something of this magnitude. And it was a great deal—perhaps too much—to request of a friend. Still, there was no knowing until she asked. "I'd like to say I'm going, so Father won't expect me in the house for a few days, and then skip the party to go do a job of work that's a bit more complex than my usual."

"Oh, Freddie." Sophie put her teacup down too abruptly, clinking the china and nearly sloshing the contents in her haste. "What are you up to now? Does Lord Smith-Grenville know about this?"

"Of course. He's coming with me."

"He's *what*? Oh, don't tell me you're planning to elope. I know I'm the worst chaperone in the world, but I simply won't have an elopement. Your mother would murder me."

Blushing to her forehead, Freddie took up her tea and took an overlarge sip to bolster herself. "It isn't. We're not eloping. We're not—he's the man my father hired to watch me, not—"

"Fine job he's doing too."

"That's what Dan said."

"Daniel Pinkerton is a fine, sensible young man, and you ought to pay more attention to his advice."

"We are not eloping. I can't say exactly what our plan is, because the less you know, the better. But I should think you'd be the last person to suspect me of planning to elope, Sophie. Where on earth did you get such an idea?"

Her friend's serene brow wrinkled the tiniest bit, the closest to a frown Sophie ever allowed herself to get. "I've seen the way he looks at you. I know that look. Too well."

"You've seen Barnabas look that way before?" Was he in the habit of mooning after young ladies? She wasn't at all sure she liked that idea.

"No, not on Lord Smith-Grenville." There was a subtle rebuke in her voice at Freddie's familiarity. A much-needed one too. Freddie should be more careful to use the man's proper title. "Although there is a strong family resemblance."

"His brother."

"Phineas." Her lovely mouth curved around the name, turning it into a sensual talisman of sounds.

They had been on a first-name basis, just as Freddie and Barnabas were and shouldn't be.

"Oh, Sophie. How?"

"Not easily. But my father was occupied with keeping his creditors at bay, and my mother took ill for over a fort-night that Season so I had an unprecedented bout of free-dom. Events I wouldn't have normally attended. Driving out with groups of friends. Wallingford seemed primed to offer for me, and I'd complied with all their instructions to encourage him, so I think they were also inclined to give me my head and let me push on to the finish. Which I did, of course."

"Eventually."

"Thomas never imagined he had my heart, Freddie. That wasn't part of our arrangement. He had someone else, you know. Someone he could never be public with. We did become friends, and we even tried for an heir before he grew ill. It was far from unpleasant, to be honest. I was faithful to him. But neither of us ever thought it was love. He and I understood one another perfectly."

Freddie suspected many marriages made do with less, and she knew her friend had been relieved to free herself from her family's clutches. Grateful to Wallingford, and happy in her new life. But it still sounded sad, deeply so, now that she knew how steep the cost of Sophie's liberation really was. She would never have been allowed to marry Phineas, but to turn him away in order to accept the ring of a man she had no hope of loving must have been unbearably bitter.

"What happened, then?"

"We met on one of those drives. Phineas was on leave and visiting a friend in London. It was as if we'd known each other all our lives. He didn't want to hear that I was already spoken for. We quarreled when he found out the engagement had been formalized, but we still corresponded for a few months afterward. He tried everything he could think of to persuade me. The next chance he got, he came again to see me. That was a few days before my wedding. It ended in tears."

"Had you told him why—?"

"No," Sophie snapped. "How would that have helped anything? I made my own choice. You want to paint me as a tragic heroine, Freddie, but I was never that. You mustn't think that way. My life is not a Gothic novel. Yes, my aunt was put into an asylum shortly after she refused a promising engagement. Yes, my parents felt free to remind me of that, and the knowledge was ominous at times. But what you've never seemed to accept is that *everyone* in the family truly believes Aunt Elizabeth is a lunatic, whether or not she actually tried to kill herself. She was never quite right, even as a young girl. And they kept me so close because they were terrified of what might happen to *all* of us if I didn't marry well, or if I started to behave as Elizabeth had and *couldn't* marry. It's not as though they were profligate. Father inherited most of his debts and saw a chance to clear them in one go. Besides, the laws have changed considerably in the last twenty years. My solicitor now says they never would have managed to have me committed, even if I turned down a proposal from the Prince of Wales himself, so the implied threat was an empty one."

"You didn't believe so at the time."

"I could have run off with Phineas. If I'd truly wanted to, I could have. I decided to accept Wallingford because I wanted to please my family and ease their circumstances. And I wanted a comfortable life for myself too, more than I wanted the uncertainty of aligning myself with a young officer I thought I loved but barely knew."

Freddie's own stakes were not quite so high. She clung to her life of luxury, true, but there was no romance attached to the other option to lend it urgency. Nor would her family suffer financial loss if she ever did make that choice. She had it easy in every way, compared to her friend. If only it *felt* easy. Her trouble was she wanted both things, her family's regard and support *and* the freedom to go forth and tinker. Finding a way to have both had become something like an obsession for her lately.

Sophie might have superb control over her emotional display, but Freddie had never perceived her as cold or calculating. Now, seeing the fine house in Belgravia, the delicate china, Sophie's muted but elegant dress in the latest style, she tried to imagine how she might choose, if presented those same drastic alternatives. True love at the price of possible penury, and the loss of one's family, who must then suffer financial disaster? Or the chance to secure everyone's future, at the cost of one young man's heart?

In a romantic novel, the choice would be obvious. True love must always win. In real life, however, the handsome young lover might not turn out to have a secret fortune stashed away, to be revealed only once he knew the heroine was picking him for the right reasons. And the nasty, grizzled, rich old husband of necessity might in fact be a soft-spoken, kind gentleman in poor health who simply didn't want to spend his final years alone. It all bore further consideration, but for now she had more important concerns.

"I am truly not planning to elope with Phineas Smith-Grenville's brother. I am not planning anything romantic," she insisted, stretching the truth a bit more than she knew she should. "I only need a few days."

Sophie shook her head, then sighed again. "Two. You can have two days. Saturday as early as you like, you can be off and do what you need to do. By Sunday afternoon you report back here, with Lord Smith-Grenville, or I'll go to your father."

TWELVE

❧❧❧

HE COULDN'T TAKE his eyes off her. At some point, Barnabas knew that might conflict with the impression he was trying to give of being a naval officer. Military men weren't encouraged to sneak glances at one another's bottoms and think lascivious thoughts, as far as he was aware.

To be fair, it wasn't *only* her bottom that drew his interest, in part because her smart, double-breasted uniform coat covered much of the body part in question, so only tantalizingly brief glimpses were available. No, it was the whole of her, the *Freddie*-ness, that appealed. The very fact that she'd orchestrated this excursion, that they were descending into a secret tunnel to explore an undersea station and possibly steal a submersible while they were at it, all because some fishermen were out of work . . . the *certainty* she projected, that this was a justified and appropriate course of action. Her conviction and bravery astounded him. The facts of her life, as she'd managed somehow to arrange them, amazed him.

She defied belief, and she put him to shame, because she made things happen instead of waiting for them to come along. Barnabas was beginning to feel as though he had only ever existed on the fringes of his own life, instead of inhabiting it fully and turning it into what he wanted. Even this job, he had taken at somebody else's suggestion. Only recently had he started to ask himself, why? Why was this search for Phineas so important to him, when even their parents had come to peace with the loss of their younger son? As yet, he had no answer for himself.

"Remember, if there are workers in the vestibule, we ignore them and move forward. Keep your eyes on the tunnel entrance, and if the velocipede is there just climb aboard and get ready to pedal. Let me handle starting it up, while you look at your papers and act disinterested."

"I'm not completely unfamiliar with engines, you know. I can strip a steam car to parts and rebuild it. I could have sorted out what to do myself, given time."

"But even I, who did sort it out, had difficulty operating the thing smoothly. Now I've had a few times to practice, while you've had none. Besides, you'll look like the senior officer. It makes sense for the junior to have to crank up the engine."

"If it's there at all. If it isn't, we'll have to turn back. We can't walk to Le Havre, it must be three hundred miles."

They'd had this argument before, with Freddie insisting on exploring as far as they could even on foot, and Barnabas refusing to venture into the tunnel again except in whatever ran on the rail. As the lift was slowing toward a halt, he finally brought out the trump. "If that tunnel really does run all the way to France, nobody would ever walk into it on foot. Where would they be going, on foot down a featureless three-hundred-mile tube? We *have* to take the vehicle or the workmen will know something is amiss. If it isn't there, we can only act surprised and annoyed and leave with all due haste."

She scowled at him a moment, then: "Blast."

The door rattled open and they strode into the vestibule, heading straight toward the tunnel. Barnabas could feel the handful of workers looking, studying them. Identifying their features for future identification, possibly. Sweat formed on his brow and he forced himself to unclench his fingers when they began to crumple the sheaf of papers he held. He heard the noise of a saw blade and then a creak of metal on metal behind him as the men resumed whatever they'd been doing.

A cart was waiting for them, and he wasn't sure whether he was relieved or thrown into a panicked despair. Either way, it felt almost like swooning. This was no humble pedaled vehicle, but a full-fledged carriage of newly polished wood and brass, with plush velvet upholstery on its benches. Brave Freddie marched straight up to the shiny, teacup-shaped thing and started turning a crank on what must be the engine casing near the base. As Barnabas mounted the step and swung himself into the forward-facing seat, the motor purred into life, much quieter than he was expecting.

"I'd love to know what's under the bonnet," Freddie murmured as she joined him, sitting opposite and perusing the control panel with a nonchalant eye. "Another Stirling engine, I'd be willing to bet, but it sounds like nothing I've ever seen or heard of. Can you reach that panel behind you on the wall? There's a flame symbol on it. I think it might activate a light. Or a fire alarm, one or the other."

"We'll find out," he muttered back, reaching for the panel and just managing to tap it with his fingertips. Tiny green bulbs guttered into brightness along that wall, illuminating an eerie path down the tracks that disappeared into the darkness.

"That's better than nothing," she said with a shrug.

"Although this time . . . ah, yes." With a decisive gesture, she flipped one of the myriad toggles on the panel, and a headlamp blazed to life. Another flick, and Barnabas heard a ratcheting sound as the carriage shifted into movement. Slow at first, probably because the engine was still heating, and it took time to build up momentum.

By the time the thing was at top speed, he longed for the relative sedateness of the velocipede. The green lights blurred into a solid line on the wall beside him. The headlamp illuminated a woefully short distance ahead of the cart and created, for Barnabas, the constant sensation that something was going to fly at his face from the suddenly violated darkness of the tunnel.

I must not be sick, he told himself over and over. *I must not be sick, I must not be sick.*

He checked his chronometer when they flew past the first set of portholes, easier to spot this time with daylight filtering down through the water of the channel. It had taken a mere twenty minutes, compared to thirty on the velocipede, to reach that point.

"Do you mind if I join you on that seat?" Freddie asked. Her voice sounded strained. "Sitting backward, I feel like something's going to loom up behind me at any moment and whack the back of my head."

He nodded, lips clamped firmly together, and slid over to make room. He'd have liked to commiserate more clearly, but feared to speak lest he lose his already tenuous control over his protesting stomach.

She took the space next to him, looking forward with a groan. "I'm not sure this is any better."

"At least we'll see it coming."

It never came. After the first quarter hour or so, the fear wore itself down into boredom. Freddie's tentative math regarding the time to reach Le Havre had been based on the apparent speed of the velocipede in reaching what had appeared to be the mouth of the Thames estuary. As she had only the roughest gauge of the actual distance, and the carriage seemed to be traveling faster than the velocipede, all she could do was guess at how long their journey would take. Four hours was her estimate.

At first, they sat, not saying much. Then the silence grew intolerable, but as neither of them had spoken in so long, neither seemed willing to speak first. Finally, Barnabas cleared his throat.

"I need to talk or I'm liable to fall asleep."

Thank God. "What would you like to talk about?"

"You. How did you learn to pick locks, anyway?"

"That's what you want to know? You could ask me anything, and you choose that? It's not very exciting. I taught myself, mostly."

"Yes, but . . . why? You said your parents didn't lock you in, so you obviously didn't need to escape."

She considered that, the earnest belief with which he'd said it and the instinctive clench of her stomach at the idea. "Just because you're not locked in, doesn't mean you have nothing to escape. I'm not trying to wax metaphorical, I simply mean that there's escaping *from* and escaping *to*. But that doesn't really answer your question, I know."

"No. You don't want to answer my question. Forget I asked."

They would be there for hours, and awkward silence would only make the time go more slowly. She might not be used to conversing this way with anyone, but Barnabas had proven himself a good listener thus far.

"It's all right. There's nothing sinister involved. It's just . . . complicated."

"We have time," he pointed out needlessly.

"All right. When the war ended and my family moved from London to Le Havre, we settled in a rather large manor house in the countryside. Huge, actually. It had belonged to some ancient, aristocratic family who'd lost their fortune, and it had been empty for close to a decade when we moved in. Father, Mother, and me."

"No siblings?"

"No, just me. And I'd spent most of my formative years in the London house, which always seemed crowded with guests and family. Everyone on top of each other. I'd never been in a house as big as the one in France, or in a place so empty. There were a dozen or so servants, naturally. But other than my governess, I hardly saw any of them. As a child, I felt very much alone there. And with my father spending so much time at his factory, and Mother often away visiting old friends or reacquainting herself with Paris, I truly was by myself there most of the time. Eleven years old. Nobody to play with, no shops or sights to see. Just miles of coastline. Every so often Father would take me to the factory with him, and it was the best place on earth. I would have happily gone every day. I dreamed of a day he might even allow me to work for him, with him. But most of the time he left me at home where I was lonely, and terribly bored."

He knew her well enough by now to smile and shake his head. "Oh, dear."

"I'm afraid so. I was an intrepid little girl—"

"This does not surprise me."

"Hush! I was too intrepid for my own good, and the only way I knew to manage fear was to be bold in the face of it. I was bored but also terrified, you see. Of that big, spooky house, especially the closed-up wing my father had forbidden me to enter."

"He might as well have laid a trail of candy to point the way."

Freddie nodded. "It's as if he had designed it specifically to entice me. I set out to explore, and it wasn't long before I came up against locked doors. There was nothing for it but to open them, and I didn't dare risk stealing the house-keeper's keys. I had hairpins, I knew the basic principles of lock design, and I had plenty of time on my hands, so . . ."

"What was your governess doing while this was going on?"

"Carrying on an affair with my father's valet. He still used one back then. I thought it quite romantic. Anyway, I learned to pick the locks, which weren't all that complicated as it turned out. I explored the mansion and conquered my fears."

Barnabas tilted his head, acknowledging her accomplishment. "And what did you find in your explorations? Treasures? Skeletons?"

"Yes, actually!" She giggled when he affected to look appalled. "Mouse and rat ones. And a tiny, perfectly preserved bird skeleton on one hearthstone. Also some furniture that hadn't been fine enough to sell or light enough to steal. A beautiful crystal chandelier shattered on the floor in an empty ballroom, because the ceiling was rotten. Fortunately I hadn't yet tried to walk in the room overhead, or I might have fallen straight through on top of all that mess. Let's see, what else? Several lovely books, most of which were full of bookworms but a few of which I was able to salvage. A forgotten menagerie of tiny clockwork toys that I appropriated for experimenting on. Most of them were broken, which turned out to be instructive. And a single diamond ear bob lodged in a crack in the floorboards of what appeared to have been the lady of the manor's boudoir."

"Real diamonds?"

"Yes. You've seen me wear them. I told my parents I'd

found the thing in the upstairs parlor, where I was allowed to be, and they praised me for having such sharp eyes. When I was older, Mother had the stones set into a pendant for me. They still don't know where I really found it. And they thought the clockwork menagerie came from the nursery cupboard."

He shook his head, equal parts admiration and pity. "That's amazing, but still . . . terrible too. Poor little thing. It's lucky you didn't kill yourself wandering around alone in all that decrepitude."

Freddie recalled the days spent creeping through the silent, dusty halls, the thrill of even the most insignificant discoveries, and the rank terror that had claimed her on a few occasions. Like the time she'd tried to shove a heavy curtain aside to let light into one of the rooms, and the rotted fabric had torn from its rod with no warning to fall on top of her. She'd screamed and screamed, batting at the suffocating velvet until the thick dust and mildew nearly choked her. In her panic, she was sure somebody had accosted her, and she struck out in front of her rather than seeking the edge of the curtain. And then by some accident she found it, and burst forth into air and sunlight, whipping the assaulting cloth away from her body in a final glittering shower of dust particles. They danced in the sunbeams long after her heart had stopped its mad racing.

Another time, she'd nearly set the empty wing on fire when she set her lantern on a chair that was too rickety to take even that slight weight. The whole thing had toppled over, and the candle had tumbled from the lantern and ignited the cobwebs between the chair legs. She'd barely managed to stamp out the flames with her feet before they spread.

"It is lucky," she agreed. "But it wasn't terrible. I learned a great deal."

"With the clockwork pieces?"

"Those too. At the time my father still liked my propensity for tinkering, and he let me bring the menagerie to his workshop. I would study what the masters and journeymen did, and apply everything I saw to repairing the toys until they were all running again. But really, what I learned from the whole experience is that I can sometimes create options where none seem to exist." And she'd learned not to let her father hear her talk of a desire to become a makesmith herself. That sort of talk had gotten her banned from even visiting the factory, much less spending time on the workshop floor. Her father wouldn't hear of Freddie sullying herself by taking up a trade.

"Is that what you were trying to teach Lady Sophronia? The lock-picking was just a metaphor?"

She reminded herself yet again to be patient. To remember that Barnabas had never truly been circumscribed in his life and simply couldn't grasp what it really meant to have no options available. To even have to create one's own alternatives. "Sophie's parents were more desperate for money than anyone but their creditors knew. She was their one hope of resolving their financial difficulties in a single swoop, and they weren't going to waste her. They polished her until she shone, they gave her everything she needed to be successful on the marriage mart, but they were more about the stick than the carrot. Not the literal stick," she hastened to assure him. "She had this aunt, you see. Her aunt Elizabeth. She'd only known her for a short time, back when she was a little girl and Elizabeth was about to make her debut. Something bad happened, Sophie never knew exactly what, and one day Elizabeth was gone. The official story was that she'd suffered from a nervous condition, and had to move to the country for her health. That her constitution was too delicate for marriage. For years, that's what Sophie believed."

"And the truth?"

"Because of her nervous condition, she'd refused to marry the man her family chose for her. She refused to marry at all. After they'd failed to convince her, they had her declared insane and committed to an asylum. And before they sent Sophie to France—which they only did to delay her debut for a year, giving them more time to come up with the money to fund it—they told her the truth. A little cautionary tale, with her 'bon voyage.' It was not entirely a lie, of course. The asylum *is* in the country. A sanitarium, really."

Barnabas was shaking his head. "That doesn't really happen in this day and age. Surely Lady Sophie must have misunderstood, or . . . perhaps the woman was simply genuinely ill. If she weren't, they never would have kept her at the sanitarium once it was clear she didn't need their care."

"You think so? An overdose of laudanum. A suicide note, in what appeared to be her handwriting. A devoted family claiming a history of such attempts. And a patient who denies these very clear proofs, and also demonstrates paranoia by implicating her family in a conspiracy to make her appear a lunatic. There's really no way to know who's telling the truth; even Sophie says the family truly believes the woman is mad. But even if she isn't, the presumption favors the people doing the committing, not the patient. Sophie's parents also made it very clear to her that a family history of insanity would only make it easier for them to repeat the process. For her own good, of course. Because she would have to be a lunatic to deny a reasonable proposal."

"Good God."

"I suspect God abandoned the case years ago. The locks weren't a metaphor for Sophie. Learning to pick them was a survival skill. In case she ever truly needed to escape. Fortunately for her, it didn't come to that." Freddie pulled her feet up beneath her, squirming to make herself more comfortable on the seat.

"Because she accepted Wallingford." Barnabas sounded dubious, still.

"He seemed by far the best alternative."

"I suppose he was."

"How magnanimous of you to allow for such a possibility."

He looked at her, clearly bruised by the touch of sarcasm evident in her tone. "I can't pretend to know what the ordeal was like for Lady Sophronia. However, I can still feel for my brother. He was a reserved and steady man, not given to dramatics. If the affair affected him as deeply as it seems to have done, caused such an upheaval that he turned to narcotics to forget, he must have been truly in love with the lady. The circumstances were unfortunate for him too, not her alone."

She nodded, ashamed of herself. Of course Barnabas thought of his brother first, as was only right. Sophie herself was inclined to remark on all the various extenuating circumstances surrounding that time in her life, giving credit wherever she possibly could. It was easy for Freddie, on the outside, to take an extreme view. It didn't really impact her directly.

"My turn to ask you a question."

Barnabas stifled a yawn. "All right."

"What will you do if you find your brother and he really is an opium addict, and a smuggler?"

"He isn't."

"But if he is?"

Barnabas's profile was impassive, stern. "If he is, at least I'll *know*. It's the uncertainty I can't live with. I don't know how anybody can."

"Will you club him over the head and try to drag him back to civilization?"

"No. I don't think so, at least. In the moment, perhaps I'd feel differently. I might make the attempt. But I still don't believe it of him. There's something else going on."

"It's nice. That you believe in him like that."

Freddie had no siblings, no close cousins, very few true friends. Even her connection with Sophie was only of ten years' duration or so. A lifelong attachment, like that between two brothers, was beyond her imagining. Who would look for her that way, live only for her to be found, believe in her despite all reason, if she became lost to the world? Nobody. Her father had his work. Her mother had her friends. Even Sophie, Freddie knew, had an occasional gentleman caller whose identity she never revealed.

Freddie had a passing acquaintance with dozens of tradesfolk and scores of the gentility, her sometimes strained friendships with Dan and Sophie, and a few stolen hours with a man she shouldn't trust as well as she did. Her body still remembered his, as though he'd imprinted on her in some secret code of touch and yearning. She was attuned to him, like it or not. She had no idea whether she liked it, but she planned to experiment further if the opportunity arose. Because he was safe and had no choice but to be discreet. And because she couldn't seem to help herself.

The wind on their faces was drying and unpleasant, inclining both of them to close their eyes a good deal. That in turn led to the inevitable sleep, which at least alleviated the boredom of the long ride under the channel.

A shrill ringing woke Freddie from a convoluted dream involving her father, a cannon, and a transparent, tentacled sea creature that seemed bent on pulling the top off St. Paul's Cathedral. As it was on land, she wasn't sure how she knew the creature was from the sea. But it was, and her father was bent on destroying it. In the dream it had seemed imperative that she stop him, but the instant she woke she wondered why, as one would think a monument-destroying amphibious sea monster would be less than desirable to keep around.

Barnabas stirred beneath her, mumbling something about the bell. Freddie realized her face was pressed into his shoulder. Sitting upright abruptly, she felt her cheek, where it was clear she had an impression from his epaulet.

"Damn."

"What's that noise?"

"Oh." The bell was trilling from the control panel, and one glance shot Freddie into immediate action. "It's a proximity alarm, I think. We must be nearly there!" She flipped switches, praying she understood the sequence correctly, and crossed her fingers waiting to see if the carriage would slow in time. If she was in error, they might be flung head over heels when the cart reached the end of its track. If that happened, it would surely draw unwanted attention, and their injuries would become the least of their worries.

To her vast relief, the carriage bled speed, losing velocity until they could see the individual green lights blip by once more. They spotted the end of the tunnel and watched it loom close, at a speed slightly greater than Freddie was comfortable with. They still had some momentum at the end of the tracks, enough to bump the carriage up in a frightful bounce. If they hadn't been clinging to the sides, they'd have been jolted loose from the seat. But the bump was enough to stop the cart, and it slid back down onto the tracks to settle quietly as the engine wound down.

"Are you all right?" Barnabas asked, raising a hand to Freddie's cheek.

She felt herself blushing as she pulled away. "I'm fine.

That happened . . . before. When we were asleep. It's from your shoulder. It should fade soon."

"Oh, I see."

"Are you hurt?"

"No, I'm quite well. So. Shall we?"

The vestibule on this end was empty, as Freddie had hoped. Construction appeared complete, and a double door of glossy dark wood graced the end of the chamber instead of a lift cage. They paused before the doors, gathering themselves. She wished there were a hope of finding a water closet beyond the portal, and wondered that she hadn't considered such a fundamental concern before embarking on a several-hour trip into the unknown. Still, there was nothing to be done about it now save exercising self-control and hoping for the best.

"Remember to look terribly interested in your documents," she reminded Barnabas, straightening his collar. He, in turn, adjusted her cap, tucking up a stray wisp of hair and letting his hand linger at her earlobe until she blushed and looked away.

"Don't forget to salute if anyone stops us," he said, breaking the tension. "And let me do the talking."

"Aye, sir!" She snapped to attention and cocked her arm sharply, and Barnabas returned the salute with a cheeky grin.

He really did look quite handsome in that uniform.

"All right. On we go."

She turned the knob, opened the door . . . and was nearly deafened as a klaxon started to sound.

Thirteen

❧

His FIRST INSTINCT was to close the door and run back to
the cart. Freddie was already inside, however, so Barnabas
could only hover in the doorway and try to restrain his panic.

"Get back," he whispered frantically. She either couldn't
hear or chose to ignore him. She seemed to be observing
the apparent chaos in front of them.

Not chaos, Barnabas realized after a moment. It was order,
urgently executed. Officers in uniforms dashed from one
console to another in the large, circular depression that
seemed to house the station's command center. He couldn't
begin to guess what all the machines did, what the printed
tapes meant, where the tangle of copper tubes and conduits
led. But clearly, the men and women of the station did know
and were operating in some state of high alarm. He didn't
blame them, as his own heart was beating at a hazardous pace.

"Echo Alert," a voice blasted over a loudspeaker, tinny

and distorted from the high volume. "Echo Alert. All hands commence quake protocol one-A. This is not a drill."

"The alarm wasn't because of us," Freddie exclaimed, backing toward the door and speaking over the din. "It's an earthquake. They're preparing for another earthquake. Look, I think they're planning to evacuate."

Indeed, the Navy personnel were peeling off and disappearing through various exits at an increasing rate. Soon the chamber would be empty.

"Let's go back."

"Excellent idea." He held the door for her but was dismayed when she stopped immediately on the other side of it once it was closed, instead of proceeding to the carriage.

"I can't believe our luck!" she shouted. The shrill alarm was no quieter on this side of the door.

Flabbergasted, Barnabas gestured toward the tracks. "I thought we were *going*."

"Don't be silly. This is perfect. Nobody should be exiting this way; they expect the carriage to be at the other end. Did you notice most of them were heading for the doorway to the right of this one? That must be the direction of the submersible docks. We can wait right here for the room to empty out, and then follow them down that hallway. They'll all be distracted. Then they'll be gone and we'll have the run of the place to find what we need."

"In an earthquake."

"It won't last long."

"But . . . an earthquake. They all seem to feel it's worth abandoning ship immediately—or station, rather—for this. Shouldn't we do likewise?"

"By what means?" She gave a philosophical shrug. "We can't go back the way we came; the tunnel probably isn't any safer than the station itself, and even if it doesn't collapse entirely we could end up trapped halfway with no provisions. And we'd be spotted as impostors in no time if we tried to join the rest on one of the subs they're using."

"It doesn't seem sensible to stay," he insisted. He knew he was fighting a losing battle. He was fairly certain he couldn't deny this woman anything, that he would follow even her most outrageous whims. Worse, he suspected that Freddie could also sense this about him.

"It wasn't sensible to come in the first place," she reminded him. "But as we're here, we might as well try to get what we came for. If the earthquake makes that possible, well . . . so now we wait for that big control room to clear out."

As one, they pressed their ears to the door, listening for any remaining hint of activity as if they might actually hear anything over the alarm bell. Freddie finally risked a peek, cracking the door open a fraction of an inch for a few seconds before closing it again.

"I didn't see anyone left. I couldn't see the whole room, though. Do you suppose they're all leaving by submersible, or by the other underground tunnel, the France one?" she asked.

"If the other side is like this one, I'd imagine submersible. There seemed to be dozens of crew members inside, and those were only the ones we could see. The carriage in the tunnel wouldn't be large enough to transport more than a few, and they'd be at risk in the tunnel the entire time. It seems as though a submersible would carry more of them and be safer. I wonder how much advance warning the—"

The ground bumped beneath their feet, a palpable and unnerving bounce. Then another, accompanied by a vibration that rattled their teeth in their heads as they tried to keep their footing.

"This seems worse than the last one," Freddie cried out, clinging to the doorknob.

Barnabas fully expected the tunnel to collapse on them at any moment. "It is worse! Let's get inside the station." He jerked his side of the door open and hurried her inside, only to stop and stare with horror at the now-unoccupied chamber. He hadn't seen much else than the scurrying officers on his first glance. Now that the vast room was vacant, Barnabas could appreciate the magnitude of the space, and the majestic proportions of its ceiling which vaulted in a framework of metal, wood and glass up into the waters of the channel itself. A seascape, directly over their heads, held off only by some shards of glass that seemed absurdly fragile from his point of view. In a delicate frame that was currently receiving sharp jolts to its base in the bedrock.

"God, that's beautiful," was Freddie's assessment.

She was correct, but only in a certain sense. "Yes, hemlock flowers are lovely too, but they're still likely to kill you if you're not careful."

"Everyone's gone, at least. I wonder for how long? The quake's already subsiding."

He started to disagree with her, then realized she was right about that. The ground gave another fitful shrug, then settled into a broody stillness. Having felt it shudder, Barnabas no longer trusted it to remain solid. A queasy uncertainty lingered with him, convincing him that he simply wasn't meant for high adventure. The rippling, water-filtered light throughout the room, while beautiful, only added to his sense of unsteadiness.

"I would hazard a guess that they're gone until after the risk of aftershocks has lessened to an acceptable degree. Of course that could mean any number of things. They could be headed back already."

The klaxon stopped sounding as he spoke, leaving him

to shout the last few words into the suddenly still room. Freddie lifted her eyebrows, clearly amused.

"We should get to exploring, then." She sounded more excited than frightened, but there was an edge to her voice that hinted at bravado.

"There's no shame in preferring to hide under a sturdy table, you know."

"Don't be silly. A table won't help us one bit if that ceiling collapses. I want to find the *Gilded Lily* so we can use it to beat a hasty retreat. You didn't think I meant us to stay down here indefinitely, did you? They are coming back eventually. Besides, it's an earthquake, for heaven's sake, Barnabas. We need to get out before the aftershocks."

That. That exact instant, those precise words, were what Barnabas would always remember as the moment he knew he was in love with Freddie Murcheson. That he would follow her into certain death if it came to that. But he thought if anyone could find a way to prevent that death, it would almost certainly be Freddie.

"Down that corridor, then."

They nearly came up on the heels of the last few evacuating crew, and another handful of junior officers jogged past them in the passageway, but nobody seemed to pay them any mind. The Navy personnel were too preoccupied with following their evacuation protocols and with vacating the station in the quickest, most orderly fashion possible.

"They must all presume we know what we're doing too," Freddie murmured. She ducked into a side passage and tugged Barnabas with her, glancing up and down the main hall to ensure nobody saw them. "They seemed to be heading down to the end, so I assume that's where the larger submersibles are docked. We can wait another moment or two to be sure the coast is clear, then look at some of the closer docks."

Barnabas registered her words, but only vaguely. He was too busy staring into the chamber next to them, whose door had been left ajar.

The room itself was unremarkable—small, carved stone walls, the same marble and wood and brass trim they'd seen throughout the station. The three wheeled chairs inside were pushed close together, a tight fit for the trio of crew who must operate the machinery that held Barnabas's attention. The equipment took up the entirety of the room's widest wall, with a bewildering array of small lamps, switches, and flat panels that somehow displayed lighted text and numbers. In the center of the wall was a larger brass panel, embossed with elaborate, fluid, concentric shapes and studded with lights. Some of them glowed red, some green. A larger green bulb occupied the approximate center of the design. It took Barnabas some time to realize he was looking at a topographical map.

He tugged on Freddie's arm, drawing her attention away from the adjacent hall and the faint noise of voices raised over clanking metal on metal. "If that's a representation of the ocean floor, and the big light is the station, what are those other lights?"

"Good *God*, that's fancy!"

"But what *is* it?"

"I have no idea, but oh, I'd love to take that thing apart." The look on her face hovered between awe and lust.

"No time for that."

"I know, I know. Well, let's see." She ventured into the chamber, studying the panels and running her fingers over some of the myriad switches as though she could read the machine's intent that way. "The lights on the chart are in fixed locations, so they can't be submersibles. Other geographical features? That seems more likely, but the pattern seems too regular. And these lines from the station to each light look almost like spokes on a wheel."

"Or arms on an octopus," he suggested. He'd thought of a spider, first, but an octopus seemed more fitting for their current setting.

"There are a good many more than eight, however." She pointed to one of the longer lines, tracing it out to its terminus in a tiny red glimmer. "This is a fresher mark in the brass. See, it hasn't darkened yet. The eight heavier lines, the ones along the main compass directions, must have been the original ones. More were added later."

"Some sort of beacons, perhaps? Part of the system they use to surveil the channel?"

"No . . ." Her curious gaze traveled on, landing on a row of shelves at the side of the room. More than a dozen small devices were lined up, each with a band of slowly scrolling paper tape and an inked needle scratching over the surface. Some were mostly quiescent, but a few bounced to and fro at a fervent pace, scrawling peaks and valleys on the tape in scarlet ink. "I think it's a seismograph."

"A what?"

"For detecting earthquakes. Remember? I *told* you, they have a way to do that. Except Father said it was all but useless in several quadrants," she murmured. "Those must be the red lights, the ones that aren't working. Oh, what else did he say? Something about warnings for tremors, needing more data but the glass octopus is being sabotaged. Barnabas, I think this is what my father was talking about. I think *this* is the glass octopus. Not an actual cephalopod, a giant seismograph."

"This is how they know when to evacuate." He eyed the machine with new wonder. "If that map is to be believed, this thing spans most of the channel. It must be the largest of its kind in the world."

"Even with parts of it out of commission. And from what Father said, it sounds as though it can not only detect but predict earthquake activity, when it's not damaged. It *predicts*."

She sounded angry now, not awed as she had been, as he still was. "Why does that not sound like a benefit when you say it?"

Freddie turned on him, fury turning her lovely face into the visage of an avenging angel. "It certainly is a benefit to the Navy. To the people in this station who know to get to safety. But what about the people on shore, the civilians? Three men died in the last quake. And that's just in London, where we hear the news almost immediately—who knows about the smaller ports, the fishing villages? Not to mention the French side. How much advance warning might they have all had, if the Navy saw fit to share what they're learning down here? How much senseless tragedy might have already been averted? From what I overheard, they think an even bigger quake may be coming, which means more people might be hurt. And my father seems to be in a position to change things and he hasn't, because he doesn't care."

"You don't know that."

"I can deduce that from what I do know. I can't figure out how this is all related to the problems with the fish being depleted, but it all comes down to the same thing. Father playing God."

"Why do you despise him?"

"Why do you defend him?"

A stalemate. And Barnabas wasn't even sure why they were fighting to begin with. It had all gone sour so suddenly.

He gestured toward the main tunnel. "I don't hear anything out there. I think they may be gone."

She seemed to come back to herself, to his relief. "Forgive my outburst. It's hardly your fault, after all."

He thought in a sense, perhaps it was. He was complicit in the system. Pointing that out was an exercise for another time, however. "Of course. And I apologize if my question was impertinent. Shall we see if we can find the *Gilded Lily* now?"

He'd raised concerns earlier about what would happen to them after the Navy discovered its submersible was missing. Freddie had never adequately addressed those concerns, to Barnabas's mind, but it hardly mattered now. They had to get out of the station some way, and taking the *Gilded Lily* seemed as good a way as any other. They'd just have to handle the consequences as they came.

"I suppose we ought to." With a last, wistful glance at the seismography equipment, she joined him at the doorway. Nobody was in the side hallway, and when they crept forward to check, the main corridor was empty as well. The station was silent, at least of personnel noises. A pervasive hum of hidden gears, the engines that kept the station habitable for humans, accompanied the pair as they scouted their way down the hall one doorway at a time.

THE ROUTE WAS more complicated than Freddie had anticipated. None of the closest doors led to submersibles at all, but to other offices, equipment consoles and work rooms. And when they finally discovered the twisting stairway around the corner at the end of the corridor, they followed it up to find a labyrinth of steel-paneled passages. The only improvement was that some of the walls had portholes, so they knew they were no longer in the bedrock but once more above the surface of the ocean floor.

"That's promising. And look, how clever!" She pointed

out one of the portholes and waited for Barnabas to catch up. "See there, at the edges of the pane? Rock and coral. And if you look over there, that hillock thing at an angle to the window? There's another porthole in there, I think, right next to that largest clump of seaweed. You can just make it out."

"The whole thing is camouflaged."

To any submersible or diver who didn't know what to look for, the entire station must look like an outcropping, a natural formation. Except for the larger glass panels over the main control chamber, but perhaps those were camouflaged too in some way that wasn't noticeable from the inside.

"The smugglers weren't flirting with danger, they simply didn't know the tunnel was there."

The massive scale of the undertaking grew more apparent as they passed through a hatchway and entered yet another corridor, this one angled downward in wide, terraced steps. At each landing, there was another hatchway. The low-ceilinged passage continued out of sight, curving as it followed the natural or manufactured terrain. Two dozen hatches, perhaps more. A glance into the porthole on the first one confirmed Freddie's suspicion. These, at last, were the submersible docks. An entire fleet, apparently, could be housed at the station, all unseen except by those with a need to know.

Like the hatch they'd just come through, the portals along the terraced passage were closed. Nevertheless, the air was distinctly briny, damper than the rest of the station had seemed. The odor reminded Freddie how deep they were underwater, how much pressure must be on the station, how strong the structure needed to be to withstand the weight. And the earthquake had jarred it badly.

"If we split up, we can find the *Gilded Lily* faster."

Barnabas shook his head. "Under no circumstances will we split up. I put my foot down."

When she opened her mouth to argue, he put a finger over her lips, then pointed down to his foot. And stamped it.

It should have made her furious, his emphatic insistence. Instead she had to turn away to hide her smile. "Very well, then. We can start here. The sub in this one looks smallish; let's take a closer look."

"It's not that I don't trust you alone." He stepped forward to spin the wheel on the hatch, pulling it open to let her pass through first. "I mean I don't, of course I don't, but that isn't the point."

"That's quite all right."

"No, no. I believe you can take care of yourself. Good God, you travel regularly in parts of London where no gentleman dares go, and you haven't had your throat cut yet, so I can only assume you have developed at least some self-preservation skills. But—oh, this isn't the one, is it?"

The submersible that bobbed in the open-topped tank before them was more bathysphere than anything else, a pudgy pod that bore no resemblance to a sleek lily bud. Freddie propped one foot on the low metal parapet that held back the water, sighing as she gazed down at the ugly vessel.

"No, it isn't. And I don't think both of us would fit in there, at any rate. On to the next one."

"It might do for a backup plan, if we can find two of them." He followed her to the next docking chamber, still talking as he worked the wheel to the portal. "But capable as you are, I would never forgive myself if I knowingly let you go off alone, and something happened that would have been in my power to prevent. I know it makes little sense. You did well enough before I arrived, after all."

She had. But Freddie had to admit it was enjoyable to adventure with a partner for once. Dan Pinkerton, bless him, had never quite been that. He'd never entered into the spirit of the thing. Despite his obvious anxieties, Barnabas at least seemed game to explore. Like a small boy, he took up the ineffectual wooden sword of his bravery and crossed into the dark forest, fully accepting the possibility of wolves.

Or, in this case, floods. The stone floor of the next dock was slick with seawater, an ominous sign. Whatever had once been docked there was gone now, and the water in the tank was level with the top of the retaining wall.

Barnabas closed the portal carefully after they'd exited. "We should hurry."

Another few of the ugly bathysphere-shaped things, another half-dozen empty tanks. Freddie's chest began to tighten, her head to ache. From the pressure, probably, but whether it was literal or figurative, she couldn't tell.

The wheel on the next hatch stuck, but when Freddie stepped in to help Barnabas turn it, he pushed back with a stiff arm. "No! Look . . ."

She looked at his face first. He'd gone a sickly shade of pale gray, and sweat beaded on his brow. "Are you ill?"

"No, not at me. At the window."

"Porthole," she corrected automatically, but turned her gaze where he was pointing. And gasped, backing away as if it might help. He followed, embracing her, placing a comforting hand on the center of her back as he tried to interpose himself between her and the danger. She had to peer over his shoulder to keep her eyes on the hatch, clinging to his upper arms for support.

Water splashed against the double pane of reinforced glass, level with Barnabas's eyes. If he'd succeeded in opening the hatch, they might have been drowned. And who could say what the deluge might have done to the station? The hatches were obviously closed, and very thick and heavy, for good reason. The docking pools clearly relied on a careful balance of air pressure to maintain their integrity. If the quake had caused a breach in the station's hull, any one of the hatches might be holding back the entire channel.

And what's more, "What if that one was the *Gilded Lily*?"

Barnabas shook his head and released her with clear reluctance, then proceeded to the last hatch before the tunnel turned at an angle. "Nothing we can do about it. If this isn't it, though, I vote we split up after all and each take one of the ones that look like oversized diving helmets."

"Agreed."

But the last hatch along that wall was operational, with no flood behind it. And there, in the pool of pressure-contained water, floated the living embodiment of the diagram in her father's office.

"The *Gilded Lily*, I presume?"

"At last!"

Grinning, she turned to him, thrilled to see that his anxiety was at least tinged with excitement over their discovery. Freddie flung her arms around his neck on impulse, too happy and relieved to care about the setting, the awkwardness, the fact that she was meant to be a male naval officer.

"Thank you," she whispered in his ear, and his arms came up around her waist as a shiver went through his body.

"For what?" he responded, bending to let his breath tickle her ear in return. Freddie's body tingled with surprised interest.

"For helping me find the *Gilded Lily*. For coming with me to scout out the station. For believing in me, even though we may both hang if we're caught."

Pulling back enough to look at her, Barnabas smiled weakly. "I'm trying not to think about the hanging part.

What do you plan to do with the submersible once you're through using it? So that we *can* avoid being caught with it in our possession, at least?"

"Abandon it. I ought to scuttle it, but I can't bear the thought of ruining such a lovely piece of machinery. Besides, I don't want to deprive the Navy of their equipment, only borrow it for a little while since they're not making good use of it. So I'll leave it somewhere they can probably find it again, under a dock or something like that. Wipe all the surfaces clean first, of course, because I've heard they have a way to take a person's fingerprints from smooth surfaces like metal now."

"I read an article about fingerprints in a scientific journal that Baron Hardison had lying about. I'd forgotten all about it. You'd make a brilliant criminal, Freddie."

"Thank you, I think."

He smiled, looking almost bashful, and bent closer. She could feel his breath against her face and wished she weren't wearing so much padding so she could feel the solid planes of his body against hers.

"I meant it as a compliment," he assured her, before stealing a kiss. Just a brush of lips, a moment of shared breath, but it was enough to make Freddie's knees go weak. She sighed as they stepped away from one another, recognizing the necessity but wishing the kiss could have gone on for longer. Maybe later, when they weren't threatened with the imminent collapse of an undersea cavern and orchestrating the theft of costly military equipment.

She searched the chamber's worktable until she found what she needed, a thick book with a cheap binding. It was a manual, filled with additional notes in various neat hands, clearly a work in progress.

"Look, Barnabas! Instructions!"

"I suppose that will help. You, ah . . . you have no idea how to pilot this thing, do you?"

He still looked distinctly off-color. Freddie didn't blame him one bit. She felt somewhat fragile and translucent around the edges herself and would be more than glad when they could finally vacate the possibly crumbling station.

"But we have the handbook, so I will in a bit. We'll start at the beginning, yes? Preoperation Checklist. Item the first: Integrity inspections . . ."

Fourteen

❧❦❧

IT LOOKED LIKE a typical warehouse built out over the dock. Sometimes Rollo's men even used it to store goods other than contraband, although only for short periods of time. But the important part of the main building, the only part Rollo really cared about, was the giant open pool in the middle of the complex. Submersibles could access it only by navigating through the channel at precisely the right intervals to avoid the Navy patrols, and then following the one narrow cleftlike passage with a deep enough draft to accommodate them and keep them hidden from any fishermen or commercial boats on the surface. Nothing came through at low tide.

There were no pleasure craft to worry about. Nobody would tour that part of the channel for the view, unless they had a particular fondness for mile upon mile of seedy waterfront construction, fishing docks and dry docks and freight yards and the nastiest drinking establishments in the Commonwealth.

When his brother still held the reins, there had always been at least some cargo in the warehouse. Dried beef, leather goods, cheeses . . . the products of the legitimate side of Lord Orm's business. His cattle didn't make him anything like the money he earned from opium, particularly once shipping costs to Europa were factored in, but that didn't matter. The respectable front was all that counted.

Rollo had no further access to leather and cheese now that the California operation had been shut down. He did, however, have an unprecedented load of opium on hand, the largest stockpile of his career. His subs met the boats, which went on to their destinations with no trace left of their suspicious freight. Then brought the goods to the warehouse, where they were normally dispersed throughout England and, via other subs, across the channel to Europa. Orm had built a black market empire, nearly cornering the market in illegal opium to the continent, and Rollo was determined to hang on to it as long as he could despite the lack of new product coming in from the Dominions. While he opened negotiations with new suppliers, he'd hoarded what he could to drive the price up.

Opium dens across the land had awaited his product eagerly at first, then fervently, now desperately. The time was right. Rollo sensed he'd pushed the market as far as he could take it, and he was set for a massive, staged delivery operation.

As soon as he eradicated the cephalopod threat. And for that, he needed all the submersibles in his fleet that were equipped to carry torpedoes. Four were docked in the warehouse already, with another one expected from France at high tide. Two more awaited his signal to rendezvous at the coordinates where they'd spotted the squid.

"What d'you call that, anyway, Mordecai? A herd of squid? A school? Maybe a flotilla?"

"Cuttlefish," Mordecai corrected him, rousing from his

sulk to engage on the topic just as Rollo knew he would. "They're cuttlefish. And . . . I don't know. I don't know, Rollo. Not a school, that's for fish. Whales are pods. I don't know what it is for cuttlefish. Or for squid."

There was always the risk, once Mord was upset, that any little thing might set him off. He was already miffed at having to wait so long to return to the nest of squid. He hadn't wanted to leave in the first place. If Rollo had let him have his way they'd still be there, counting and observing the monsters. Then someone had let slip that Rollo meant to do away with the creatures, and Mord had been in a proper stew ever since.

Rollo had seen Mordecai pull wings from flies and study their dying throes. He'd kept his young friend from performing equivalent operations on kittens and was fairly certain he'd been unsuccessful in saving the lives of many rats and mice who had gone to their untimely deaths in Mord-inflicted agony. But Mord liked these sea creatures. Found them peaceful. Didn't want them to die.

Sometimes—just sometimes—Rollo thought Mordecai was more trouble than he was worth.

"Can we let one live, Roland? Just a small one, like?"

That was the problem. Moments like that one, Mord staring at him with those huge, hopeful eyes, looking to him for help. Trusting him, as terrible a specimen of humanity as he was. Mord looked up to him, without even fearing him as most sensible men did. Mord had no sense of that kind. He feared many things, but not Rollo Furneval. And Rollo could never resist the allure of having somebody, even as wretched a somebody as Mordecai, trust him implicitly.

"All right. But only a small one."

"Can we bring it home?"

"I don't see why not. If somebody were clever enough to

devise a net we could deploy from the sub. Something that wouldn't snag on the propellers or be in the way of the torpedo launchers, mind you."

"I can! I know! Do you promise?"

"Yes, I promise. But it'll need a tank. You'll have to take care of feeding it and looking after it."

"I know what to do. I'll do it, you wait and see, Rollo!"

Mordecai ran off to work on his scheme, slamming the office door behind him. Rollo had no doubt his childhood friend would come up with a brilliant mechanism that would find all sorts of applications unrelated to the capture and keeping of live cephalopods. And the invention process would keep him happily occupied for hours and conveniently out of the way while Rollo devised a plan with the other submersible pilots.

"Barmy bugger," Edwin scoffed from the corner of the office, where he sat whittling a figure from a hunk of driftwood. He kept a special knife just for that, along with those he used in the course of his employment.

"Barmy, to be sure. I've never known him to be one for the gents, however. You don't want to know about his tastes as regards the fairer sex."

"Aye, I'm sure I don't. You really gonna let him trap one o' those things, Mr. F?"

"Indeed I am, Ed. Pet squid. Never know when that might come in useful, eh?"

Ed snorted. "It's a cuttlefish."

Rollo turned toward the corner, observing his minion silently until the large man grew visibly uncomfortable under the scrutiny. "Perhaps I shall assign you the task of feeding the new pet, Ed."

"As you say, sir. Though I'd hate to deprive Mord of the pleasure and the chance to learn some responsibility."

"I'm fairly sure Mord would derive great pleasure in figuring out how to feed the squid with you."

A sharp knock interrupted them. If Rollo had been a different sort of man, he would have laughed out loud at the look of exaggerated relief on poor Edwin's bulldoglike face.

"Come."

Young Finn leaned into the room, holding the doorway by his fingertips as though the floor might lurch beneath his feet or otherwise betray him at any moment. As always, Rollo was struck with the thought that the man must have been a proper little sailor at some point in his life, as he seemed to have a permanent set of sea legs.

"Nearly high tide, sir. Remy telegraphed a few moments ago, says he'll be docking within the hour."

"He'll need to refuel and reprovision?"

"Aye, sir. And arm his vessel."

"He's been running defenseless? We need to remedy that in future. No telling how many of these creatures are out there aside from those in the . . . herd. The new policy will be to eradicate the monsters on sight. Right, tell the pilots we assemble in an hour to debrief. Then do a perimeter sweep. Make sure all the lads are awake and where they ought to be. We don't want somebody sneaking in through the fence while our attention is on the water."

"Aye aye."

"Do you know what a group of squid is called, Finn?"

To his surprise, the young man nodded, pausing on his way out the door, "A shoal, sir."

"Really? A shoal of squid."

"I believe so, yes."

Beneath the shaggy overgrowth of hair and faintly ridiculous mustache, behind the patch obscuring one of Finn's eyes, a keen brain lurked along with a sense of the absurd that the young man couldn't always hide. Sometimes, as now, his good eye gleamed with barely suppressed humor out of proportion to the circumstance. Rollo knew the man's value, but he also held a deep natural distrust of those who spent such effort hiding their true nature. In many ways, he preferred the brutal simplicity of an Edwin, or the blatant lunacy of Mordecai, to this sort of useful but clandestine personality.

"That'll be all."

Finn nodded and was gone.

"A shoal of squid," Edwin repeated, shaking his head. "Fancy that."

"Where do you suppose he learned it?"

This question was beyond Ed's capacity, however. The behemoth simply shrugged and resumed his carving. Rollo couldn't tell whether the figure was meant to be a dog, a bear, or some sort of tiger. Whatever it was, it was lumpy and ugly, not unlike its creator.

One hour. In one hour, he would assemble the captains of his fleet and make a plan to find the shoal of squid—or cuttlefish, as the case might be—and eliminate all but one small one. Further clearing the path to expand his business into Europa. He would be one step closer to a future in which he, Rollo Furneval the bastard, achieved if not greatness, then at least a more distinctive level of infamy.

"But how does it generate the oxygen?" Barnabas asked again. "How do we know we won't run out? The tank doesn't seem nearly large enough to last us both any length of time."

Freddie had absorbed enough of the instructions to pilot the sub out of the dock and away from the station, but once Barnabas had taken over poring through the manual, he'd insisted they surface and regroup before going any farther.

"The tank is just a backup. The primary air source is a by-product of the heating process. It's a chemical reaction," Freddie repeated patiently. "As long as we begin with sufficient zinc, manganese dioxide, and potassium chlorate in these canisters here to keep the engine powered—the gauges all show nearly full now, you see—we'll have sufficient air for breathing."

"For how long?"

She pulled the book from his hands and flipped through the pages, searching for a definitive answer. The guide was far from easy to follow. The vessel was evidently a work in progress, and the original fuel delivery system had been altered. The current design had been noted by hand, in the margins and over heavily crossed-through passages. Rough sketches and cryptic formulae were appended here and there with no discernible logic. The gist, however, was clear enough.

"We ought to have at least eight hours. Although I'm not sure what happens when the submersible isn't moving. I don't know if the engine keeps enough baseline heat to generate sufficient oxygen if it's idling. Or how long the reserves will last if it's turned off altogether. Perhaps we should assume that if we need to stop for any length of time we'll have to surface again and unseal the hatch. That way we can reserve the oxygen tank for a true emergency."

"I don't feel quite well," he responded with a frown. In truth, he looked quite ghastly, as the tiny craft bobbed in the choppy water of the channel. Freddie understood perfectly and was filled with an odd urge to coddle him, but her sympathy was extremely limited by pragmatism.

"Don't you dare be sick. Or if you are, do it now over the water, before we close the hatch again."

She wanted to get underwater again. It felt too exposed on the surface, surrounded by the revealing glare of sunshine on water on this unaccountably sunny day. The large subs full of Navy personnel might return at any moment. Or a smuggler might be rushing through the deeps beneath them as they floated dithering over the minutiae of the sub's workings. The strangely noisy hiss of the whitecaps under the cheerful breeze, the odor of salt fish and the attending movement were all surface phenomena as well. Below, everything had been steadier, quieter. Barnabas would no doubt feel better once they returned to the relative safety of their cruising depth.

He certainly sounded anything but steady now. "Get below and fire the engine back up. I'll just . . . enjoy the fresh air a moment longer."

"It isn't fire. It's a—"

"Just . . . go."

She wouldn't think about it too closely. Laying the manual flat on her lap, she followed the sequence to heat the steam engine back to running capacity. By the time she was ready to engage the gears and set off, Barnabas had secured the hatch and returned to his seat on the floor of the small cargo area behind the pilot's chair.

As they dove below the waves, heading in the direction of the estuary mouth, Freddie passed the book back to him. "See if you can determine how the hydrophonic array works. I think the controls are there on the wall in front of you."

The pilot's area was already crammed with equipment. The panel of instruments and gear opposite Barnabas appeared to be a late addition involving a periscope sight, a series of control levers and a set of brass ear trumpets. The manual was unclear as to how to approach it.

"This whole section is terrible. Whoever wrote it in had a very poor hand as well as a distinctly loose grasp of proper grammar and spelling."

"True. Excellent illustrations, however. Look at the diagram on the back flyleaf."

"Ah. Oh, I see. This isn't bad at all."

She heard him flipping through the pages, toying with the controls. Before her, the murky water obscured the long view, and she had to trust the instrument panels to tell her they were heading in the right direction and maintaining a safe distance from the channel floor. It was difficult at first, observing the gauges and ignoring the scanty physical evidence. After a time, however, she found herself drawing inward, cycling her attention through the various panels in a comforting pattern, the dials more real to her than the world outside the safe bubble of the submersible.

"What should I do if I find something?" whispered Barnabas after a particularly long and quiet interval.

"Tell me which direction it's in so I don't run us afoul of it, I suppose."

"It's right . . . there, over there." It took her a moment to realize he was pointing, another to follow the direction of his finger and shift her focus back to the world outside the cockpit. "Look, don't you see?"

Of course she saw. It was huge and ungainly, a whale of a vessel compared to their own sleek craft. Painted in watery striations of blue, green and brown, with a poorly executed yellow poppy on its pointed nose. Freddie quickly adjusted speed so as not to pass it by. The big sub was evidently going in their own chosen direction, and she'd nearly overtaken it.

"I don't see any hydrophones on that one."

Until Barnabas said this, she'd been in a mild panic, assuming the other sub could "see" them as clearly as they saw it. He was correct, though; the massive vessel seemed to sport no special listening equipment like their own. Nor had it altered its course when they approached. Keeping behind it, they might as well be completely invisible.

"What if it isn't going anywhere useful?" Barnabas worried aloud. "We could run ourselves out of fuel and never learn another thing about the smugglers' location."

It had been a little over three hours since they departed from the station. Freddie was having trouble converting knots into miles, but she thought they must be reasonably near the English side of the channel by now, and surely there were only so many places the smugglers' sub could be heading.

"Look at the size of that thing," she pointed out. "It can't dock just anywhere. It seems to be traveling in the same direction we were, which suggests to me that it came from France as well. Besides, what's our other option? To wait about until some other clearly demarcated smuggler's vessel comes along instead?"

"Fine, then. But stay well back. And keep an eye on the instruments. I say if we seem in any danger of running empty, we make for the nearest available piece of land and abandon ship."

"Fair enough."

Perhaps.

But the more pressing problem, in the end, wasn't an insufficiency of fuel. It was the challenge of continuing to follow the sub once they neared the coastline. The captain of the smuggler vessel clearly knew what he was about, for he seemed to have no difficulty maneuvering his seemingly unwieldy craft through a narrow gap between two rock shoals, then into a sort of groove along the channel's bottom, a winding course of obstacles that left Freddie's nerves jangling and her knuckles sore from an overtight grip on her submersible's controls.

Then, there was an even shallower stint, dangerously near the surface, and finally the bit that nearly had her abandoning the entire enterprise. They had to weave through a labyrinth of massive pilings, all of which confounded the hydrophones and other instruments as well. She proceeded on faith and hubris, and when the course cleared again she was so relieved she almost followed the other sub straight up to the water's surface.

"No! Retreat, retreat!"

"What? Oh!"

Maneuverable as it was, the *Gilded Lily* couldn't reverse course with no preparation. Freddie throttled back hard and prayed as the ship drifted perilously close to a piling, pitching higher in the water while its momentum bled away. She didn't want to attempt to navigate backward, so she executed a hasty turn before engaging the main propeller again and slipping away between the piers to what she could only hope was a safe enough distance from where the smuggler had docked.

"There were four more of those things in there." Barnabas seemed to have gotten the hang of the hydrophone mechanism. "One of them was the one we saw our first time in the tunnel, I'm sure of it. It had the whiskers."

"Five submersibles. That's a large operation for blockade running, isn't it?"

"They could be supplying the whole of England and the European seaboard with opium, with a fleet like that. But submersibles have a limited range, and we know the opium must have originated in the California Dominion. At least Orm's did. Perhaps whoever is running the operation now has a new supplier. But either way, he'd need to be receiving shipments over longer distances than subs could manage. There must be ships involved, also. Perhaps even the steam rail in Europa. It goes everywhere now, faster than lorries or wagons and far cheaper than airships."

"We still need some sort of evidence, though. And I know where we are in the water, sort of, but I've no idea how to find the same place on a map of the shore. We need to go up and find some landmarks."

Abandoning the earpiece and levers, Barnabas leaned over the pilot's seat, one hand on Freddie's shoulder for leverage as he pulled forward to examine the instruments. She'd grown so accustomed to his presence a few feet away that she'd forgotten how close the space truly was. Inches apart, they'd been this whole time. His hand burned even through layers of uniform wool and cotton, and his breath teased her ear when he bent closer to peer through the glass up into the sun-dappled water.

"There. Go back into the pilings, but bring us up underneath one of the docks where it's widest. Where a warehouse is, but not one with an opening in it." She complied, hands more certain on the controls now, and the little vessel broke the surface in an uneventful few seconds. "Nobody should spot us under here, and you can stay with the sub while I can climb out under the pier and if need be, swim to a better vantage point."

"Or I can go, while you stay with the sub. I brought a change of clothes too, you'll recall."

"You'd drown in seconds once that bolster under your coat got waterlogged." He poked a finger at the padding over her belly, and Freddie stifled a giggle. The disguise was ridiculous in that respect, she'd be the first to admit.

"Fair enough."

"Why a portly lad? I've been wondering. It seems an odd choice for a costume you wear so much. It can't be comfortable."

He'd kept his fingers there, brushing the fabric, when she

expected him to pull away. Flustered, she gave him the truth before she could think better of it. "If I pad my middle it helps to hide my bosom. Somewhat. I mean I still have to . . . people get an overall impression of plumpness. As long as they don't squeeze me I'll never be found out. And when I'm in my usual clothing that particular feature seems to be the first thing men notice. I don't mind, really. I suppose it makes it even less likely anyone will recognize me."

"I did," he pointed out. He seemed to have moved closer, despite the interfering presence of the chair. Entirely too close, really.

"Yes, but you didn't know me."

Barnabas chuckled, a soft round breath of a laugh that filled her senses and made her skin come awake to a host of sensations. She felt as though the stifling air of the sub had sprung to life and started caressing her, taking liberties.

"Does that make sense?"

"It did until I said it out loud. At any rate, the costume is a helpful illusion. And it makes me feel more the part, if I know that nobody can see me under all that batting."

"I can," Barnabas admitted. His voice dropped to nearly a whisper. "Your illusion has spent its power with me."

"So even with all that extra stuffing, you still look at Freddie the tinker or Fred the officer and see Frédérique, the half-French temptress with the splendid figure?" she teased, trying to lighten the mood.

"I'm afraid so. In fact, it drives me more than a little mad to look at Freddie the tinker or sailor. I not only know what's under the stuffing, I know that when you're dressed this way you're not wearing a corset."

She had to tip her head back to see him properly. "We really shouldn't be discussing my undergarments, Lord Smith-Grenville," she sighed. "We have smugglers to spy on."

"It's not so much the undergarments as the lack thereof. We shouldn't be doing a lot of things, Freddie," he pointed out. "You shouldn't be running around dressed as a boy or spoiling ball gowns with engine grease; I shouldn't be thinking about your lack of a corset while helping you steal government property and chase dangerous criminals. We really shouldn't be extorting one another. And yet . . ." He trailed a finger down her cheek, then carried on from her chin straight down her neck to the divot between her collarbones. It was shocking, almost literally, as though he were electrified and her skin had become a conduit for that energy.

"And yet?" No use trying to keep a level voice. It was as shaky as the rest of her.

"Yet we keep doing all those things. It says something about us both, I suspect."

"I'm sure it does." She wanted him to move his hand and he did, as if he'd read her mind. Just a stroke, gentle but assured, fanning his fingers out and letting them curve under the fabric of her lapel.

"And don't let's discuss what I'm thinking about whenever I see you in trousers," he added, sounding damnably calm. His hand, though, was trembling. And so was his other hand, which had somehow arrived at her hip. In fact, it had all turned into an outright embrace at some point.

"Well, we seem to be on the subject just now anyway." She didn't know how she could speak; it must be some reflexive action to throw a quip Barnabas's way to keep the conversation going.

"No, really. We shouldn't discuss it. I'm having a difficult enough time maintaining my composure as it is."

Her next quip was silenced aborning by his lips, finally— when had it become a question of finally?—claiming hers.

Fifteen

HE WOULD HAVE preferred to remain in the submersible, kissing Freddie and avoiding any possibility of encounter with potentially hostile smugglers. At the very least, Barnabas wished they'd considered bringing waterproof weapons, as he was now stuck with traipsing about the enemy lair bearing only a penknife with which to defend himself against the criminals inside.

On the other hand, once he'd fallen from the understructure of the pier into the shockingly cold water and had to swim his way out from under the warren of dark, algae-slick columns, the idea of his being attacked on sight for not belonging seemed less likely. He'd traded his uniform for the rough clothes he'd worn to accompany Freddie on her tinkering job, and now he could have been any dripping, miserable fool wandering the docks after an accidental dunking. Surely it was a common enough sight that nobody would give him a second look, unless it was to laugh at him.

Shivering, wondering what his life had become and feeling generally put-upon, he crept along the narrow edge of pier between one dilapidated building and the water, resisting the instinct to go sideways with his back pressed to the wall. From the corner of that structure he could almost reach out and touch the fence that separated Orm's warehouse from its neighbors. At least he could only assume it was Orm's establishment, the one under which the poppy-emblazoned smuggler sub had docked.

The docks were quiet, nearly deserted, only an occasional gull cry or slap of water breaking the afternoon calm. Sounds of a barroom, drunken good humor and a shrill fishwife of a barmaid, drifted in from a few streets over, but the building Barnabas stood by seemed empty and quiet.

The silence of Orm's place, however, seemed active and ominous. He heard footsteps behind the fence. The creak of shifting weight on the planks of the pier, but not so much as a whistle from whoever walked there. No conversation or sounds of industry. When the walker seemed to have passed, Barnabas risked a peek between the fence boards. His limited view showed him only more sad, weathered gray wood.

Emboldened, he gripped the top of the fence and hoisted himself up, feet scrambling for purchase, until he could rest his weight on top of the boards and have a good look in either direction.

To his right was the empty, windowless prospect of the warehouse's side wall, with the broad span of walkway between it and the fence.

To the left was the corner of the warehouse and the waterfront beyond, and Barnabas had just decided to venture in that direction when a man rounded the corner, stopping with a look of near-comical shock that Barnabas could only suppose was a mirror of his own expression. Horrified, he tried to slip back off the fence, only to lose his balance and flip forward instead to land at the unexpected watchman's feet.

"Here now, you shouldn't be on this side. There's a sign that says no admittance! Now I 'av to take you in to Mr. Edwin, and none of us'll be happy."

From his vantage, the poor guard looked as taken aback as he was, and more anxious about the prospect of dealing with Mr. Edwin than concerned with any danger Barnabas might actually pose. But he was armed with a vicious-looking club and seemed ready to call for assistance, so Barnabas steeled himself to either flee back over the fence or fight his way free.

He stopped by some instinct when the boy—for he was young, this apparent criminal, and obviously green—looked over Barnabas's head with a squint against the sun's glare and then relaxed, sudden relief palpably altering his apple-cheeked face.

"Mr. Finn! This one was slithering over the fence. I ought to stay on my watch, do you want to take him in?"

"Happy to, Nick. I'm sure nothing would please Edwin more. But look, what's that over there?"

The newcomer pointed to the water; young Nick gaped in that direction, then slumped into Barnabas's lap, felled by Mr. Finn's expertly wielded blackjack to the head.

"Sorry about that, Nicky. Well, well. You've just made my day considerably more complicated, I'll have you know. Come on, back over the fence before we're spotted."

His rescuer bent a knee and cupped his hands together, and Barnabas took the chance without thinking. He used the assistance to vault back over the fence, stumbling and pitching over onto his knees on the other side too. The other fellow was over a few seconds later, executing a neat turn at the fence top and landing on his feet, soft and agile as a cat. An eerily familiar cat.

"You'll need to get up. We mustn't linger. What kind of conveyance did you come in? Is there a chance it's been spotted?"

Barnabas couldn't believe his eyes, but he couldn't ignore his ears. He knew that voice better than his own, even if it seemed at odds with the roughly clad, scruffy, patch-eyed pirate who was speaking. For a moment he was so overcome he couldn't answer; the conflicting feelings welled up to clog his throat, to cloud his brain with years of unspent emotion. Relief, joy, anger and betrayal, all vying for first place.

The pirate extended a hand, hauling him to his feet and frowning. "Did I arrive too late? Did Nick get in a blow to the head I don't know about?"

It couldn't be. But it was.

He flung his arms around the pirate, not caring if all the smugglers in the world were bearing down on the other side of the fence.

"Phineas!"

His brother succumbed to the embrace for only a second or two before pushing him away none too gently. "Yes, yes, but we really ought to have this reunion at a more opportune moment, when there isn't quite so much risk of imminent death. Or pneumonia. Christ, you're drenched. And now so am I."

Barnabas laughed because he would have sobbed otherwise. There was little humor in the short, ugly sound. "You heartless bastard."

"Shhh! Your carriage, where is it? Or did you swim down the river? It smells that way, I must tell you, Barnabas."

"Neither. I came by commandeered submersible." He couldn't understand the vague pride that swelled in him when he made this disclosure, surely more the feeling of a younger brother to an older. The wish to please, to impress. Or perhaps just to remind his sibling that he too had unexpected resourcefulness.

Phineas didn't seem impressed, but the facial hair and eye patch made it difficult to tell for certain.

"Just lead the way. Quietly."

FREDDIE HAD PROMISED to wait inside the sub until she heard Barnabas's prearranged coded knock on the hatch. She had given that up after a few minutes and leaned on the rim of the open hatch instead, with her feet braced on the back of the pilot's chair and her head and shoulders in the breeze. Not that there was much breeze under the dock, just an occasional stirring of the fetid air that brought a moment's coolness at the cost of a fresh wash of fish and rot. And worse odors she refused to put names to.

When the trapdoor dropped down mere yards away from her head, she gasped and nearly lost her footing attempting to duck out of sight. But it was Barnabas, identifiable by his dripping wet trousers. He swung from the rope-and-plank ladder that had come down along with the door, then navigated a tricky scramble onto the nearest crossbeam, making room for the next climber, a development even more unexpected than having Barnabas return from his venture after only five or so minutes.

"What are you doing? Are you mad? That trapdoor is inside somebody's business establishment, anyone could have seen you. And who is that?"

"Shh! The warehouse above is empty. Nobody saw us, but they'll hear you if you keep that up. Fire that thing up, we need to leave with all due haste." Barnabas made room on the beam for the other man, who jumped across after closing up the hatch behind them. He wore an eye patch and directed a fearsome scowl at Freddie as he followed Barnabas over the intervening puzzle of woodwork to reach the submersible.

"All three of us? We'll never fit. And he's a pirate."

She pointed at the stranger's eye patch as clear evidence. Barnabas shook his head and waved a hand, dismissing her concern. He maneuvered himself into the hatch and dropped down, pulling her with him and bracing them both against the moment of turbulence as the sub took the shift in weight. "All will be explained in the fullness of time, Freddie, but we must go *now*."

As if to punctuate his demand, a distant shout and a rumble of footsteps erupted above them. Freddie cast a final baffled look at the newcomer, then flung herself into the seat, engaging the fuel tank and readying the engine. "Secure the hatch. This is still warm, it'll only take a moment."

"Hatch secure," the stranger volunteered. He was squeezed into the back of the cargo area, looking entirely too long and gangly.

"Check it, Barnabas."

"I think he knows how to secure a submersible hatch, Freddie. Probably better than either of us."

"Is he the acting captain of this vessel, Barnabas?" asked the pirate in polite, cultured tones that in no way matched his appearance. Something about him tugged at her mind, even as she tried to focus on the sub's controls.

"Is . . . I suppose so. One might say that."

"Then you check the hatch."

Freddie smirked. "Thank you, whoever you are."

He didn't respond. Not all *that* polite, then. Barnabas, grumbling, fidgeted behind her—checking that the hatch was secure, she assumed. Although now she trusted the stranger to have done it properly in the first place.

"Why did you say the *acting* captain?" She fiddled with the ballast controls, taking the submersible down and angling toward the open water beyond the pier. "Why not just the captain? It's my submersible, I'm piloting it, who else would be in charge?"

He chuckled, and she had to stop herself looking to make sure it wasn't Barnabas responding. They sounded freakishly alike. That was what had bothered her a moment earlier.

"I know you can't be the captain, and I know it isn't your submersible. It's the Royal Navy's submersible, and you and Barnabas stole it. Your uniform is real enough, but you're no more an officer than my brother."

"Brother?"

"Mind your trim."

"Oh!" She steered away from a looming hulk of algae-draped wood and into an avenue of thick pillars. "You're Phineas! He found you! And you're not an opium fiend after all, how lovely."

"Phineas found me," Barnabas corrected. "I've no idea if he's an opium fiend—"

"I am not."

"Or whether he's truly working for the smugglers instead of the government now—"

"Of course I'm not working for the smugglers. But just a moment, I have to ask . . . are you a *girl*?"

Freddie understood he was no longer speaking to Barnabas. "Even if I am, I'm still the captain. What gave it away, though?"

"Understood. You said it was lovely I wasn't an opium fiend. Not the usual turn of phrase I associate with young male officers. But I had my doubts, anyway, looking at your hair. Bits are coming down from under your cover."

"Cover?"

"The hat."

"Oh, I see." The bobbed hair, while performing brilliantly under a standard hat, was less manageable under the smaller, streamlined model worn by naval officers. Now that Phineas had mentioned it, Freddie was aware of wispy curls tickling behind her ears and over the nape of her neck. She would have to invest in more pins, and possibly try some pomade next time.

Barnabas cleared his throat, reinserting himself in the discourse. "As we're discussing subtle verbal signals, Phineas, I have to point out you said you were not working for the smugglers. You did not say you were working for the government."

Phineas chuckled again. "Blast. I was hoping you could tell me. *You're* working for them now, aren't you? That was my impression, anyway. I've kept tabs. One of the clerks for Father's man of business in London is secretly working for me as well, so I see a great deal of his correspondence. When I learned you were on your way to Rutherford Murcheson, I made what seemed the obvious assumption. If anything I was expecting you to show up sooner."

"But don't you *know* if you're still working for Murcheson?"

"I did know. However, when I was taken to the Dominions by Lord Orm's crew last year, my last communication to my superior at the Agency went unanswered. Next thing I knew, my name showed up in an article in the *Times* about the ravages of opium abuse in Her Majesty's military, and I learned that the Navy had informed our parents I was missing and due to be discharged in absentia for addiction, moral turpitude, and suspected treason."

"They never discharged you, to my knowledge."

"But the letter was sent. I'd been working for Murcheson for months already at that point and been into several opium dens as part of my investigations, so the suggestion of addiction was part of the cover story for my absence from my post with the Navy. Murcheson didn't warn me of that before I agreed to work for him, I hasten to add. Then the cover story made it pitifully easy for them to explain away my disappearance. My name was published on a list of accused deserters. And Murcheson ignored my efforts to check in. Even once I was back in London and learned he was here as well, he took no apparent notice of my attempts to contact him."

He sounded more jaded than horrified. The abandonment hadn't surprised him, Freddie thought. Her father's involvement didn't surprise her. "Why do you suppose that is? That he ignored you?"

"Bear in mind I'm only telling you this—or rather, telling Barnabas this—because I've reason to believe Barnabas is caught up with the same Agency, the same point of contact. I can't assume it's coincidental. I fear Murcheson plans to use my history against you, Barnabas. To discard you too, the moment you cease to be useful to him. He'll claim addiction runs in families, I'd wager anything on it. He always viewed me as disposable; I just didn't know it until it was too late."

"But weren't you supposed to be investigating the opium smugglers?" Barnabas queried. "Why would Murcheson toss you aside for continuing to do that?"

"I was already embedded as an operative working for Orm's men in London a few years ago, trying to piece together the supply chain for the rash of new opium dens spreading across London and the French coast. Working on one of the smugglers' submersibles, primarily. I'd made contact with them in one of my forays into the dens. Then Orm himself came for a visit. Ostensibly he was there for his cattle ranching concern, but the real motivation was a push to strengthen his European operations. Pinpoint new lieutenants to take the smuggling deeper into the Continent, find new markets. And handpick useful talents to bring home with him. I was taken off my sub and informed I'd be returning to the Dominions to join one of Orm's personal airship crews. This wasn't presented to me as a choice, you understand, but a fait accompli.

"Evidently, my other employer was uninterested in supporting an operative so far from home, regardless of the quality of information I might supply. He had no brief to track the opium ring to the Dominions. Not then, anyway. His authority didn't extend so far. He'd have had to pass my handling along to either the New York or Salt Lake City bureaus, and he would have lost the credit for anything I uncovered after that point. Easier to cut me loose, cut his own losses. And in some small amount of fairness to him, I never did receive official approval to shift my base of operations halfway around the world. I had to leave Europa before I heard back from him. Not that I could have done anything else without risking my life unnecessarily, but Murcheson did technically go by the book when he pronounced me a rogue."

Barnabas was obviously appalled. "But Murcheson would never have done that, thrown you to the wolves that way. There must be some mistake."

Freddie knew better. "No, that sounds exactly like something Father would have done."

"Father?"

The shift in his tone was palpable, ominous. Freddie focused on her navigation for a few moments, finding and following the deep groove leading back out of the estuary to the channel's deeps. The pause gave her a chance to collect herself, her thoughts. "I'm not just *any* girl. You needn't fear he'll hear anything back from me, however. I don't work for the man. And I should point out I'm the one agreeing with you regarding his professional ethics. On paper it all reads sensibly, and he'll never do anything to endanger his reputation. Or his family, for that matter. He's an excellent father in that respect. But outside of that, he doesn't care who he hurts."

"Who do you work for, then?"

A prickle on the side of her neck when she turned her head was Freddie's only warning. Phineas was holding a slender, wicked blade to her throat. He kept it where it was, letting the point dig into her skin, until she looked back at the console with a calm born of such extreme fear she simply couldn't comprehend it.

In her brief glimpse, she'd seen Barnabas gaping from his brother's face to the knife, clearly unable to form a response to the unexpected turn of events.

"I work for myself, Mr. Smith-Grenville."

"As a planted society darling? A sweet, simple aristocratic angel nobody would ever suspect? That's his favorite type."

At that, she had to snicker. "I'm very far from that type, sir. No, I work as a tinker-makesmith."

"A—what?"

"A *tinker*. I go out on a pony trap full of tools, dressed as Fred Merchant the tinker, and hire my services to people with broken equipment. Engines mostly, some clockwork, you know. The occasional defective printing press."

"Mechanical spit dog," Barnabas reminded her.

"That was a first."

"I'm horribly confused," Phineas responded, but he eased the knife away.

Barnabas shifted into her line of sight just long enough to place a proprietary hand on her forearm. Not interfering with her steering, just offering his support. "She's very good at what she does. She can fix *anything*."

Oh, bless him. Bless him a thousand times over for that.

"And the classified, eyes-only submersible? Your father just happened to let you take it for a spin, did he?" She knew it wasn't the case, but he sounded like he was still holding the knife to her throat.

"Oh, no, you were quite right about that. I stole it."

"And you just happened to know how to pilot it."

"I'm a quick study. And I had the manual." She pushed the book over her shoulder as evidence. "One engine is much like another, so once you add the up and down aspect of navigation through the water it's not terribly different from driving a steam car or anything else. Was your airship so different to operate from a submersible?"

Phineas took the manual. After a moment he responded, some of the tension easing from his voice. "I suppose it wasn't, at that. I wish I'd had a book to study; that would have made the transition a good deal easier."

Now that they were all less fraught, Freddie noticed another less than pleasant element in the sub's close atmosphere. "Good heavens, what is that *smell*?" Rotting vegetation with a hint of hot pigsty, was her best guess, but she could hardly say that aloud. "It's quite unpleasant."

"You saw me take a dunking," Barnabas reminded her. "Never go for a swim in the river, even the mouth of it. And especially not under a pier."

"Must we go very far? You'll leave a permanent odor in the cabin if you're in here too long."

"We ought to return to Tilbury and collect the cart."

She sighed in exasperation. "We can't take this all the way to Tilbury. The river's too shallow there. Even if we didn't run aground or get our propeller fouled in something, we'd be sure to be spotted before we found any safe place to dock. And where would that be, in Tilbury? It's a bustling port, not like the one we came from. We can't just tie the *Gilded Lily* off under my father's shipping pier and hope nobody notices it."

"Why did you have to steal it in the first place?" Phineas sounded genuinely curious. "And why bother with a sub? If the Agency wanted to surveil inside the factory there are far easier ways to put a man—or woman, begging your pardon, miss—on the inside. The whole enterprise is run on whims and guesswork. Rollo Furneval's men fear him, but they've nothing like the rabid terror that Orm commanded from his minions. They make mistakes constantly, the discipline is quite lax, and I'd think some basic observation would have revealed that."

"*I* didn't steal it," Barnabas assured his brother. Freddie rolled her eyes, unseen. He'd certainly assisted. "And my assignment isn't related to Orm's operation, or this Carnival fellow."

"Furneval. Then what the hell are you doing here? Again, pardon, miss."

"I followed Miss Murcheson."

"Why?"

"That was my assignment."

She didn't think he was *still* following her because of that, but again she thought better of saying this aloud.

After a dubiously long silence, Phineas leaned over Freddie's shoulder, taking in the navigation panels. "Once you're out of the trench, bear north. I'll work a heading out for you. You're absolutely right, we can't go to Tilbury. But I know a place on Mersea we can risk. You should have sufficient fuel. And once we're there, we can work out what on earth we ought to do next."

Sixteen

To the extent that Barnabas had a plan anymore, none of this had gone according to it. He'd imagined an emotional reunion with Phineas, and either a revelation regarding the true nature of his brother's work or perhaps a filial epiphany and renunciation of the demon opium from which Barnabas had rescued him.

Instead, Phineas had rescued him and seemed to be taking charge of their little operation, with Freddie according him a respect that had nothing to do with the knife he'd briefly held to her throat.

God, she'd been brave. Never batted an eye, just kept piloting and talking calmly, doing what she needed to do. Had he anticipated hysterics, fainting? He was no longer certain what to expect from a girl. Freddie had taken his existing notions and tossed them out on their ears. He knew plenty of strong, capable women already—the Baroness, for one, and Eliza Pence for another. Not to mention his own mother, who'd have brooked none of that knife nonsense, thank you very much. But Freddie's responses just seemed remarkable, because everything she did was remarkable.

He didn't care for the way she listened to Phineas without challenging him. It was an issue for another time, however.

They were nearly to Mersea when he remembered to ask Phineas about the sabotage and whether he'd played any part in it.

"Sabotage? There's been no sabotage."

"But the seismograph. We saw the chart, all the spots where it's out. Freddie heard her father talking about somebody sabotaging the glass octopus."

"She just *happened*—"

"Yes, I just happened to hear him," Freddie interjected. "Because I was in a secret compartment, eavesdropping. I'm not proud of it. But he did say they're having trouble with early detection of the quakes because of sabotage. It's why Father wanted another sub besides the *Gilded Lily*, to test a larger hydrophonic array. To find the saboteurs. So we *know* about them, and I'm not at all comfortable with knowing you're lying to protect them."

Queasy, unsure who to believe, Barnabas looked to Phineas for his reaction. "There was a quake while we were down in that station thing. The alarm did sound, but with very little lead time for the crew to escape. Perhaps that's normal; I mean it's astonishing enough they can detect it in advance to begin with. But then we saw the control panels for the seismograph, with so many areas marked in red. It seemed to back up what Freddie had relayed from her father."

"I don't doubt any of that. I'm sure the seismograph is in shambles, but it isn't smugglers. It's giant squid. Or perhaps cuttlefish. Cephalopods, anyway. Gigantic, glowing ones that can also apparently camouflage themselves until they're all but invisible. They've been attacking boats as well, and . . . why are you looking at me like that?"

"Oh, Phineas. I was so hopeful. But it was opium after all, wasn't it? All this time. You're going to be a ruined shell of a man. Mother will be devastated."

"Good *God*. I'm not hallucinating the squid, Barnabas; they actually exist. And I'm not an opium addict. I've never actually used the stuff at all, except the occasional dose of laudanum tincture when I was ill as a child. Same as you."

"But . . . giant squid that are invisible but also glow?"

"A whole shoal of them, yes. Apparently the camouflage properties are common to those creatures, and the glowing may be some sort of communication or perhaps a method for enticing their prey. I've been doing some reading up in my spare time. One of Rollo's men is a savant of sorts, with all sorts of arcane knowledge about animals. He's utterly mad, and a little frightening at times, but he has quite the library stashed in his quarters, and he lets me take books out in exchange for toffees."

Barnabas saw his little brother there, beneath the disguise, the earnest and deeply *good* brother he'd protected for so many years. Of course it would be Phineas who found a secret library, who established a currency of sweets with its lunatic keeper, like placating a fairy-tale monster in order to steal its treasure. That childlike wonder, wielded with adult power, helped him navigate the treacherous waters he'd elected to live in. For a moment the idea of Phineas back in the real world was jarring. Where would he fit in, after all this time? Would he even *want* to return? But since he had biffed one of his boss's men on the head and potentially exposed himself to save Barnabas, did he really have any choice? It wasn't as though he could return to the smugglers.

Freddie seemed more concerned with the practicalities of the moment. "So the smugglers aren't *doing* the sabotage, but they probably aren't displeased by it either."

"Not when it's happening to the Navy, no. But the squid don't discriminate. They've taken down more than one of our boats—Furneval's boats. They seem to be attracted to the flashing signal lanterns, and by 'attracted' I mean 'inclined to do damage.' Which might explain their attacking the sensor points of the Glass Octopus as well. The seismograph, that is. It uses light to communicate the seismic data from the collection points back to the central terminal. I gather the idea was to make it invisible to hydrophones and the like, but it seems to have acted as a beacon for these creatures instead. Furneval wouldn't mind that part if they left his fleet alone, but as it is he's decided he'd rather destroy all the squid to ensure his own operation's safety. He's assembling his submersibles to do that."

"That could benefit the Navy even more than it benefits him," Barnabas pointed out.

"What's his time frame?" Freddie asked.

"Soon. He's probably meeting with the pilots as we speak. Or perhaps not, if they've discovered I'm missing by now. Somebody's bound to run across Nick eventually and raise the alarm. I really should have . . . well, but perhaps he won't remember enough to hurt us."

"You should have what?" Barnabas demanded, though he didn't think he'd like the answer. "Should have rendered him incapable of remembering anything?"

"Should have killed him, yes. It would have been the smarter thing to do. Leaving him alive created more risk for us."

"But you don't like wet work," Freddie said softly.

"No, I do not. You really are your father's daughter, aren't you? No wonder you didn't seem to mind my knife at your throat. You never believed I'd use it."

"Oh, I minded. I'd forgotten all about the wet work business until now. And I suspect you would have used the knife if you had to. You have used it, haven't you?"

He didn't answer. It didn't matter. Barnabas could see the truth all over him, see how haunted he was by it. But that too was probably an issue best dealt with at another time. "We're getting close to Mersea Island, aren't we? Are you going to navigate from where you're sitting, Phineas, or steer us in yourself? Might be simpler." And might demonstrate trust and teamwork, going both ways.

"Miss Murcheson is doing just fine. I'll navigate. Where do we go once we're ashore, though?"

"Won't you want to check in with somebody, even if it isn't Murcheson? Make an official report of what you know about the smugglers?"

Phineas snorted, the ends of his ludicrous mustache puffing away from his face. "When I do report in, it'll be to my old commanding officer, Admiral Nealy. But if I show my face now, after all this time and with no solid evidence about Furneval, they'd hang me as a deserter without even listening to what I have to say. No, my first priority is to stop Furneval from eradicating all the squid, that's the pressing problem. After seeing the creatures, and going back over the maps, I believe it's a mistake to kill them. I'd need better information to be sure, the kind I could've gotten from the Glass Octopus. Specific times and so forth. But it almost seems as though the attacks have started to *precede* the tremors. Not just in a general sense, but specifically, one by one."

"Invisible, glowing, *clairvoyant* squid?"

"They're very intelligent, but I don't think they're cephalopod spiritualists, no. I think they may be acutely sensitive to the vibrations, that's all, and able to detect them earlier than even our instruments can. But don't you see the progression? The Navy builds the station, then installs the Glass Octopus some time later. The system works, the lights go off, and some time after that, after a period of unusually high seismic activity, these creatures start to make themselves known. They see the lights flash every time a tremor begins, then over time they begin to attack the lights as they're triggered. And now to attack them before they have a chance to go off."

"So they *are* sabotaging the thing?" Freddie asked.

"I don't think so. I believe they may be attempting to communicate, to express their alarm over the impending quakes. Or perhaps they think the lights are causing the quakes, and they're trying to stop them. I'm not so sure they're being deliberately aggressive, though it's obviously had that effect. It warrants more study, is all. We might even be able to use the squids' quake prediction ability to our advantage. But not if Furneval takes a drastic approach like slaughtering them all. Besides, we can't be sure there's only the one grouping of them. Killing some may only anger the others. He doesn't look ahead well, Furneval."

"Why not go to the Admiral, then," Barnabas suggested again, "and have him apprehend Furneval before he gets the chance to do away with the squid?"

Phineas sighed. "Because I've been in the military, and I haven't forgotten what that's like. Look, from the smugglers' intelligence, Furneval gathers that the Navy still thinks it's sabotage by either political enemies or smugglers. I've seen nothing to tell me they have any idea about the squid. The Navy appears to be focusing all their efforts on hydrophone development to catch the malefactors, but they don't have sufficient funding, so their equipment is still on too small a scale to be useful, even when they cooperate with other agencies to pool resources. Then of course there are the internecine disputes about whether to continue operating Atlantis Station at all, continue the soft blockade at all, now the war is over. The Glass Octopus is a primary reason for keeping the station open, because it has scientific value beyond military applications. But the funding for that project doesn't extend to experimental sound detection equipment for nonseismic purposes on military vessels. It's all complicated. Nealy and Murcheson are both having to juggle to pay for everything, so they can keep all their toys. They have tunnel vision, literally and figuratively. Furneval killing the squid off would only mean one less financial worry for them, and for Atlantis Station. They wouldn't gamble that the squid might prove useful in the future; they'd let him do his hunting before they brought him in just to spare themselves the expense."

Barnabas could hardly believe what he was hearing. "Phin, you *have* to turn yourself in! You have a head full of knowledge about a major opium smuggling ring, and every reason to think the smugglers will come after you once they realize you're missing. You left a witness whom you knocked out to save an intruder, then absconded. They'll *know* you're up to something. Going to either the Agency or the Navy is the only way to protect yourself. Besides, it's your duty, isn't it?"

"Turning himself in? That makes him sound like a criminal," Freddie protested. "Father may have ignored him, but to my way of thinking he's still an agent of the Crown and he should be able to decide for himself how best to serve his mission. Which isn't necessarily over. Besides, Father seemed to suggest that there's a bigger quake coming, that the scientists have somehow been able to use the Glass Octopus to predict that. But what if these creatures could do an even better job of warning us? Isn't that worth investigating? If Phineas tells the Navy what he knows, either they'll go after the smugglers too late to prevent the squid from being slaughtered, or they'll go after the smugglers and *then* kill off the squid anyway because the one thing they know is that the squid are responsible for the damage to the Glass Octopus. The squid will be just another threat to eliminate. That's what they *do*. And none of that will happen quickly. There would be more funding squabbles first, probably, more arguing about who gets credit for what. If a larger quake is on the way, people ought to be warned. The system needs to be repaired at the least, and improved if possible. Time might be of the essence, and the smugglers won't be wasting it arguing about the budget. They ought to be stopped, and quickly."

"Blast." He didn't want their logic to be correct. He wanted to get Phineas safely to the proper authorities and return Freddie to her home, and for himself he wanted a hot bath with a set of clean, dry nightclothes at the end of it. In the chilly, dank air of the miniature submersible, his soaked garments had remained sopping and odoriferous, and he had been shivering so long he was growing physically exhausted from it. Most of his thoughts centered increasingly on how pleasant it would be once he was dry and warm and had a stiff drink or two inside him. "When are they going after the squid, then? How long are we talking about?"

Phineas shrugged. "They won't argue the budget, but there will be plenty else for them to work out. As long as a few days, possibly. At least one of the subs still needs to be fitted with a torpedo launcher. A few of the others will need some repairs to make sure they're truly seaworthy for an extended trip with a possibility of having to fire weapons or take serious evasive actions. It's hard on the structure of the sub, all that jolting. He'll want a thorough check to make sure the ship-to-ship communications are functioning properly as well, I'd imagine. Usually those things get taken care of over time, not all at once, because apparently the fleet's never been assembled like this. Furneval doesn't have many dedicated sub mechanics, so it will take them some time to work through it all. Which still leaves us with the question of where to go once we're ashore."

Barnabas drew his knees up to his chest, trying to conserve what little heat he was able to generate. "Anywhere I can obtain a bath. Or even a warm blanket."

Frowning, Phineas peered into his face, then picked up one of his hands by the wrist. "Your lips are blue, and your words are slurring a bit. Your pulse is strong, and you're still shivering, which are both good signs. I don't think you're hypothermic, it isn't quite cold enough in here for that, but there's no need to take chances. Here, take your shirt off and wear this." He stripped his jacket off and held it out for Barnabas, who eyed it suspiciously.

"Do I need to fear fleas?"

"Can beggars be choosers? Quickly, while it's still holding some of my body heat."

It was just one more humiliation to add to the list. One more didn't matter at this point. He peeled off his tinker's shirt and vest, wanting to whimper at the sting of the sub's channel-cool air on his exposed, damp skin. But Phineas was right. His jacket, though scruffy and dubious in appearance, was deliciously warm from the second he pulled it on. Large, though, all through the shoulders and at the sleeves. His baby brother had grown taller and broader even since his last Navy uniform was fitted. Smuggling had apparently treated him well in some respects.

"Sadly, we have another swim ahead of us. There's a long

pier on the western side of the island that should provide us enough depth and cover to escape detection, but once night falls and the dock is clear, we may need to swim to shore. I've no idea if there's a ladder or stairs. I won't hold out any hope for a fortuitous trapdoor either."

"So," Barnabas summed up, "we'll all be soaked in sea-water, freezing our . . . selves, and stranded in an unfamiliar fishing village in the dark."

"But there's good news. Just across the road from the pier, there's a tavern."

NOT ONLY WAS there a tavern, but Phineas seemed on quite friendly terms with one of the barmaids, a young woman of roughly Freddie's age with buoyant yellow curls and dimples. She seemed less than happy to see him, however. No sooner had they walked into the common room than she was shuffling them right back into the hall where the other patrons wouldn't see them. Not that any of the pub's denizens looked interested in anything other than their pints, but Freddie supposed any of them might be a covert operative, just as Phineas was. She might have to start viewing *everyone* with suspicion, in fact.

"Mr. Finn, you shouldn't be 'ere!" scolded the tavern wench. "It's the constable's night to come in for a pint, you know that. And Father's home already, there's no transacting business here tonight. What can you be thinking?"

"Alas, fair Marie, I could stand to be parted from you no longer."

Freddie rolled her eyes when the girl broke into a giggle.

"Oh, and you know it's just plain Mary. You do have a way with words, Mr. Finn. But 'ere, you're soaking wet! What on earth?"

"Soaking wet and in dire need of assistance from a kindly soul, good Mary. Do you have a room for us? I have coin."

"Up the stairs with you. And you two. Oh wait, you're dripping *everywhere*. I'll need Lizzie to come after us with a mop and pail."

Once Lizzie was summoned, mop in hand, Mary led them up to a snug room on the top floor of the inn over the pub. Though small, and hardly quiet with the barroom noise filtering up, it had a fireplace and a view of the shore. And one large bed.

Oh dear.

Per Mary's copious instructions, Lizzie laid a tidy fire in the grate, then disappeared to fetch hot water and spare blankets, leaving the three to parse out their boarding arrangements. More than anything, Freddie wished she could have a few moments alone with Barnabas to consult him on his preferences about sharing information with his brother. Sadly, those moments were not forthcoming. Furthermore, Phineas seemed to have forgotten one of his party was of the opposite gender. This, despite the time he and Barnabas had just spent treading water outside the submersible while they waited for Freddie to change from her uniform into her tinker's clothes. As soon as Lizzie left the room, Phineas started stripping off his drenched shirt. He had his trousers half off his hips before Barnabas's fervent throat-clearing and hand-waving stopped him. Fortunately he'd kept his drawers in place.

"Are you having some sort of fit?"

"No, Phineas, we can't disrobe. Not in front of Miss Murcheson."

Sighing, Phineas stopped removing his trousers and shifted a chair in front of the fire, draping his shirt there to dry. Freddie had to appreciate the magnificence of him as a physical specimen, though she could do without his hot-and-cold personality. His scraggly mop of hair and idiotic mustache took a fair number of points off, as well.

"I don't want you to catch your death," she said magnanimously. "Perhaps I could face the wall. You two carry on."

"We can't."

"You have to get your clothes dry somehow, Barnabas. Be practical. It's not as though I'll peek."

Would she peek? Naturally. She was quite interested to see more of Barnabas in particular, and he was still covered by Phineas's big coat and uniform trousers. Turning her back, she perched on the edge of the bed and removed her hat, sliding pins from her hair until she could shake the whole thing loose.

"Your clothes are wet too. You're dripping on the bedclothes."

"Just the edge here. It'll be fine. Hurry up, so I can take my turn. It's cold this far from the fire."

In truth, it was such a small room that the fire quickly warmed the whole thing. When she removed her jacket, the muslin shirt beneath began to dry almost instantly, though the many layers of padding beneath and the wool trousers did not. Itchy, wet wool aside, she was quite content as she combed her fingers through her hair and stole glances at the gentlemen, who stripped to their drawers and huddled by the fire. Barnabas was quite as fit as Phineas, but smaller and smoother all around, like a slightly miniaturized and less finely chiseled version of the same model. Freddie liked that. He looked manageable. Phineas, with his brooding eye and stony muscles, looked like a treacherous rock that a woman would crash her ship into. She didn't want to crash. Barnabas, hapless and eager, had a sunny lighthouse smile for her at the strangest times, and it always made her feel she knew what to expect with him. Guidance and reliability, although she wasn't sure that was what he intended. Freddie hadn't been aware of a need in herself to be led or steered, or to rely on anybody for their smiles. But she must have those needs, because clearly Barnabas met them and she felt the better for it.

She tried to imagine returning to her work rounds with Dan instead of Barnabas on the pony trap. Stoic, occasionally sarcastic, prudent Dan. He was huge, strong, the better guardian by far in a tight pinch, and not a bad right hand when a stiff bolt wouldn't come loose or something needed the heavy mallet. He was the sensible choice for a companion, but the picture wouldn't form in her head. It was all Barnabas now, smiling and sometimes looking vaguely awed when she repaired something that seemed hopelessly broken. Or trying to trick her into leaning over so he could better ogle her bottom. She always had trouble keeping a straight face when he did that. It was necessary, though, because if he knew that she knew, he would stop. And Freddie quite liked being ogled by Barnabas, although of course she could never admit that to him. One didn't.

One didn't accost gentlemen in their chambers late at night either, of course, and she had done that. Would like to do it again, should the opportunity present itself. If only Phineas would go chasing the barmaid.

He seemed happily ensconced before the fire, though. Barnabas, more restless, stretched his arms overhead, leaning from side to side to work out muscles that had to be stiff from his long, freezing stint in the sub. Freddie felt much the same, and she had been dry for most of the trip. It would be a lucky thing if Barnabas didn't catch cold or, worse, experience a relapse of his recent influenza.

"We should have Lizzie bring up some hot toddies," she suggested through a veil of hair.

"Stop peeking," Phineas admonished without turning.

"You're a bit full of yourself, lad." She let the street creep into her voice, drawing the mantle of her adopted manhood around her.

"Not really. Not at the moment, anyway."

"Phineas!" Barnabas whirled on his brother, staring up at him aghast.

Unable to help herself, Freddie cackled at Barnabas's shocked expression, the way he'd propped his hands on his hips like an angry nursemaid settling in for a good long scold.

"Oh, Barnabas, I don't care. I hear worse on the streets nearly every day I'm out working. At least your brother has some hint of subtlety."

"I am mortified for all of us," he retorted. "This is the decline of the British Empire, writ small right here in this room. Gentlemen cavorting unclad in front of young ladies, and those same ladies laughing at ribald remarks, all after engaging in any number of illegalities all the day long. Not to mention relying on the goodwill of a smuggling front operation for hospitality, if I'm not very much mistaken."

"No, you got it in one, brother. I do have coin to pay the fetching Miss Marie, however. I'm not entirely larcenous, nor does her goodwill extend to housing dangerous criminals free of charge."

"Do you come here regularly?"

"The less you know of my activities, the better. But . . . it's a point of contact, yes. One of many. Furneval vaguely remembered me from before my untimely departure to the Dominions; he'd heard nothing to make him distrust me while I served his brother Lord Orm, so when I returned with Orm's token he took me into his confidence to a degree I found frankly alarming. He's not the most stable individual to work for. Although he's a vast improvement over Orm, I must admit."

"From the things Matthew Pence told me about his ordeal with Orm at El Dorado, I can believe it. It sounds like a waking nightmare."

"It was hell," Phineas said curtly. "I'd rather not discuss it." He set himself to rearranging the clothes in front of the fire, pulling the second ladder-back chair over from the room's small table. A gentle steam had begun to rise from the garments, and with it the smell of wet wool, and cotton that had been worn far too long between washings.

A scratch on the door alerted them to Lizzie's return. Freddie snatched up her hat and shoved her hair into it as best she could, but the serving girl paid her no mind in any case. It was a busy night, and they'd been lucky to get this room, which had been the last one available. All this she told them in a steady, amiable stream as she set down the armload of clean, coarse blankets she'd brought and poured the ewer of steaming water into the waiting basin.

After agreeing to return with hot toddies, the girl left as quickly as she'd come, leaving a sudden silence behind her.

Phineas finally broke it, pulling his trousers from the chair back and tugging them on, though they were clearly still damp. "Give me one of those blankets. I need to talk to Mary's father, and then I'll probably find a place to sleep in the stable."

"But why? Isn't it safer if we all stay together?" Barnabas countered. "Not that I'm arguing, if you think it's best to go. But you needn't think you *must* go, just on account of . . . well."

His brother raised his eyebrows, looking from Freddie to Barnabas until she felt herself blushing. Pretending great interest in the rearrangement of her hair, she turned away from the men.

Phineas cleared his throat. "I have a reputation to uphold as an opium trafficker who is unfortunately and notoriously a user of the product himself. I'll see old Bob at his cottage near the tavern, and ask if he has anything I can purchase to ease me to sleep. I sincerely hope he does not, as otherwise I may have to pretend to smoke it. That's difficult to do without actually smoking it. But in any case, he wouldn't expect me to take the product back to my compatriots to share. It would not be remotely in character. Ergo, I go alone and sleep off my shameful excess in the stable. From where, I should mention, I can more readily observe the shore and road, and remain at liberty if it turns out that Furneval's men are on our trail. They'd be most likely to come after us here in the inn, because of my established preference for the lovely Marie. If I'm elsewhere at the time, I can then come after them, thereby apprehending them and rescuing you."

"You're leaving us here as *bait*?"

"Would you prefer to go bunk with the livestock? I can remain here in the comfortable room, and I'm sure Miss Murcheson and I can come to some sort of agreement regarding the sleeping arrangements."

Barnabas didn't answer. Freddie risked a peek and saw that his jaw was white, strained, and his fists were clenched so tightly she feared he might draw blood from his own palms. After a few seconds of staring one another off, Phineas spoke again, swinging the blanket around his broad shoulders like a shawl. He hadn't bothered with a shirt or shoes.

"Sleep well, brother. And you, Miss Murcheson. I'll be back at dawn."

Seventeen

❧❀❧

"HE KNOWS, DOESN'T he? Somehow he knows."

Privately, Barnabas agreed with Freddie, but he shook his head anyway. "He just wanted to be alone. Even if he suspects, it's not as though he's likely to tell anyone. By the time he got to that part of the tale, he'd already be either in the stockade or possibly promoted to rear admiral. Either way, I doubt we're in much danger. And his misanthropy is our good fortune."

Good fortune, or a temptation sent by the Devil? Barnabas wasn't at all sure he believed in the Devil, but this scenario could have been handcrafted by the old sinner expressly for the purpose of ensnaring a young man's soul.

A room. A bed. An entire night to spend there. And Freddie, studying him with those remarkable green eyes, with half a smile playing hide-and-seek at the corners of her mouth between sips of hot toddy.

She was dressed as a boy. She was quite possibly more

than a little mad. They had been impersonating military officers, stealing government property, were probably being hunted by smugglers and maybe also facing encounters with giant, rampaging squid things.

He'd never felt so happy or content. So sure of what he was doing. Which made no sense, because objectively Barnabas was aware he had no idea what he was doing, with any of this. Not the job he had been assigned, certainly. Not anything he'd ever planned to be doing with his life, or even contemplated as a set of options. He *ought* to be horrified by the entire situation.

"What are you thinking?" Freddie asked.

"I'm thinking about . . . you." It was more or less the truth.

"Not sure I like that, with the look on your face just then. You can't have been thinking anything very nice."

"How did I look?"

"Baffled. Do I baffle you?" She frowned, as this was clearly a matter of grave concern.

"Only in the best possible ways. I do sort of wonder what comes next, however."

"I find it more than a little worrisome you don't *know* what happens next. Of the two of us, you're really the one who ought to know."

"No, no," he laughed, moving a step closer. "That part I know. Minx. I mean after all this is over. Assuming neither of us is dead and I'm not thrown in prison, and we both go back to our lives. Or do we? Is that what you want? Is it even what I want, because I honestly have no idea at the moment. It's as though, where once I looked ahead in my life and had a general idea of how I expected things to go, now I find I can't even picture what lies in store. I'm not sure whether that should make me feel liberated or petrified."

"Instead of thinking about how it *should* make you feel,

maybe let yourself think how it actually *does* make you feel. That seems a better place to start."

"Do you know your future? Can you see what you think it'll be, I mean?"

She considered it a moment, then shook her head, frowning. "It's that same problem with *should*, I suppose. I was the pot calling the kettle black, wasn't I? I know all the types of futures I should want, the ones that I know are available to a woman such as myself, and it ought to be a simple question of choosing between them. It isn't, because none of them seem remotely palatable, but I have no idea what to picture in their place. It's as though I don't have a wide enough frame of reference even to imagine what I want yet. I don't know what my possibilities ought to be."

"You'll have to make new ones, then." He wanted to see her try. Wanted to see the world she might construct, given free rein to do so. And he hoped there would be room for him in her orbit. "You're still in wet things, I've just realized."

"So I am." Her frown vanished, but she tried to hide her smile behind the hot toddy. "I'm probably headed for a nasty case of pneumonia."

"We really ought to do something about that."

"Yes, but what?"

"Fortunately for us both, I know what happens next."

He took the still-warm mug from her hands, placing it carefully on the table by the bed, and drew her off to stand in front of him. The buttons of her shirt seemed to melt open under his fingers, but he stopped cold when he saw what lay beneath once the shirt dropped to the floor.

Padding. Layers of it, bandaged into place. All sodden, heavy, and now dripping seawater onto the floor by his feet. "I'd forgotten all about this. How can you stand it?"

"At least it's kept me warm. Here, I'll do that."

He plucked at a knot where she'd tied a bandage off. "No. I'll unwrap you."

It sounded more intriguing than it turned out to be. In truth, the bandages were tricky to remove, and the prurience Barnabas had started out with was quickly subsumed by more practical thoughts. Such as whether to find a knife and simply cut through the entire mess, saving time and effort. Freddie refused to allow this, however, as she needed the stuffing and wrappings intact to wear again the next day.

The soaked linen seemed to have congealed where it was knotted, however, and Barnabas was yawning by the time he got the first one untied and began unwinding it, passing the wad of bandage around Freddie's midsection with quick, efficient movements. She was already at work on another knot and kept having to move her arms out of his way. It made an odd ballet, the two of them working at cross purposes until they found a rhythm that allowed them both to operate.

"This is a great deal less lascivious than I had hoped it would be," he complained, when he realized there was still another bandage left to work on, besides the one Freddie had started on. The last one tied off near her hip, and Barnabas dropped to his knees to attack it once he'd dropped the first bandage on the hearth to dry.

"I imagine any sinful impulse left will be completely annihilated once the padding is off, because I'm sure I smell frightful under there."

"I smell like fortnight-old halibut myself, so I'm positive I won't even notice."

He really only heard the *under there* part of what she'd said, because it reminded him that beneath the tricky padding and fiddly bandages was a naked girl, a naked *Freddie*. More than worth the bother.

She was, however, sadly accurate regarding the smell. It

centered on the bag of cotton-wool-stuffed muslin that formed the basis of her figure-transforming disguise, but clearly the source was the skin beneath. He'd envisioned revealing her torso and immediately conducting a sensual exploration prior to shucking off her trousers. Instead, despite the astonishing visual appeal of her smoothly curved waist and high, small, rose-tipped breasts, his first impulse was to suggest she wash first.

"Ugh. I told you," she said before he could figure out what to say. She stepped from between him and the bed and went to the washbasin, grimacing as she lifted her arms to scrub with the scrap of rag draped over the side.

Barnabas remained where he was, enchanted with the play of the firelight on the muscles in Freddie's back. Beneath the ugly impressions left by the constraining bandages, her skin was smooth and fair, and when she twisted to clean the other side, she resembled a Greek marble. He couldn't think which one. He could hardly think at all.

The braces she'd slipped from her shoulders earlier dangled at her hips, framing the view. Without their support, her trousers had slouched low to hang from her hips, accentuating the graceful sweep from hip to waist. His body responded to the angles and particularly the arcs of hers, hardening while his eyes lingered everywhere she was softest.

"Those trousers are still wet too," he reminded her helpfully.

"Perhaps you'd like to help me with them."

He would. Nothing would please him more.

When he stood to cross the room, however, he glimpsed Freddie's face in the small mirror over the washstand. Eyes squeezed shut, bottom lip caught between her teeth. It was not an expression of lustful anticipation, but anxiety. Because she was, he remembered all at once with the sick thud of painful reality slipping back into place, not actually a brazen, daring, smuggler-defying submersible thief. Not just that, anyway. Primarily she was a young, sheltered virgin who was quite possibly making heat-of-the-moment decisions she would later regret.

She'd said it herself: She didn't know what she wanted her life to be. He could only assume the rejected plans included everything obvious and conventional, such as marriage and motherhood and helping a husband manage a small but reasonably profitable estate in the Hudson Valley. Everything, in short, that a man like Barnabas could offer. And if she wasn't prepared to do that, should he really be doing anything like taking off her trousers? His conscience told him no. His still-stirring erection and the tingling in his balls indicated there was room for debate.

Cautiously, he wrapped his arms around what he deemed the safest portion of Freddie's anatomy, her waist. It was a mistake. As soon as his chest came into contact with her back and he felt her sigh against him, he knew his conscience would lose the argument, and for the worst reasons. He wanted to keep holding her because she felt like she was already part of him. Knowing he could never keep her should make him back away, not squeeze tighter.

"We don't have to do anything next, you know. Not if you're not sure."

She wrapped her arms around herself, placing her hands over his forearms. "Don't you want to?"

He shifted his grip lower, pulling her hips toward his, pressing his length against the exquisite cleft of her backside. "Of course I want to. I've wanted to all along. I want to every time I look at you. If wanting were all that mattered, the world would be full of naked people coupling on every street corner. Nothing else would ever be accomplished. In fact there probably wouldn't even *be* street corners."

Her giggle registered against him, delightfully vibrant against his body as well as to his ears. "Good, then. Because how often in my life can I expect to be stranded in a rustic inn overnight with a beautiful man who doesn't mind that I'm wearing trousers?"

Barnabas trailed her waistband with his fingertips, finding the placket and unbuttoning the trousers in question. "Are you just using me because I'm convenient for playing out your little fantasy?"

"Convenient *and beautiful*," she reminded him.

"I ought to be offended."

The wet wool didn't slide off; it had to be tugged and coaxed. They were both laughing by the time he finally yanked the garment free of Freddie's foot and held it up with a triumphant "Ha!"

She grinned at him. Standing there, in a pair of damp cotton drawers that hid nothing.

"Ha," he said again, letting the trousers fall from his fingers. They thumped to the floor, surprisingly loud.

"Shouldn't you put those in front of the fire?" She smirked and started for the bed, flipping the counterpane back and climbing on while he retrieved the fallen trousers and spread them carefully among the collection of slowly drying clothing.

When he turned, Freddie had already made herself comfortable, propped on one elbow and watching him. Her feet were tucked under the sheets, but the rest of her was gloriously bare. She had removed her drawers at some point while he wasn't looking. He had a fleeting moment of disappointment about that until he lost himself gazing at the swatch of auburn that decorated the crease where her shapely thighs met. Very shapely. Luscious, even, all creamy velvet and plump curves. Then that dip at the waist, and the delicate shell of her ribs, visible beneath her skin when she breathed just so. Vital, arresting. Her breasts were smaller than they appeared when she was clothed, objectively probably too small to properly balance out her magnificent derriere. His were not objective eyes, however. To him, she looked like everything he'd ever desired.

"Stop *staring*."

"But there's so very much that's worthy of a good, long appraisal."

"Barnabas?"

"Mmm?"

"Stop staring and come to bed."

SHE'D USED UP her audacity, and as Barnabas stepped closer to the bed, Freddie closed her eyes and tried to slow her breathing to something approaching a reasonable rate. It was little use. She could anticipate his approach, gauge his proximity as though her body had come equipped with special Barnabas hydrophones she'd only recently activated. She knew the second before the mattress dipped under his weight, and opened her eyes as he smoothed her hair back from her forehead.

"I shouldn't have cut it, should I? It makes me look like a boy."

"Nobody could possibly mistake you for a boy. Not without your boy suit, anyway. Certainly not right now."

"You're staring again."

His gaze tracked down the line of her body, lingering here and there. "As I said. Worthy. I want to memorize every inch of you."

He'd taken his drawers off while her eyes were closed. Not that they'd concealed much. She could see all of him now, though, the length of his penis pressed against his thigh as he leaned in, the way the hair thickened in a dark line down from his belly.

She'd seen a naked man once before, a wandering drunk on some crooked lane in London, who'd inexplicably peeled off his clothes in the middle of the pavement while belting "Rule Britannia" to a mostly amused crowd. He'd had a fine bass voice, a barrel chest the size of an actual barrel, and whatever manhood he'd possessed had been shrunken by liquor and obscured by his prodigious belly.

Then Dan had slapped his hand over her eyes and made her promise not to look in that direction while he steered the cart around the disturbance.

This occasion wasn't remotely like that one. That man didn't even seem like the same species as the lovely, finely drawn creature before her now. She decided Barnabas must have his own category, one in which distinctions like clothing or nakedness were simply irrelevant. He was beautiful no matter what he did or didn't wear. The unclothed version did have some interesting features, of course.

Freddie closed the distance between them, tracing the long muscle in his closest thigh with her fingertips. He hummed at the contact, his dark eyes fluttering shut like a shy maid's. Like her own had, she supposed. But he didn't protest, so she reached farther, shaping her hand around his erection. It was firm and hot, and felt more muscular than she'd expected. Springy and resistant. She could assign it no corollary on her own body to help her understand its ways by association; she'd just have to learn it from scratch.

Barnabas stopped her before she'd got very far, removing her hand with great care before shifting position to lie alongside her on the bed, head on his hand, mirroring her. But his other hand was already busy, brushing against her ribs then up to cup a breast. She expected something more, a witty remark most likely, but he didn't say a word, just tossed another smile her way and then bent his head to suck.

His lips and teeth felt like a series of small miracles on her flesh, pulling sensations from her that she hadn't known existed. Something about the wet heat, and the intimate connection of a mouth to a nipple or the sensitive skin surrounding it. Something about the way his dark hair slanted across his forehead, obscuring his eyes until he looked up to meet hers.

That was too much. She couldn't look at him with him looking back and his mouth still on her like that. She closed her eyes and laid back, letting novelty and delight wash over her as Barnabas went exploring. Her breasts, thoroughly, until she was almost ready to push him off to escape the attention but at the same time realized she never wanted it to stop. Her neck and ears, in a series of tiny nibbles that left her spine zinging with joy and had her twining her legs around Barnabas's hips in an effort to wriggle even closer. Which was impossible, because he was already lying on top of her, but she had to try anyway. Then he worked his way down, all hands and mouth and the spirit of discovery, until he settled between her legs.

"We really should have called for a bath—"

"I don't care."

"Yes, but—"

"Shh."

When she would have said more, he licked her. *Licked*, from the veriest crux of the cleft between her legs up to that higher, keener spot. A slow, meandering line of liquid warmth and intention that took all her arguments and threw them out the window. She was reduced to breathy sighs, to wordless utterances that she could only hope conveyed her absolute approval of everything he was doing with his tongue, his lips and eventually his fingers too. Carefully, methodically, he unlocked her secrets until she lay open and revealed, allowing herself to give in to trust. When it finally grew to be unbearable, the eager pressure too much to withstand, she almost cried. She didn't want it to be over. But Barnabas grazed his tongue over that aching spot again, and again and again, and worked another finger inside her and she came, slow and hard and sweet. Her legs trembled, even though they had no weight to support. But her soul soared, stronger and steadier than ever.

"Was that all right?"

How could he even need to ask? "Quite."

"Oh. Good." His lips brushed one quaking inner thigh, triggering a minor aftershock in the surrounding regions. "Never done that before."

She wanted to come back with a snappy remark, but her brain seemed turned to candy floss and fireworks. Not an unpleasant state by any means, but not conducive to witty repartee. "Weren't you going to . . ."

"I wanted to make sure you were all right first."

Sweet. But she'd had a climax, not a debilitating illness. "Now."

"Are you sure—"

"Now."

He didn't rush, despite her command. He crawled over her, kissing his way up, until he was in more or less the appropriate position, but he paused there. Freddie opened her eyes and stared up into his face, struck by a wave of tenderness. It was dear to her, that face. *He* was dear to her. She was glad to be doing this with him, regardless of what happened afterward.

She didn't know where he mustered the patience or forbearance, but he entered her slowly, clearly fretting over her well-being even as he gasped at the pleasure. Limp, sated, she let him set the pace, and was aware enough to be grateful for it. Nothing hurt much, counter to her expectation. A slight twinge when his restraint failed him for a moment and he

pushed forward the last bit all at once. Then only more pleasure, happy friction between them, and the wonder of discovering that her body had been designed to do this thing all
along. Completed, she felt completed, not so much by Barnabas as by the act itself and the fact of their doing it together.

He buried his face in her neck and began to work his hips,
not quite as gently as he'd started, and it was all the good things
in the world together, all at once, right there in her arms.

"This is why people keep having babies," she murmured.

Barnabas chuckled, his breath hot on the skin below her
ear. "Please tell me that isn't your plan here."

"God, no. I meant in the abstract."

"Right." He braced himself up on his elbows again to look
her in the eye. It should have been embarrassing, like when
he watched her while he sucked on her breast, but somehow
it wasn't. This was a fine position for a conversation, apparently. "I mean to withdraw. Before I—*Lord*, that feels good."

"Before . . . oh. All right."

"Freddie . . ."

Whatever he'd meant to say, he lost track of it on his next
thrust. A shiver went through him, and she clutched him
tighter as he sped up. Faster, deeper, like a compulsion, the
sensation overtook him and he had no choice but to follow
it to his finish. A final moan—thrilling, primally wonderful
sound—and a thrust deeper than before, and then he yanked
away, ending with his face on her belly and his hips aimed
somewhere between her knees and ankles.

His hair was flopping in his face again. Freddie combed
it back so she could watch him return to the world, which he
did with a smile she'd never seen on his face before. She quite
liked it, as long as he never took it outside the bedroom. He
could fell unsuspecting women at fifty paces with such a look.

"Beautiful," she whispered.

His words slurred when he answered, as though he were tipsy on pleasure. "I think you're supposed to call me handsome."

"I don't do what I'm supposed to."

"Fair enough. But I think everything you do is wonderful. And I'm not just saying that because—"

"I know. I think you're wonderful too."

He propped one fist under his chin, getting a better angle to contemplate her. "I wish it didn't sound sad when you said it."

She swallowed back the tears that threatened to prick through. Those pesky, unwarranted tears again. "It's not sadness. Nothing about you makes me sad. Least of all this."

"Wistful, then. Least of all this? Do you suppose we could do it again sometime?" He reached up with the hand not under his chin, toying with the ends of her hair where it curled around one ear. It was such an affectionate, familiar thing to do. For a moment Freddie wished she could make a whole life of this. Just her and Barnabas, a room with a bed and a fire. Perhaps smelling less like the mouth of the Blackwater River and more like something romantic and fresh, such as clear ocean air or the aroma of a rainswept meadow.

"Of course. But we really should wash first."

"Agreed." He pushed up and away, sitting on his heels and surveying the wreckage they'd made of the bed. Blankets thrown to the floor, sheet in utter disarray, a generally questionable air to the whole scene. Barnabas nodded at the wadded linens next to him. "It's a disaster."

And it would just have to remain a disaster. Freddie crooked a finger at him, and he slid down next to her, trapping her legs between his and wrapping his arms around her. She snuggled against his chest, one hand curled against the soft mat of hairs at the center of his breastbone, and decided that rainswept meadows were probably not all that fragrant anyway.

Eighteen

❦

FREDDIE DIDN'T ASK where Phineas had obtained the velo-cimobile. It seemed safer not to question it, simply to climb into the precariously attached sidecar and hope the thing didn't fall to pieces before they had traveled half the fifty or so miles from Mersea back to Tilbury.

Between the chattering growl of the engine and the wind in their faces, conversation wasn't possible between Freddie in the sidecar and Barnabas, clutching to Phineas's waist as he straddled the main seat behind him. She was practically alone with her thoughts for the three hours to Tilbury, which was plenty of time to do exactly what Mrs. Pinkerton would have once forced her to do, waggling a finger in her face until she did it.

You sit right there, young lady, and think about what you've done!

And so she did.

She had expected to feel transformed, somehow, as though something wonderful but at the same time cataclysmic had happened. Indelibly altered, perhaps marked in some mysterious way. Instead she felt more or less the same as she had before making love to Barnabas. Clearer about her reasons for wanting to do it again, certainly. A trifle sore between the legs, perhaps, though not from any rending of her maidenhead but from simple muscle strain. It had been ambitious of them to engage in that sort of romp, after sitting for hours in a cold submersible, then swimming to shore in clothes that grew heavier as they grew soggier. That was the sort of thing she wouldn't have known to consider before, of course. The athleticism. The sheer physicality of the business. The surprising and pleasant absence of any rending whatsoever. He'd been so careful, so considerate.

She peered at Barnabas, taking a moment to admire his profile, much of which was obscured behind the thick goggles and leather helmet he wore. She and Phineas were similarly outfitted, so even if Barnabas had looked her way, the tinted goggles would hide her eyes and her undoubtedly foolishly tender expression. She knew she wore that face because she could feel it. And she wanted to feel Barnabas again, perhaps finishing what they'd had to call a halt to this morning. His warm skin against hers, the delicious friction of the hair on his thighs rubbing against the smooth backs of her legs, the sweet grind of his hips into her bottom as they both woke up. Already sliding together, meshing, as if they'd never stopped.

Then Phineas had knocked.

Did he look at her differently when he entered the room, see her new status on her face like a brand or a scar? It was impossible to tell. He hid behind that eye patch, as usual, and the alarming facial hair. Of course, he'd also left them alone in the first place, so perhaps he just assumed they'd already been engaging in . . . that.

Intercourse, she told herself boldly, refusing to accept her mind's attempt to censor itself. *Carnal knowledge. Sexual congress.* She'd always thought "sexual congress" sounded like a particularly naughty method of government.

Fucking. She'd heard that one plenty of times on the street, sometimes from the prostitutes who liked to proposition her and Dan when they passed by. He always tried to instruct Freddie to look away—"Avert your eyes," he'd say—but she was fascinated by the women. Saddened, also. Their faces grew old long before their time, and she couldn't help but notice how quickly they seemed to come and go on the landscape. A few months, perhaps a year, then some other girl would be there on that corner, a cheap, bright shawl wrapped around her shoulders. Quick to catch the eye, quick to fade as the season wore on.

Had they done that, really? Fucking? It didn't feel like what those young women sold. That commodity seemed shameful, feral, soulless. The human equivalent of the back of the butcher's shop, something necessary but fundamentally unpleasant and far better left unseen. What she and Barnabas had done was beautiful, every minute of it. She couldn't bring herself to feel any shame about it.

He was looking her way. She told herself it was the landscape that held his attention, but when she looked to his goggles, he smiled at her. He held one hand toward her, bravely releasing half his death grip on his brother, and Freddie stretched to brush her fingertips against his. One second . . . two . . . and then the velocimobile hit a larger-than-usual bump and Barnabas was clinging for dear life with both hands again. But still grinning.

She had almost hoped that the act of lovemaking would effect some change in her, make her want things that would be more convenient in her life. As if penetration could somehow carry with it a new pattern for thinking, for wanting, in realms that had nothing to do with the bedroom. But Freddie still didn't want to settle down on some piece of land and have babies for the sake of having babies. Or, heaven forbid, as some sort of family duty. She wanted to carry on exploring the ways of the flesh with Barnabas, and she wanted to keep working as a tinker. Those two things, in equal measure. She could think of no life that would afford her the opportunity to do both.

But still, it had been beautiful. She didn't regret it, even if her heart grew heavy as they drove into Tilbury to find the steam pony trap waiting where they'd left it the day before. The town was Sunday-quiet, and only a few strangers passed as Freddie unchained the pony from the old hitching post she'd secured it to. Barnabas topped off the boiler while Phineas stoked the furnace, and they were off within minutes on the second, much shorter leg of their journey to Sophie's house.

Freddie drove because, as she explained, driving helped her to think and she could do with a little bit more of that.

"Where exactly are we going?" Phineas demanded when they turned onto the street that would take them to Lady Sophronia's carriage house.

"I told you. To a friend of Freddie's." Barnabas was afraid of what might happen when Phineas learned the truth, which he was bound to do any moment now. "Somebody who helps her lead her double life of fancy dress balls and tinkering about in fishmongers' shops."

"You mentioned a footman, and his mother the former nursemaid. This is no retired servant's neighborhood. My God, are you attempting to take me to the girl's own house? To Murcheson himself?"

"It isn't my neighborhood either," Freddie assured him. "Calm yourself. As Barnabas said, this is the home of a friend."

"I see. A friend. One you trust, I sincerely hope. I think I know this house. Surely it's under different ownership now, though."

Wallingford had purchased the house for Sophie when they were married, according to Freddie. If Phineas recognized it as hers, that meant he'd been here after the wedding. Pining after his lost love, no doubt. He'd already been working in deep cover by then, but he'd taken the risk to come to Wilton Crescent.

There was every chance this might not go well.

"I believe it's under the same ownership, actually. In a manner of speaking."

"Oh, dear," Freddie mumbled.

"You're taking me to Sophie Wallingford. You actually expect me to go into that woman's house asking for succor? And then what, she'll lend me some of her husband's clothing for a new disguise? Somehow I don't think it will fit. You might want to consider a better class of friend, Miss Murcheson."

Perhaps they should have gone to the Pinkerton home. But Freddie had insisted, and he had agreed, that Dan's mother was already in enough danger of discovery. Sophie, at least, had resources to defend herself if she was accused. And her consent in the whole affair was certainly better informed than Mrs. Pinkerton's.

"When I'm dressed like this, it's Fred," Freddie reminded Phineas. "Whatever sordid history you have with Sophie, that's irrelevant to the current situation. Either I report to her, or she reports to my father. I'll leave it to you to figure out which is the wiser alternative at this point. But figure it out quickly, because we're here."

The pony juddered to a halt by the carriage block, and a young groom dashed out, only to pull up short when he saw the rough conveyance and its rougher denizens. "'Elp you?"

"You're new here," Freddie remarked, hopping off the trap's seat. "Run fetch Digby and Taylor, they'll know what to do."

The boy ran off, and the seasoned grooms arrived in his place a moment later to spirit the trap away and usher the disheveled trio into the house, where Jacob, the senior footman, awaited them. Disapproval was plain on his face, but he kept any censure to himself as he led them to the green parlor. Sophie Wallingford was there, pacing and wringing her hands, and she swept across the room with a glad cry when Freddie crossed the threshold.

"Another quarter hour and I'd have sent Daniel straight back to your father to send him looking for you. I never dreamed you'd be this long." She moved as if to embrace Freddie but stopped when she got within a step of her, one hand rising to her nose as if to protect it. "Good heavens, that's . . . pungent."

Freddie snorted. "This is nothing compared to how it smelled yesterday. Poor Jacob would have turned us away entirely."

"Won't you come in and, um." Sophie was clearly torn between manners and practicality, but the latter won out. "Come and stand while we talk. Lord Smith-Grenville as well, I'm so glad you're back unharmed. Oh, and who's this?"

Barnabas followed Freddie into the room, only to see Daniel Pinkerton stationed in one corner, arms crossed over his massive chest, scowling like a gargoyle. He wore his rough clothes, which made him look even larger than he did in his employer's livery. The big man looked so fierce Barnabas actually flinched when he saw his expression. But Dan barely registered him. His eyes were on Sophie, who was transfixed by the last person to enter the room.

"My lady." Phineas inclined at the waist, a half bow almost more insulting than none at all.

Not for nothing was Lady Sophronia known for her composure. Her eyes widened a moment. Her slender throat bobbed in an obvious swallow, her mouth pinched too tightly for that same instant. Then as he watched, the signs of strain seemed to melt away, leaving only the cool, beautiful statue in their wake.

"Mr. Smith-Grenville."

After the most horrible moment of silence Barnabas had ever experienced, Sophie turned away and Phineas coughed into his hand and everybody else took a collective breath.

"Dan, what are you doing here? It's not your holiday, or your half day." Freddie didn't seem concerned, more curious, but something about Pinkerton's expression sent Barnabas's hackles up.

"Supposed to be driving you to the country and back, miss, remember?"

"Oh, of course."

"Daniel has been very worried for you, Freddie."

Barnabas thought the man looked more angry and sullen than worried, despite Sophie's charitable characterization. They might have done better to bring Pinkerton along on the escapade, to keep him involved if he wanted to be. On the other hand, if he'd been there, last night would have never been possible. On balance, Barnabas found he had no regrets about leaving Dan behind.

"It's thoughtful of you, Dan. We're back on time, however,

so there's no need to worry anymore. About anything except arranging a nice bath."

"I'll see to it," Sophie assured her, but Dan spoke up.

"I'll see you home, miss. We can bring you in the back and straight up to your room. If I send a boy now you could have hot water waiting for you."

"I never go home like this, you know that," Freddie reminded him with a frown before turning back to Sophie. "I'm sorry for bringing all this down on your head, Sophie. It all became more complicated than I ever dreamed."

"Doesn't everything?" She didn't look at Phineas as she said it, but the subtext was palpable.

Fearsome though Dan looked, Barnabas was inclined to side with him. He wanted to see Freddie home safely, bathed and in bed. He was exhausted, so he knew she must be. And the sooner she returned home, it seemed to him, the sooner the risk of her father discovering her hijinks disappeared.

When he approached him, however, the footman's scowl deepened to a murderous glare. Dan spoke before he had a chance to, in a low tone that didn't carry to the others. "She didn't mention she'd be out all night. I thought she'd be here, not halfway to France or wherever you took her off to. Overnight. Young impressionable girl."

Well, that was really too much. "I would hardly call—"

"And the two of you, you brought danger to this house. No, not him." Dan waved a dismissive hand toward Phineas. "Whatever his story is, I can tell his bark's worse than his bite. I mean Mr. Murcheson. You know as well as I do if he decided to, he could crush Lady Sophronia Wallingford like an insect, and all the money in the world wouldn't protect her. Not if he thought his daughter had been put in peril, and Lady Sophronia had helped. You know what he is. And after last night, I know what you are. *My lord.*"

Barnabas didn't know what he was himself, these days, but he knew enough not to ask Dan for his opinion on the subject. "Miss Murcheson has had a very long, tiring two days. If you believe you can get her home discreetly, dressed as she is, I'll urge her to take your offer. That way we'll all know she's secure, and we can all stop worrying."

"I'll still worry," Dan assured him. "But aye, if you can convince her."

The deciding factor was the number of bathtubs with water laid on in Sophie's house. Two. One for Barnabas, who could think of only one thing he'd ever anticipated more keenly than that particular bath. And one for Phineas, who had spoken scarcely another word since his arrival, other than to offer to leave on foot and find an inn or hostelry where he could bathe in peace.

"You'd have to walk for hours from here to find an inn that would let you in the door," Barnabas pointed out. "You can hardly stroll into Claridge's looking and smelling like that, even if you had the money for it."

"I do, as it happens, have the money for it." But Phineas couldn't argue that his presentation was less than desirable at the moment.

"Phineas and I will stay," Barnabas decided for them. "Once he's had a wash, Phineas can find a hotel, and I can come along to Murcheson's house. Meanwhile, Pinkerton will see Freddie safely there. After breakfast tomorrow we'll go driving, and Phineas can meet us in the park. We can regroup then."

"We need to get back to—" Freddie clamped her mouth shut, eyes cutting to the side to find Sophie. She must have recalled that Lady Sophronia knew nothing of the details of their outing. Nor would it be prudent to reveal them at this time, with the mood already so fraught. "We need to retrieve that *thing* from where we left it, and attempt to stop that event we discussed yesterday from taking place."

Phineas nodded. "You can both have a rest. I'll stoke up the trap later and go in search of more fuel for . . . for the thing. Then I'll go back to fetch it. Go for your drive after luncheon, unfashionable though it may be, to give me plenty of time. I think I know of a closer place that can accommodate the thing. We can meet and embark from . . . wherever that is."

"I'm not sure I trust you with the thing," Freddie said with a scowl.

"I was entrusted with it by its rightful owner, long before you ever laid eyes on it. I'll take good care of it, rest assured. Make sure it's safer from prying eyes than it is right now too."

"It certainly sounds as though you all have a full day before you tomorrow," Sophie said wryly.

Barnabas concurred. It sounded like a busier day than he was up to, but he supposed he would have to manage. The only way out at this point was through, although through *to what* he had no idea. Wasn't sure he wanted to know.

"You need to rest too," he reminded Phineas. The dark circles under his brother's eyes were not part of his disguise, nor was the slump in his shoulders. He'd had two hard days and a rough night in between. Far rougher than Barnabas's own night, which had not quite been restful but indecently comfortable. "You look ready to drop. And we ought to talk."

"I suppose we must, but not tonight."

Dissatisfied but sensing it was wiser not to press, Barnabas left off for the moment and nodded to Dan. "What about Miss Murcheson's things? Will you tell the house they were sent after her? Won't it arouse suspicion if she doesn't return when her luggage does?" She had packed as if for a weekend of frolic in the country, which evidently required an enormous steamer trunk.

Dan shrugged. "We'll bring it with us. Miss Murcheson can play the part of the lad I took pity on in the street and paid tuppence to help me carry the thing upstairs. If she keeps her head down, it should work well enough. As long as nobody gets within sniffing distance."

Barnabas wasn't sure it sounded like a good plan at all, but his own head was swimming from fatigue and Freddie's eyes were drifting shut as she swayed gently on her feet. He wanted to do something, kiss or hold her, even touch her. But what they'd already done was dangerous enough. Bringing it to everybody's attention was out of the question. For now, at least.

"Rest well, Freddie." He allowed himself that much, and earned a smile in return.

"The same to you. Both of you. And thank you, Sophie. You're a true friend."

"I'm not so sure. We can hash it out another time, though. See she gets home safely, Daniel."

Pinkerton tipped an invisible hat and opened the parlor door for Freddie, who gave Barnabas one last, long look before following the big man out of the room.

Nineteen

꧁❧❦❧꧂

SHE WAS TIRED, deservedly so. That was the excuse she gave herself later on, anyway. But Freddie still thought she should have suspected something was amiss from Dan's broody silence, in place of his usual broody lecturing. Or by the absence, which really ought to have been conspicuous, of any servants in the carriage house, or the garden, or the kitchens, or anywhere else on their journey from the mews to the door of Freddie's room.

Or the mere fact of the bath laid on for her there, steaming hot and enticing, so she needn't wait a moment to get clean. And supper, still warm under its cover even when her bath was done, a comfortingly large serving of roast beef and Yorkshire pudding, with a slice of berry tart for afterward. A cup of tea or some lemonade wouldn't have been unwelcome, but she was too tired to call for it. The wine somebody had thoughtfully poured was more than sufficient, for all it was a bit stronger and sweeter than she had expected.

So tired. Hardly had she finished the meal than she fell gratefully into her bed, and into what she expected to be a restful, well-earned sleep. Instead she dreamed of swimming through black water, filthy and thick, knowing she must surface to breathe but terrified of some unnamable *something* she knew was waiting for her there. And later, of chasing Barnabas and Phineas down an endless dock, but her feet wouldn't move, and when she opened her mouth to call out to them, no sound would come out.

It was not a peaceful night. She awoke to a noon-bright room, a foul taste in her mouth, and the feeling that she had forgotten something important.

The tub was gone, as was the supper tray. She hadn't heard them being removed, but now a tray with breakfast sat on the small round table by the window. Sadly the teapot was cold and the tea appeared too stewed to be drinkable. The toast and kippers were also stone cold, as though they'd been sitting there for some time. Her stomach was uneasy anyway, and she pushed the stuff away.

Ringing for a servant seemed to accomplish nothing, and after waiting several minutes—brushing her hair out and pondering what on earth to wear to go on a drive through the park culminating in a submersible ride to find invisible squid—she decided to peek out the door to investigate. No need to get herself into clothes yet and go looking for help if one of the girls happened to be dusting right outside her bedroom.

The door wouldn't open. It wasn't just stuck either, as sometimes happened on damp days. When she yanked hard on the knob as she turned it, and at the same time kicked a certain spot near the hinge, nothing useful happened. Nothing even budged. She hadn't really expected it to. It was not a damp day, for one thing.

She peered through the keyhole, but saw only the blue

striped paper on the hallway wall opposite. A glance under the door confirmed that the key had not simply fallen from the lock. Not that it should have been there in the first place, as she rarely bothered to lock her door and certainly hadn't done so the previous night, but she would rather test all avenues before accepting the awful truth. At last she tried folding a slip of heavy paper from her writing desk and slipping it between the door and frame. Sliding up from the floor, the paper was stopped by the door catch, as she'd expected. But continuing up, she encountered another obstruction a few inches higher. Something on the outside of the door frame, that was very solid and that she was certain she would have noticed had it been there before.

Freddie cast her mind about for some other alternative, some other truth to frame these facts with, other than the unpleasant one she didn't want to accept.

She was bolted in.

Her stomach lurched as the realization set in, and she had to sit for a moment while the fog of sudden, intense anxiety cleared from her head. Soon it occurred to her that the fog was not all anxiety, and a dawning suspicion made her lift the lid from the teapot again and dab one finger in the liquid. Tasting the smallest amount possible, she tried to analyze. Tea, of course. But honey-sweet, not her preference at all, and beneath the honey was a subtle, wretched bitterness she had apparently failed to recognize in last night's wine. Laudanum, or something as like as made no difference. She spit as much as she could out of her mouth into the napkin, wiping her tongue with the linen until no trace of the medicine remained. No wonder she'd slept through half the day, unaware of the meals being traded out or the lock being installed on the outside of her door.

A look at the clock on her mantel confirmed that it was

nearly lunchtime. In another hour or so she ought to be taking her drive with Barnabas. Being locked in her room was going to make that far more difficult to accomplish.

"Damn you, Father!"

She considered ringing the bell again, pulling the cord until she got some sort of response. But that would really only create annoyance for the servants, not for her father, who might not even be in the house. And it also assumed he hadn't disconnected the bell, anticipating her attempts to summon someone. Should she ring it, just in case that was what he was expecting her to do, to make him think she was that predictable and throw him off track when she did something wildly unexpected later?

And what exactly might that be?

The pessimistic voice in her head took the opportunity to remind her, also, that she really deserved no better treatment than this, and was lucky her father hadn't had her thrown into a stockade somewhere. Or perhaps Newgate. She wasn't really sure what his relationship was to the military, or whether he had the authority to throw anyone in a stockade, but he could certainly have turned her over to some sort of authority for any number of crimes she'd committed. Which did he know about? She'd stolen things, broken into a classified military base, stolen things *from* the classified military base . . . really she'd done quite a lot of illegal things, lately. Normally her stealth and subterfuge were merely employed to allow her to pursue her chosen line of work. Since Barnabas had arrived, however, things seemed to have taken a decided turn for the larcenous and vice-ridden. Not that he'd encouraged any of it, except a few of the vices.

He'd been against the rest of it from the start, of course. That was the basis of his employment. In their last few encounters, though, he seemed to have forgotten all about that. And really now that she was looking back and trying to clarify her hindsight, shouldn't that be suspicious in itself?

Somebody had to have tipped off her father to trigger this incarceration. He'd obviously known when precisely she would be back. The hot bath and meal, perfectly timed. The drugged wine, already prepared. And then the locksmith who'd evidently been plying his trade here in the middle of the night. It all spoke of preparation, premeditation.

Just as she'd tried to find some other explanation for the locked door before accepting it as truth, Freddie scoured her mind for other possibilities, other ways her father could have learned she was up to more than her usual no good. Phineas had come into the picture only recently, and if he'd been pretending not to know her in the sub yesterday, he'd done an excellent job fooling everyone. He couldn't be her father's man still. He didn't even know whose man he was; he'd said as much himself. And even she hadn't known she'd end up at that particular dock at that particular time. Not Phineas, then.

Not Sophie either, she knew in her heart. Sophie might care for her, might want her to avoid dangers both physical and moral, but she would never give Freddie's secrets up to a man who might lock her in a room because of them. It simply wouldn't occur to her to even consider such a thing. Besides, Sophie had had years to develop a tolerance for Freddie's doings. She'd volunteered to help in the first place, and urged Freddie to find her own path if the one offered to her was too bleak to contemplate. If she'd wanted to change things, she could have simply stopped abetting the sneaking about. The same was true of Dan. And neither of them had anything to gain by ratting her out. Quite the opposite. They were best served by preserving the status quo, dubious though it had been.

Although there had been that odd exchange between Dan and Barnabas, at Sophie's house. She hadn't overheard it, but Dan had looked thunderously displeased and Barnabas wore his smoothest, mildest, most harmless expression throughout. Giving nothing away.

Change. That was what it all came down to, the fixed point her mind kept circling. The status quo had clearly *not* been preserved, so what had changed? What new element had unbalanced the delicate machinations by which she had maintained the structure of her life?

Her stomach clenched again as she focused in on what had to be the truth. There was nothing else left. Barnabas had known her whereabouts and her plans. He'd helped her, followed her, been vocally concerned about her safety, and she'd trusted him with . . . well, with everything. But now he had found his brother, and they had the smugglers to foil and the squid to save, and what if Barnabas had grown *too* worried at the prospect of Freddie accompanying them? That was the kindest slant she could give it, that he'd meant well. She could almost bear it if she thought that was the reason, that he'd turned Freddie in to her father to protect her. Bear it, but not forgive him.

Because the alternative . . . Freddie wrapped her arms around herself, trying to hold herself together as panic and anguish came crashing in. If he had played her for a fool, strung her along to get to his brother and the smugglers, turned her in to get her out of the way once he'd served his own ends—*and* stolen her heart in the process, not to mention her maidenhood—she would have to get out of this room. And she would have to find Lord Barnabas Smith-Grenville. And she would have to punch the treacherous smile right off his beautiful face.

* * *

"BARNABAS."

Something wiggled his foot, and he snatched it to safety under the covers, trying to find his way back into his dream. It was a lovely dream, featuring a nebulous but alluring fantasia of Freddie, naked in a clean bed, with her legs parted just enough that he could almost see—

"Barnabas."

And it was gone.

"Bloody fucking *hell*, Phineas."

"You were supposed to go back to Murcheson's last night. You fell asleep in the bath instead. Fortunately the butler came along and heard you snoring."

Barnabas had a vague memory of a groggy conversation with the butler, and of being shown to a room, but he couldn't have attested that it was *this* room, or to any other particulars of the evening. He no longer smelled like dead fish and sewage, though, and he counted it among his blessings that he had evidently finished the functional part of the bath before he fell asleep.

"Well done, Lady Sophronia's butler." He sat up and rubbed his hand over his face, grimacing at the stubble and at the sleep sand caught in his lashes. "What time is it?"

"Half past eleven. You slept for nearly twelve hours."

"Blast. How can I return to Murcheson's now, after being gone all night and half the day? How do I explain it?"

"Mrs. Wallingford already did. She sent a note saying you'd injured an ankle getting out of the carriage to assist her down when it stopped here, and she'd insisted you remain here while she summoned a doctor to examine you. Later, of course, she sent another note stating that the doctor had recommended you stay in bed with the offending limb elevated for at least a night and a day."

"Murcheson's house isn't two miles from here. I could've traveled that. She made me sound like a bloody Jane Austen heroine."

"It seemed believable. She also invited Freddie to take luncheon with her today. She should be here within the half hour, so get dressed."

He was wider awake now, and the full peculiarity of the situation was dawning on him. Phineas was standing next to the bed. Phineas, whom he hadn't seen in years until the mad adventures of the past two days. Having a conversation with him as if it were the most normal thing in the world. He continued to look like a pirate, however.

"Why are you still wearing that ridiculous thing on your face?"

"My fine mustache?" Phineas twirled one of the long, tatty ends around his finger.

"*That* is disgusting, but I was referring to the eye patch."

His brother touched the patch, the rakish charm vanishing from his face. "*That* is to keep the sun from my eye." He lifted the edge of the thing briefly, and Barnabas winced at the sight of blood red where white should be, and a scrabble of short, vicious-looking scars fanning out from the corner of the lid. "And to keep from frightening the innocent."

"I'm far from innocent."

"As I'm well aware."

"What *happened*?"

"I attempted to rescue a kitten from a tree. It was the wrong kitten, and very much the wrong tree."

"You could have just told me it was none of my business." Barnabas flipped the bedclothes away from his legs, then flipped them back when he realized he was naked. He wasn't sure how he was ever going to face the butler again. "Where did you get the clean clothes?"

"Mrs. Wallingford procured them."

His brother lifted a pile of garments from the chair in the corner, tossing them to Barnabas and taking a seat while he dressed.

"Not her husband's?" Barnabas couldn't resist, especially as Phineas kept pointedly emphasizing the lady's marital status rather than her rank.

"Neither of you mentioned she was a widow."

"We hardly had time. Honestly it didn't occur to me until later. Would it have made a difference?"

Phineas scowled, gesturing down at himself, then waving a hand at his damaged face. "Probably not. You're a terrible spy, you know. I thought I ought to mention it, in case you planned to continue in this career past this one assignment. Assuming Murcheson doesn't have you hanged at some point in the near future, because you've made such a botch of this first job already. Watching his daughter. I just know he jokes about that assignment. It's a scut detail."

It was a fair point, one that Barnabas had made to himself already. But Phineas was his *younger* brother and that sort of talk couldn't be allowed to go unanswered. "Says the one-eyed former spy who fled the country in the middle of his own undercover job, apparently in a fit of pique because the girl he fancied had married somebody else. And is that supposed to be a pirate costume, Phin? An airship pirate? How can we possibly tell? You're still short one wooden suction-leg and a grapnel hand, not to mention the parrot. Somebody might not understand that you were a pirate, without those additional cues. The eye patch, unkempt hair and surly disposition simply aren't definitive enough. Though the striped shirt you had on the other day was a superb defining touch. You might consider knocking out a tooth or two."

"Bastard."

"Don't disparage our parents like that." Barnabas knotted his tie before shrugging into the jacket Phineas had thrown his way. The clothes fit surprisingly well, though they were plain. Sophie apparently had a good idea of men's sizing. "Perhaps we can get something to eat before we go to find the squid. Wait, why are you here at all? I thought you were going to Mersea to retrieve the *Gilded Lily*. Did I dream that conversation?"

Chuckling, Phineas stood and headed for the door. "Last night I went for a walk and discovered that Lady Sophronia had a very nice single-chair dirigible in her carriage house. Not to mention a comfortable steam car. I borrowed them for a little while, took the steam car to the place I planned to dock the *Gilded Lily*, then flew to get it and took it to its new dock. Deflated the airship and drove the steam car back here, after making a few stops for supplies. I returned a few hours ago and had a short rest until I got bored waiting for you to wake up on your own. Really, the trip was ridiculously easy compared to when we made it."

"It all depends on who you're borrowing from, it seems. I must say you've had an admirable night and morning, doing all that while I was sleeping like the dead. You must have the constitution of an ox. What stops did you have to make?" He stepped into his shoes and bent to tie them before following Phineas. They were the ones he'd had on the previous day, unfortunately, and were still damp with a disreputable air about them. Somebody had at least attempted to clean them and restore their polish, however. Sophie really did have a top-notch staff.

"Villesandro's Fine Voltaics, of course. For zinc and potassium chlorate. Where else would you find them?"

Squishing down the hall, Barnabas shrugged. "Of course. Naturally."

"Then a printer's, for the manganese dioxide. I had to ask around a bit to find a fellow who specialized in colored plates. Hope I have enough of the stuff. Of course the real problem will be keeping the potassium stable until we can get it to the submersible. Where it may or may not blow us to kingdom come when we actually attempt to use it."

"Did you memorize the sub's manual?"

"I could have, but I didn't have to," Phineas said, as they tramped down the stairs side by side. "I wrote most of it."

Twenty

❧❦❧

Daniel Pinkerton stood in the hall near the foot of the stairs, bearing an envelope. He appeared to be there in his official capacity, as he was wearing livery, and he studiously avoided Barnabas's eye as he passed him the missive with a perfunctory bow. All formality.

"M'lord."

"Good morning, Daniel."

Two of Sophie's servants were at work nearby, one visible through the front parlor door, dusting, and another busy cleaning the large mirror down the hall. Although her people had demonstrated remarkable discretion thus far, Barnabas had no idea how far her trust extended. He kept his voice low as he addressed Daniel, while he pulled the envelope open and withdrew the contents.

"I take it you delivered Miss Murcheson safely last night. My thanks again."

"I did, sir."

"Regardless of what you must think, my intentions toward her are—" He stopped for a moment, unsure what his intentions in fact were. Whatever he might want, things were muddled by the things Freddie didn't seem to want. He wasn't sure where that left him. "They're not dishonorable."

"Yes, sir. Begging your pardon, but I was told I needn't wait for a response. I must return to my duties. M'lord. Sir."

He gave them each a nod and was out the front door before Barnabas could think of what to say.

"Cheeky," Phineas remarked.

"Not usually. He's a good lad, but he's under the impression I've sullied Miss Murcheson, and he's not happy about it."

"I was laboring under that same impress—"

"I'm going to marry her," he said abruptly, glaring at Phineas, daring him silently to say another word. He had no idea where it had come from, that declaration. But it felt true, and by God he would knock his brother to the ground if he kept going on like that.

"Duly noted. And probably for the best. Why don't you read your letter? It seems to have come from the young woman in question."

It had. And it was baffling.

Dear Lord Smith-Grenville,

He had to read that a few times, confused by the formal address. Too late for that now, surely. Was somebody reading over her shoulder when she wrote it?

Dear Lord Smith-Grenville,
    After my arrival home last night, I received word of your unfortunate circumstance. I hope you will accept

my sincere well-wishes for your recovery in light of what I must now convey. My father has learned of our adventures in the tunnel below the channel. He has convinced me of the extreme dangers of this enterprise and the luck we had in escaping unscathed. He has explained the severity of my crimes—and yours—and I now understand how wrong I was to undertake such activities and encourage you to stray so far from your own duties. I have agreed to limit my excursions in future to those venues most appropriate for a young, unmarried woman. To aid in this, I shall soon be moving to the country.

Father has indicated your employment will be ending as I will no longer be in need of your supervision. I wish you the best of luck in all your future endeavors.

Please also relay to Lady Sophronia that I must decline her kind invitation to luncheon, as I am suffering a headache.

She'd ended with "Sincerely, Frédérique Murcheson." If there was one thing this letter lacked, it was sincerity, of that much Barnabas was sure.

"This is some sort of code. Or he forced her to write it. *Something.* It makes no sense," he insisted to Phineas after reading the letter aloud. "I have to go see her."

"Shouldn't you be planning to flee the country? Look, you have a narrow window of opportunity here. Murcheson apparently believes Sophie's excuse about your ankle, that's all well and good, but he's going to do a great deal more than just dismiss you from his Agency if he knows you were down in that tunnel with Freddie. At the very least he must assume you've been a horribly incompetent employee to let her get that far. And it sounds as though your Freddie's had a fairly extreme change of heart. From the tone of that note, it's only a matter of time before she tells him the rest, and he learns you were actively assisting her. Working very much against his direct orders."

"She would never—"

"And if she tells him *all* the rest you won't be safe in Europa or the Dominions either. South America might give you a fighting chance. It *might*. But not if you dither away your lead time."

"What do you mean, *all* the rest?"

"I'm certain we both know what I mean, Barnabas. Are you really going to make me say it aloud?" Phineas raised his eyebrows expectantly.

The inn. The night they'd spent together. "No. Of course not."

"Perhaps this letter is code, although I can't think for what. Or perhaps, and this seems more likely to me, a young girl got into trouble far over her head and, when confronted by the primary authority figure in her life, realized what a dismal fool she'd been. Realized the risks she'd taken by exploring things she shouldn't. And of course Murcheson wouldn't have told her if he was sending people to arrest you. Whether or not that letter is genuine, you have to get out of here before they show up."

He'd known Phineas all his life, and only known Freddie a short time. Should he weigh his own irrational hope against the opinion of his brother, whom he trusted, and who after all was only taking the letter at face value?

He read the letter again, trying to see it objectively. Phineas's version of things did make more sense, didn't it? From the stories Freddie had told him, her father's approval meant more to her than she would ever admit directly. Even in her effort to escape Murcheson's control, she had sought to prove herself to him. And she'd never spoken to Barnabas of the future, of a life they might share together, had she? Far from it.

They were still at the foot of the stairs. Barnabas gripped the ornate wooden finial on the post for support, trying to steady himself against the crushing fear that his brother was absolutely correct.

"She said—no, it can't be that."

"Can't be what?"

He swallowed, forcing back a painful lump of some emotion he couldn't bring himself to name. "She said I was *convenient*. And beautiful. But—"

"She called you beautiful? She's such an odd girl."

"I think . . . I think she *used* me."

Phineas's silence was deafening. Meanwhile Barnabas's mind kept offering images of Freddie, each smile, every dimple, but seen now through quite a different lens. Friendly and eager, because that had been the best way to seduce him. Honest to a fault, because she'd seen it was getting her everything she wanted. What would be the point in lying? She'd told him what he was to her, and he hadn't listened. He'd heard what he wanted to. Not surprising, as evidently he'd been listening with his cock, not his heart as he'd convinced himself.

He'd come all this way, he thought he might have found some sort of strange, stolen happiness at last, and instead he'd been slapped in the face with his own inadequacies. By a girl in trousers.

A beautiful, convenient girl in trousers, who'd sown him like a wild oat.

"Is this what it felt like?" he asked his brother. "Is this why you had to leave everything?"

"No. That part comes later, when you see her married to another man."

It cut him deeply enough now, just thinking about it. Actually witnessing that would be too deep a wound to survive. But he owed Freddie Murcheson one thing, at least. His brother, back by his side. If nothing else good came of this wretched trip to England, he had still managed to salvage Phineas from the wreckage.

"What are you going to do now?" he asked him. "Go to the Admiral? Or to Murcheson?"

"The *Gilded Lily* is still waiting," Phineas reminded him. "It's fast and maneuverable, more so than you've seen. Miss Murcheson didn't know all its capabilities. I'm going to take it and do what I can to disperse the cephalopods before Furneval and his subs can get to them. At least it will forestall the slaughter until I can think of something better, and perhaps the distraction will buy enough time to allow the station crew to repair the Glass Octopus. I'll start at the coordinates where we found the squid shoal before, then use signal lanterns to try to draw them away. I don't know if it will work, and I suspect there's a fair chance one of the creatures will catch me and put an end to me. And you're off to South America, so I suppose this is good-bye."

He'd lost Freddie, or rather learned that he'd never had her to begin with. He'd lost his job, or would as soon as Murcheson caught up with him. Barnabas wasn't ready to lose a brother today on top of all that.

"It's not good-bye. I'm coming with you."

MORDECAI HAD BEEN busy.

Sometimes, Rollo was pleased with the things his friend

accomplished when he grew busy. But many times, and Rollo feared this was one of those, nothing good came of it.

He had squinted down through the sluggish, slopping brine at the queer assemblage of poles and mesh attached to the side of the small submersible as it departed the concealed warehouse dock, and thought, *This will end badly, I just know it.*

"You promised," Mord had reminded him when he showed him the contraption, because for all his eccentricities the little man knew Rollo very well. He knew that Rollo sometimes needed reminding of his promises. He knew Rollo was capable of breaking promises too. But not the ones he made to Mord, never those. Not yet, anyway.

"I did."

"This one's fast and little. We take it out, three of us, and when we find the baby cuttlefish we come alongside and just scoop it in!"

"Scoop it in?" The cage contraption was a cube about the height of a man on each side. Having seen the squid things move, Rollo was skeptical that the submersible could get close enough to scoop one into a trap that small, but he wasn't about to express that skepticism to Mord.

"Just *scoop* it right in," Mord had repeated, attempting to illustrate the method with his arms. "Scoop. Like that. Then the cuttlefish gets swept along, see, and it can't escape because it can't swim faster than the sub."

"At some point the submersible must stop. What then?"

"By then the baby's tired out. We drive the sub back here, some divers hop into the water to rotate the cage, tie a net on top for a cover, and Bob's your uncle."

"And if all goes according to plan, we then have a baby cuttlefish in our submersible dock?"

"I'm designing a tank for it. A *tank*. Such a tank, you wait and see."

Rollo feared he knew already. He recognized the light of lunatic genius in Mord's eyes. Such a tank would be large and costly, and must be left behind if ever they had to abandon this place in a hurry. Leaving the authorities to wonder, no doubt, about the mental stability of one Rollo Furneval. Because who kept a giant blinking squid in an opium warehouse? But then somebody would realize the tank's cobbled-together pump solved some heretofore unsolvable problem of hydraulic engineering, or find that the glass was of a structure never seen before, because Mordecai did things like that. Rollo had tried to get him to do it on command, but that wasn't how his friend operated, and he'd learned over the years that serendipity was all he could hope for. He kept his promises, he kept Mord happy and occupied, and occasionally it resulted in something spectacular. Even more rarely, it turned out to be wildly profitable, which was what really mattered to Rollo.

This didn't feel like wild profit in the making, but he'd let it play out and see what happened. Perhaps the squid would turn out to be a source of an ink nobody had ever seen before, or be filled with a rare chemical he could claim exclusive rights to. Or there might turn out to be a lucrative market for enormous cuttlebones.

The spotter had spied the inbound sub only two hours or so after it had left the dock. Relieved, Rollo waited by the secret dock, along with the two unhappy gentlemen he'd selected as divers. Young, fit, with sound lungs, but infinitely replaceable, both of them. They shivered in their combinations as the sub approached, though it was a fine day. When the cage rig scraped along the edge of the docking bay, Rollo looked into it and had to laugh.

"I think you'll be safe enough," he told the lads with a snort.

The bolder of the two leaned over to have a look, and chuckled in relief. "That's all?"

The cuttlefish was a baby indeed, and what was more, Rollo suspected it hadn't survived its capture and subsequent journey. It clung like a scrap of colorless rag to the roof of the cage, the part that would be on one side once the boys twisted it about. They jumped into the water fearlessly once the sub's engine had stopped and the propellers were still, and had just begun to grapple with the cage when the vessel's hatch opened. Mord popped out, hair in every direction, eyes so wide the white showed below his irises.

"Is it still there? Do you see it?"

"Oh, it's still there."

"Take care with those latches. Don't startle it," Mord called to the divers, only one of whom was at the surface to hear him.

"I think it's had all the startling already, Mord. I don't think it's possible to startle it any further."

"They're very sensitive."

The second diver surfaced, shaking his wet hair from his eyes. "It's unlatched. I'll go back under and pull up, you go hand over hand from that pole to this.

Between them, they managed to spin the cage and secure it, under Mord's watchful eye, to the hooks he'd anchored in two of the pier's supports. To finish the job, they slid the final panel of mesh into place on top of the cage. By the time it was all secure, the sub was moored as well, and as soon as he was off it Mordecai ran along the dock, flopping onto the boards with his face hanging over the edge, nose to the wires of the top panel.

"Is it moving? Has it changed its appearance?"

"Nah," one of the divers said, reaching a hand underwater toward the side of the cage where the bedraggled marine creature still clung, its freakish tentacles woven through the mesh. "I think it's having a nice rest."

He flicked the water close to the animal with his fingers, causing hardly a ripple on the surface, and no reaction from the cuttlefish. His mate laughed, and splashed a handful of water at him.

"See how you like it."

"You're going to frighten him," Mordecai muttered darkly.

Ignoring his warning, the first boy braced his hand on the cage, cupping his other hand to send a proper volley back to his friend. That was his mistake.

"Oy! The little bugger's got me!" He grabbed the dock, attempting to pull free of the creature's suddenly active tentacles. "It's stronger than it—ow! Fucking hell, it bit me! Get it off me, get it off!"

"Just swim away," his colleague said, paddling to the dock and clinging there, safely away from the cage. "It's a baby, just swim away from it!"

"Get it—aaah! Ahh . . ."

He dipped under and came back up struggling, obviously from more than the ducking. Rollo watched closely as the boy's body went into convulsions, thrashing so violently that he actually rose in the water and finally broke his hand free of the cuttlefish's embrace. Too late, obviously. His body jerked for a few seconds only, then went limp except for the spastic movements of his terrified eyes. The second time he went down, he stayed under, only bubbles marking his passage from the world of the living to whatever lay beyond.

The other boy gaped, too shocked to even consider a rescue. Nor did Rollo recommend one. The cuttlefish had taken its due, and he eyed it with a newfound respect.

"Interesting."

"Neurotoxins in the saliva!" chirped Mord, who was practically wriggling with excitement as he watched his new pet relocate itself, then change color to blend seamlessly with the mesh on which it rested. "Thank you, Roland!"

"Anything for you, Mord."

"I think I'm going to call him Albert."

In his watery new home, young Albert shifted his tentacles once more and began to emit a soft, pulsing glow.

Twenty-one

❧

IT WAS MIDAFTERNOON by the time Rutherford Murcheson finally visited his daughter's locked room. He was safe enough entering, and they both knew it, because he'd taken almost everything out of the place that might serve as a weapon. She might use the mantel clock as a bludgeon, but the resulting outcry or thud would be sure to alert the gigantic henchman outside her door. His name was Maurice, she'd learned when he carried in her luncheon tray. He seemed nice, but she suspected that wouldn't last long in the face of an attempted escape by timepiece.

At least that meal and its accompanying beverages had been blissfully free of opiates, as far as she could tell. Still, when her father came into her room and closed the door behind him, she said what she'd been planning to since that nasty breakfast surprise.

"Father. Would you like a nice cup of tea? Or perhaps some wine?"

It fell flat, probably because it had sounded too studied. He just raised his eyebrows at her and pulled out the second chair, joining her at the table.

"The mutton wasn't bad at all at luncheon; did Cook send that up for you?"

"Don't speak to me of mutton."

"Would you rather I speak of the likely consequences for theft of a military vessel, should the Navy or the higher-ups at my own Agency ever learn of what you've been up to?"

"You have higher-ups?" Somehow she'd envisioned her father at the top of the heap, the bodies of his foes strewn beneath his feet.

"Oh, yes. Everybody does. Even you, my little tinker. You've just managed to escape their notice thus far. What, you thought I didn't know?"

She had thought that, yes, but it hardly seemed to matter now. "If you knew, why didn't you stop me?"

"You were enjoying yourself." He shrugged, then traced an aimless line on the tablecloth with one finger. "You were always so talented at makesmithing, you know. You could have become a master, given time. Not that I would have allowed my daughter to go into a manual trade, of course, but I thought it did you no harm to play about with clockwork animals and the like. It was really your mother who insisted I stop taking you along to the factory. But she isn't here, and this hobby gave you something to do. You've always been at your worst when you're idle too long. As long as Daniel was with you or, heaven help us, some unfortunate agent of mine, I thought it was safe enough. Safer than some of the things you might be out doing instead, anyway. I was right too, until Smith-Grenville came along. I should have known better than to take on another one of those. They're not to be trusted, as I suspect you've now realized. The elder is no better than the younger."

She thought of the things Phineas had said, the different perspective he offered regarding his reliability and why he'd done what he'd done. And thought too of the timing. The trouble had started before Barnabas entered the picture, hadn't it? But again, it didn't seem important anymore to pick out the details. She could spend a lifetime trying to sift the grains of truth from the beach of lies, and still never learn a way to make Barnabas not be faithless. He *had* to be the one who'd betrayed her.

"You can't keep me here forever."

"I can keep you until you tell me where my damn submersible is."

"I have no idea where it is," she said truthfully. If all had gone according to plan, Phineas had moved it from Mersea, but she hadn't been thinking clearly enough the previous evening to ask him the new location. She'd expected to speak with him today, of course. "I know where it was last night, but it's long gone from there by now."

"Freddie, this is no laughing matter. That sub carries vital surveillance equipment. You know there are still smugglers carrying opium in the channel; everyone knows it. Well, that sub may help us track the smugglers. Stop the illegal opium trade. That would benefit us all."

She would have believed him if she hadn't already known the truth. She never would have suspected. He was that good, that smooth, and he sounded as if it meant so much to him.

"You want the *Gilded Lily* back to help you protect the seismograph. Because if that's destroyed, if the Glass Octopus is ruined past all usefulness, Whitehall won't pay to support your undersea station anymore." There, now he knew that she knew, and they could simply be open with one another. "I laud your efforts to further the cause of science, but the Glass Octopus is wasted if you're not going to use the information it provides to warn the general public about impending quakes."

"I ought to throw away the key to that door. I might too, if you don't return the *Gilded Lily.*"

Freddie pushed back from the table and stood up, pacing toward the window, wishing for fresh air. "I don't have it on my person, and I truly don't know its current location. As of last night, it was on Mersea Island. If I knew where it was now I would tell you, because I don't care anymore. About much of anything, really. But you should know it isn't the smugglers sabotaging your precious seismograph, so hunting after them won't solve your problem. I'm surprised Lord Smith-Grenville hasn't already told you that, since he was so forthcoming with information."

"What do you mean? And of course they're the saboteurs. We've already investigated the French, so thoroughly they're probably still having nightmares about it."

She knew before she spoke what it would sound like. She told him anyway, consequences be damned. "It isn't the smugglers, and it isn't sabotage. The sensors are being disabled by enormous cephalopods who may or may not be interpreting the flashing lights as some sort of signal or trigger related to the earthquakes. There's a chance they may be able to *predict* quakes, better than even your equipment."

"Cephalopods."

"Yes. Giant ones. Like squid, or perhaps cuttlefish."

"Cuttlefish."

"Yes. Oh, and they can turn invisible. Camouflage themselves, I mean, on any sort of surface. And sometimes they . . . glow."

She waited for him to repeat *glow* but he never did, just stared her down for several long painful seconds before sighing. Heavily. That special, Father's-disappointed sigh she remembered so well from her youth. *Sigh.* Father was disappointed that she'd eaten all the tea cakes, leaving none for the other children and giving herself a bellyache. *Sigh.* Father was disconsolate regarding Miss Finnegan's report on Freddie's shameful conduct during lessons. *Sigh.* Father simply didn't know what to do with a girl who wouldn't stop opening up his steam car bonnet and removing vital bits to examine them without telling anyone.

The sigh was uncalled for here. She was telling the truth about the squid or cuttlefish, and about the fact that she didn't know where the *Gilded Lily* could be found. It was somewhere between Tilbury and the channel, she hoped, with Phineas at the helm doing something to keep the smugglers from accomplishing wholesale cephalopod destruction. But that was as far as her knowledge extended.

"It's all true. Eventually you'll see."

He stood up, straightening his coat. "Knock on the door and inform Maurice when you're ready to tell me what I need to know. The longer you take to capitulate, the worse it will go for you in the long run. Oh, and you might want to start packing your trunks, if you're looking for something to do. I've purchased a small home in the countryside just a stone's throw from Windermere. You'll be moving there shortly."

"You're *banishing* me?"

"To the Lake District," he pointed out. "It's beautiful."

"I won't go."

"What sort of life can you afford on your tinker's wages? And what if the makesmith guild decides on a crackdown against the unlicensed tinker-makesmiths sometime next year, next month, tomorrow? How will you support yourself then?"

"I'll hire myself out as a French tutor." She could do it too. Her French was as good as any native's. Although she was iffy on the specifics of grammar in her almost-native tongue, which might prove a deficiency. "Or I'll think of something else."

"Freddie. Darling, I love you and I'm sorry you feel your life is so circumscribed. I'm sorry too that your ideals have to be shattered so harshly. I'd like to use the Glass Octopus as the basis for a public warning system, of course I would. But it isn't up to me, and politics is a complicated business. A truly intractable Gordian knot. The sooner you learn that . . . well, I won't say you'll be happier, but you'll waste less time worrying about it, once you accept that it can't be changed."

"It can. People change things all the time. Systems, ways of thinking, whole governments."

"Freddie."

She returned his gaze, feeling so miserable she didn't even protest when he embraced her awkwardly for a moment, giving her back a pat for good measure before releasing her.

"There, there."

"Thank you."

"By the way, don't suppose you can co-opt any more of my servants, or try to play on old sympathies. Mr. Pinkerton served me well enough, but he let you lead him astray for a good long time before coming back to his senses. I'm grateful he did come back, as I wouldn't have had you risking your life and poking in affairs that are none of your concern, but of course I had to terminate him. A man who deceives you once will always do it again given the chance. You don't keep a dog who bites his keeper's hand."

Terminate . . .

"But—you *can't* have. You killed him? You monster!"

Murcheson looked at her, questioning, then shook his head. "Oh, Freddie, don't be so melodramatic. I terminated his *employment*. And told the staff to stop sending our mending to his mother for piecework. He's a strapping young ox with a pleasant face and a good leg; he'll quickly find another position. I'll even provide him a character. As long as the household is far away from here, and nowhere close to the Lake District. You know I'm surprised to hear you defending him, after he tattled on you. Very magnanimous of you."

"Magnanimous how?" But her words trailed off, and her father didn't appear to have heard.

It was Dan.

Murcheson was already at the door, knocking for Maurice. "Go to Windermere. Oh, and I'll be sure to let you know how Lord Smith-Grenville's ankle is faring, as I'm so sure you'll be concerned. I'll be sending someone to arrest him for treason this evening, once I've made sure he isn't going to lead me to anything useful if left to his own devices. Though *useful* and Smith-Grenville don't seem to go hand in hand. Hch. Staying at Lady Sophie's for the doctor to visit, and refusing the five-minute carriage ride from there to here on the grounds of a twisted ankle, I'd be inclined to call him a delicate violet of a fellow. But those flowers have a graceful appearance, don't they, for all they're so short? So let's call him Clumsy Violet when we look back later and have a good laugh about all this. Well, Smith-Grenville probably won't be laughing, of course."

Because she had no idea what he was talking about, other than that Barnabas was apparently still at liberty, Freddie said nothing and tried to think what it could all mean. Her father seemed to take her silence for further sullenness, and it didn't seem to faze him. When the door opened he slipped out quickly, and Freddie caught a glimpse of Maurice's bulk before she was once more shut in with her thoughts.

Barnabas hadn't been injured when she left Sophie's. Had he remained there all night, instead of returning to his room here as they'd discussed? What possible reason could he have?

It didn't matter. She could find all that out in good time. Because it hadn't been Barnabas who betrayed her after all. It had been Dan. And while Dan might have wanted to protect Freddie, that couldn't have been his only motivation.

She smacked herself on the forehead. "I've been an *idiot*!"

An idiot with a practical set of skills. Freddie swiftly dug in her wardrobe, pulling out the sack in which she hid her usual work clothes. In minutes, she'd changed her simple muslin day dress for a pair of trousers and shirt, sturdy brogues and the new cap she'd found to shove her shortened curls into. It fit tighter than the uniform cap had and held all the stray locks in quite nicely.

She didn't have the padding and bandages, and she considered making do with some sort of substitute, but in the end she decided against it. The trousers were loose, but her braces still held them up, and time was wasting.

Even *sans* padding, however, she could instantly see that her first hope of escape was no hope at all. She'd had no fire since that morning, owing to the warmth of the day, so the hearth was cool enough to stand in. But when she really got her first good look up the chimney, she could see that she would never make it all the way to the roof that way. The house was old enough that the flues had hosted their share of chimney sweeps' apprentices, in the days before mechanical sweepers and clockwork flue-scouring devices became the norm. But even on her slimmest day, Freddie had never been built like a sweep's boy, and the already narrow flue took at least one jog and very likely decreased in size before it reached the open air.

That left only one option, the one she hadn't wanted to take. Crossing to the closest window, she studied the hasp and padlock that had been installed while she slept, a later discovery that had fueled a good half hour of enraged weeping. But she'd railed more at the symbolism than anything else. If her father had thought to place the lock outside the window, that might have been more difficult, but he'd been foolish enough to put it on the inside. The lock itself was simple enough, thirty seconds' work to pick.

It was the part once she got outside the window that might be tricky. Aside from the decorative sills and lintels at the windows, the white exterior walls of the house were smooth, offering little purchase for questing feet. There was a drainpipe at the corner of the house, and in theory she might shimmy down that, but the pipe was at least three feet from the window with nothing to grab in between. Then three stories down, clinging to the side of the building directly over the garden fence with its wickedly pointy spikes at the top.

She knew the climb would be a challenge, because she had tried it once before and failed, as her father well knew. It was before the household had moved to France. She had been eight years old then, bent on running away from home over some imagined injustice. Her downfall had come at the end, when she tried to spring clear of the fence and drop the last half story or so. Falling clumsily, she'd caught her skirt on one of the spikes, then swung face-first into the fence and concussed herself against the wrought iron, or perhaps against the flagstones when her skirt gave way and she dropped the last few hand spans to her final landing place. She'd also dislodged two teeth in the process. A gardener had spotted her, wandering bleeding, gap-toothed and dazed, and she supposed they must have patched her up and summoned a doctor but she couldn't recall much of that part. Only the long interlude afterward during which Mrs. Pinkerton was her constant companion, and both Mother and Father had perfected what was evidently to be a lifetime of sighing in disappointment.

Father must have known she could easily manage the small padlocks he'd put at the windows. He'd taught her how locks worked in the first place, after all. But he hadn't expected her to try escaping that way, anyway, so he hadn't invested time or money in a more secure solution. If he'd gone for bars, she would have been well and truly stuck. As it was, she had but to fiddle with the lock, slide up the sash, and wait until the coast was clear.

The irony, she reflected afterward, was that they had both been thinking the same way, judging by the capabilities she'd demonstrated as an eight-year-old girl. A woman of twenty-one has a substantially longer reach, stronger legs and enough common sense to spot where the pipe brackets were before she started her descent, so she would know what her toes were reaching for and the approximate distance until the next one. And this particular woman was also wearing trousers, no layers of fluffy skirts to get in her way or snag on the fence.

She had just dropped to the pavement side of the fence and straightened up when a bobby strolled around the corner, whistling and twirling his billy club. Constable Tucker, a friendly sort who had been a familiar sight around the park for as long as Freddie could remember. She bent on one knee and started retying her shoe, heart racing as she tried to figure out what to say if he spoke to her or, worse, recognized her.

But other than a laconic "Evenin'" as he passed, Constable Tucker paid her no mind at all.

"Evenin'," she squeaked back, and took off in the opposite direction at a brisk walk, forcing herself not to look back.

She wasn't sure about her second stop, but she knew where she was headed first. Sophie lived less than two miles away, and it was possible Barnabas was still at her house, nursing an injured ankle. And Freddie knew exactly what to do with a Gordian knot.

Twenty-two

❦

"You're going to kill us both, Phineas."

"Not if you keep your elbow out of my blasted ear."

"I can't help it. Your head is in the way. This thing wasn't designed for two pilots, especially not in the dark."

"If we turn the lights up any further it might attract the cuttlefish. I'm uneasy about the lighted dials being too bright as it is. And you're not a pilot. At the moment you're not even being a very good hydrophonics man."

Barnabas was attempting to operate the *Gilded Lily*'s hydrophone controls from a kneeling position, bracing his side against the back of the pilot's chair so he didn't fall over whenever the submersible changed speed or direction. He was not happy about doing this, but had little choice as he had no idea how to pilot the vessel. He'd at least used the hydrophonic array once before, though only to spot a very large submersible. He had no idea whether he'd be able to decipher the subtler indications of anything smaller, such as a rampaging cuttlefish. And he was trying to do it all through the impediment of a massive hangover, the direct result of his attempt last night to block out every memory of Freddie Murcheson. It hadn't worked.

"This is the location. I don't see any movement. Can you make anything out?"

On the periphery of his screen he saw some of the vague glimmerings that he'd gathered meant something was moving nearby. Nothing substantive, though.

"Not so far."

"Mord couldn't spot them either at first. Then the sub stirred them up and they moved. Keep looking. I'm taking us closer."

"Must you?"

Phineas didn't answer right away, but Barnabas heard a sharp intake of breath and pulled his face from the equipment to see what his brother had discovered.

He gasped as well. "Are they . . ."

Phineas nodded. "Blinking, yes. And we're right on top of them."

"Oh, dear God."

Through the front and side portholes, Barnabas could make out with his naked eyes what the hydrophone had missed. The creatures were everywhere: curled over the nearby rock formation, spread over the ocean floor, nestled in among the kelp. By their shapes and colors, they would have been invisible to the unsuspecting observer, completely camouflaged. Some dozens of animals, many larger than the vessel that floated among them, and they could have been part of the ocean landscape itself if not for one thing. They were all pulsing, glowing then dimming in a gentle rhythm like a heartbeat. *Blink blink pause. Blink blink pause.* In perfect unison.

The eeriness made him doubt his little brother's sanity anew when Phineas said, "I think it will be all right."

"How can this possibly be all right?" Nothing would ever be all right again, but least of all this.

"Without the light, I don't think we're disturbing them. It's odd they're not moving at all, though. You'd think the water pressure from the propeller would stir them up. I'm going to try to back out slowly, see if I can get some distance."

"Yes." That part, Barnabas could support. "Distance would be a very good idea."

"Then I want to try something. Get back on the hydrophone array."

"I don't want to try anything, other than retreating."

"No, I think this will work. This is far enough. Now I need a light, but something small. With a switch, preferably. Or something I can cover completely with my hand. Do you still have that stupid crank torch, by any chance?"

"If it's so stupid, why do you want it?"

"Are you *positive* you're the elder brother?"

Barnabas started to hand the torch over, reluctantly curious to see what Phineas had in mind. His brother cupped his hand over the end of it, holding it steady with the other hand and pointed at the front porthole, and told Barnabas to start cranking. He wound the gadget dutifully until a halo of light shone on his brother's palm.

Meanwhile, Phineas had started counting, watching the cuttlefish and matching their time until he was matched to their tempo. "On, on, *off* . . . On, on, *off.*"

"Tell me you're not going to do what I think you're—"

"Shh . . . *off.* On, on, *off.*" He uncovered the light and let it beam forth, shifting his hand to cover it at just the right moments. "On, on, *oh my God it's working.* Where are you going? Don't stop cranking! Barnabas, come back."

The creatures had responded, peeling slowly away from their hiding places and approaching the submersible in slow, undulating ripples of light and color. There was no apparent aggression. If anything, they looked curious, but they seemed to be keeping some distance. Phineas kept his frantic chanting up, keeping himself in time, and Barnabas bent over the hydrophonics array to see what they looked like on the screen now that they were in motion.

"The torch will stay lit for several minutes. Keep going. Oh, *now* I see. You know, I think a few of them may have been moving before, but I thought it was kelp."

"Barnabas, I just thought of something . . . on, *off* . . ."

"What?"

"What happens when I stop?"

"Uh. Well. Don't stop. Damn."

He would have thought of something eventually, he was certain of it, but it turned out not to be necessary. When he glanced at the screen again, he saw a set of ovals, crisp and distinct, closing in from the south. And just as he lifted his head to share this news with Phineas, the squid stopped blinking, suddenly and simultaneously.

"Cover it up," he shouted as the creatures began darting this way and that, becoming easier to spot as they grew more agitated. "Cover the light, Phin!"

"Oh, right!" Phineas stuffed the torch under his shirt and wool jumper, effectively blocking the beam while freeing his hands. "Why did they do that, I wonder?"

"Wonder no more. I think the smugglers have arrived. We didn't move quickly enough."

They had, in full force and with lights blazing. The cuttlefish swarmed toward them, a seething mass of tentacular rage, and Phineas gave chase. The nimble little sub outpaced the cephalopods and passed the enemy subs completely, but then Phineas cranked the controls hard and pivoted to observe the battle taking place.

Torpedoes, it seemed, were not the most effective weapons against cephalopods the size of gunboats. These enemies didn't flee, they charged, and before a single shot had been fired at them they had attached themselves directly to the brightest parts of each of the poppy-bearing submersibles. The portholes, the headlamps, the floodlights that swept the seabed. And they began to rend, and squeeze, and use all their considerable might to extinguish every one of the offending lights.

"Let's back away again," Barnabas suggested, when it was clear the animals were in no need of their help.

"Right. Turning tail seems like another good choice."

But just as he maneuvered the craft around, Barnabas spotted one piece of flotsam that distinguished itself from the others. It was bullet-shaped and had propellers, and it sped past them before they were sure what they'd seen.

"An escape pod," Barnabas realized after a moment.

"I'll wager it's headed to the same place we are."

Unfortunately, the cephalopods had the same idea.

PROVIDENTIALLY, SOPHIE'S PERSONAL airship was overpowered for the size of its small basket. If it hadn't been, it never would have supported the weight of Sophie, Freddie, and Daniel Pinkerton—even at relatively low speeds, and even the fairly short distance between Sophie's home and the dockside warehouse of Rollo Furneval. But they made it work, Freddie and Sophie squeezed together on the seat and Dan clinging to the back like a small boy stealing a ride on a carriage.

Dan had returned to Sophie's, mournfully repentant, after

Freddie's father had dismissed him. He'd done it for Sophie, he confessed. Given up Freddie, the sister of his heart, in the hope of protecting Sophie, the lady of his dreams.

When Freddie had knocked—pounded, really—on Sophie's front door, it was Dan who answered. She greeted him with all the feeling she'd been troubled by that day, in the form of a closed fist straight to the nose.

"I deserved that," he said from the floor. The punch had caught him off guard, which it shouldn't have, and done more damage than Freddie expected. To both of them.

Sophie's housekeeper *tsk*ed at Dan's profusely bleeding nose and instructed him to hold a handkerchief to it while she tended Freddie's split knuckles. He explained himself in snuffled syllables, pausing occasionally to groan.

"You deserved a lot more than that," Freddie said when the housekeeper turned her attention to the big man again. "If you hadn't done it for Sophie I would never speak to you again."

"To protect you too, miss. I don't like to see you running around with that troublemaker. Tinkering is one thing, but the rest of it . . . it's just not fitting for a young lady such as yourself. You don't know what men are like."

He blushed, ducking his head so as not to meet her glare.

"You've done more to teach me what I have to fear from men than Lord Smith-Grenville ever could, Dan." It was true. This, the well-meaning assumptions about what was best for her, the taking action on her behalf without consulting her for her own opinion and preference on the matter, this was what she didn't want from a man. Didn't need.

"He's a blackguard."

"He's a lovely gentleman who's been put in an uncomfortable situation—by me, I hasten to add—and has made the best of it. With a certain amount of gallantry, to boot." Dan attempted a scornful noise, but it put too much pressure on his nose and he ended in a pitiful whimper. "Yes, gallantry. You could take a lesson or two."

"Enough bickering, please," Sophie intervened. "Daniel, I take your gesture in the spirit in which it was made, and I applaud you for that. But you see, I'm well aware of the risks I take by helping Freddie. Always have been. I've chosen those risks, nobody's coerced me. It wasn't for you to take the decision on yourself."

"Aye. I see that now, my lady."

"Be still, you," the housekeeper admonished, before she gave his nose a tweak to straighten it. Dan roared, and Freddie couldn't help the sense of satisfaction she gained from it, like reliving the punch. Mean-spirited, perhaps, but Dan's behavior had been egregious.

"He locked me in my room," she told him. "A big bolt I couldn't undo from the inside. And ridiculous padlocks on the windows, although of course I managed that part quite easily. I had to leave my own house by the drainpipe, Dan. The drainpipe."

"I truly didn't know that part of it, miss. What he had planned. Not until he called me in to dismiss me. I thought he'd just lecture at you or send you back to your mother for a time."

"No. He was trying to force me to go live in the Lake Country, in an isolated house where I could come to no trouble."

It was Sophie's turn to make a derogatory noise. "I would give that arrangement a fortnight at most before somebody came to grief from it. But Freddie, you silly thing. You know you can come live with me if you need to. You could teach me to be more scandalous. Lately I feel I've missed out on too much of that."

As Sophie Wallingford was the least scandalous person imaginable, Freddie took her words with a grain of salt. But she appreciated the sentiment and the offer, nevertheless.

"You're a darling, and I love you. But right now I don't need somebody scandalous, I need somebody with reliable transportation. Fast too, by preference. I couldn't get here in time to go with Barnabas and Phineas on the *Gilded Lily*, but this is the perfect time to reconnoiter Furneval's warehouse if he and most of his men are off trying to kill all the cephalopods, so—" She glimpsed their dumbfounded expressions and cut herself off. "Never mind. It's complicated. I'll explain along the way. And hopefully we'll run into the Smith-Grenvilles at some point, because they obviously can't return to your house when they're finished, any more than I can."

And so as the sun set, they rose over the rooftops of London's most fashionable portion and headed east toward one of its roughest.

ESCAPE POD MAINTENANCE hadn't ranked high on the list of duties, and Rollo made a mental note to remedy that if he lived long enough. The thick, mildewy funk in the cramped bubble-sub might not kill him, but the aging fuel ingredients might well have had he not noticed the fast-rising gauge in time and realized the potassium sulfate was burning far too hot and fast.

He'd swiftly adjusted the rate but had no idea if the resulting level would produce enough oxygen to sustain him safely—the controls were not calibrated properly for the new rate—and no way to know if the fuel and oxygen would last him for the race back to the warehouse. The one thing he wouldn't compromise was speed.

The tiny military vessel, clearly marked as such by the

stenciling on its side, might be more maneuverable than his current mount, but he was fairly certain he had the advantage at a dead run. The pod was built to move quickly in the direction it was pointed, if not much else. If he could make it to the warehouse, he could make a stand. The Navy vessel could hold only two, maybe three at the most, and he was a decent shot. If he caught them coming out of the hatch, the whole thing could be over in seconds. They'd be most vulnerable then. It was a brief window of opportunity, but to his panicked brain it seemed the safest course of action. He had no idea how far behind him the enemy might be, or whether the two pathetic guards he'd left on the warehouse would even be close enough to help him. He might have a few seconds to prepare upon landing, perhaps as many as several minutes. If he ran, even just to his office for more weapons or ammunition, they could have time to split up upon leaving the sub and use their surroundings as cover. He wouldn't know their full numbers then, a distinct disadvantage. Of course he knew the warehouse better and could hunt them down, but still one or more might live to report back on the warehouse's location and contents. So he must be ready to disembark, then turn and fight immediately.

He nearly lost control when he entered the trench pointing toward the dock. Not an insufficiency of oxygen but a surfeit, if he read the signs correctly. Too much at too high a pressure. His lips were tingling, twitching, and what started as a faint ringing in his ears swiftly grew unbearable, sickening even. He was too busy steering the craft by that point to take time adjusting the oxygen level. The last leg was the trickiest. Dead straight down the trench, which deepened as it neared the dock. Then crisscross through the piers, in a sequence of turns he had to pray he remembered correctly despite the gathering darkness and the confusion that had begun to addle his brains and cloud his vision.

When he finally steered around the last row of barnacle-encrusted columns and saw the familiar rectangle of light overhead, Rollo wept with joy. There was no one there to see, after all. No one to witness his weakness and shame and giddy relief.

He ascended to the dock level faster than he should, shoving the controls toward their neutral position and scrambling to the hatch. His ears popped and crackled as it opened, a burst of bilateral pain that helped jolt him back to greater lucidity.

Carelessly he tossed the mooring loop over the hatch's valve handle and pulled himself up the ladder to the deck. Unsteady, still queasy, he caught sight of a glimmer under the water beside him and whirled, expecting the Navy sub to surface. It was no sub, though. He'd forgotten about Mord's squid creature, which kept up its steady pulse of light in a pattern he now recognized. *Blink blink stop. Blink blink stop.* From far off in the channel water, they'd spotted the same pattern of light and dark for a few moments before it ceased abruptly and the world turned into a nightmare of watery fury as the creatures attacked the fleet. Exactly the same beat, despite the distance between little Albert and his shoal mates. Whatever that flashing meant, it couldn't be good.

"Albert." He walked to the beast's cage and crouched at the edge of the dock, glaring into the mesh over the top. "Time for you to stop that."

And time for Rollo Furneval to break a promise to Mordecai Nesdin. Mord was most likely dead, though, ripped from a sundered submersible by a rampaging cuttlefish. So really, it didn't matter anymore what happened to Albert.

He started to withdraw his revolver from the inside pocket where he'd stashed it, despite the various pilots' admonitions against bringing a firearm into a pressurized submersible. Rollo never went anywhere without his favorite weapons. But with his vision still blurred and a concern about how submersibles could sometimes look smaller than they really were, crew-wise, he didn't want to waste any bullets on Albert. He glanced around him, looking for a gaff or something else useful to hook the creature with, keeping the water in the corner of his eye lest the pursuing Navy sub—or, though he didn't expect it, any survivors from his own fleet—break through. With his woozy attention thus divided, he almost failed to notice a more pressing threat—three intruders creeping straight onto the warehouse dock through the office door.

Twenty-three

❧

"You didn't *kill* him, did you?" Sophie whispered as the skinny, watch-cap-clad man toppled to the dark ground just beyond the feeble circle of light on the wharf at the warehouse's entrance.

"'Course not, m'lady," Dan assured her.

Freddie wasn't so sure, as the poor guard had banged his skull hard upon landing after Dan's single punch to the jaw, but she kept her worries to herself. "Should we see if there are any more, or just try to get in before they come 'round?"

Dan and Sophie shrugged in unison, a moment that would have been comical if it weren't for the inherent danger in the situation. They looked to her as if for guidance, so she felt compelled to contrive some.

"Right. Dan, you have your pistol? Good. Go peek around the corners of this building, just a glance down the pier on each side."

"And shoot anyone I see?"

"God, no!"

"Oh, right, because the noise would draw attention. That's clever, miss."

Freddie sighed. "No, we don't want to shoot anybody because . . . well, because *we don't want to shoot anybody*. Not if we don't have to. The pistol is just in case." She considered adding, *Use your judgment*, but decided against it.

Dan sidled along to one corner, pistol cocked, and whipped his head around to check for enemies. A split second's look apparently assured him the coast was clear on that side, and he began creeping to the other side of the broad building, back to the wall, as Freddie and Sophie looked on.

"Dan. At the rate you're going, we'll be here for days," Freddie urged.

"Oh. Right, sorry." He peeled himself from the wall and moved more quickly to the opposite corner, though still on tiptoes.

"I still don't see what help we're going to be against an army of smugglers, Freddie."

"Not an army. A few dozen at the most, according to Phineas. And if they've gone to attack the cephalopods, most of them may be out in the channel somewhere. Only one sentry outside the warehouse—"

"Two," Dan reported softly from the corner. "I don't think this one'll be much trouble for us, though."

Joining him, the women peered around the corner and observed another rough-clad man. This one was slumped against the side of the warehouse, cap pulled over his eyes and an empty bottle lying on its side next to him.

"Leave him, then. Now keep a lookout, while I figure out the lock."

Reasoning that the wide double doors would be too noisy

if opened, Freddie chose to work on the smaller, but more imposing lock on the smaller door next to it. It was no lightweight, simple warded padlock or even a typical pin-and-tumbler door lock, but a formidable-looking chunk of brass engraved with the name of a prominent locksmith. For a moment or two, it gave her pause. She'd brought her usual tools, a set of slender instruments that had started life as a decorative hairpin and a dinner knife, respectively. They would be useless against a tubular lock with pins on more than one side, or one of the custom models produced by that particular artisan, who famously kept a "challenge lock" on display in his workshop. That lock had been beaten, after many decades of unsuccessful attempts by all manner of folk, but only by another gifted locksmith, working with a full range of tools over the course of two days.

But luck and Furneval's earlier choices were with her. This lock might look unpickable, but it turned out to be no more than a standard model, hiding in a daunting case. Somebody had fooled either Furneval or whoever commissioned the work, for this was almost certainly not the doing of the locksmith whose name was on the device. After a minute or so of patient work, the pins fell into place with a soft, satisfying click that Freddie felt more than heard, and she turned the knob in triumph.

"We're in."

The room they stepped into was dark, as night had fallen while the three were in the air. Dan, who occasionally smoked a pipe, produced and struck a match by the light of which they were able to spot a lantern. There appeared to be gaslights as well, but Freddie didn't want to start flipping switches lest they draw attention to themselves with no need. After Dan lit the lantern she held it high, turning in a slow circle to survey the space.

"What are we looking for?" Sophie asked, recalling Freddie to their earlier, interrupted conversation.

"Anything. Opium. Incriminating documents, ledgers . . . anything."

"Bloodstains," Dan suggested.

"I suppose. Although I don't know what—"

"No, I mean here. You're standing on them."

Freddie froze, then stepped carefully back from the dark splotch that marred the already somewhat filthy wood floor. "It looks just like at the butcher's."

"Aye. And see here, these scrub marks? Somebody's been after cleaning it, but there was too much already soaked into the wood. This was no paper cut. Somebody died here."

She swallowed her gorge and reached for Sophie's hand, offering comfort. Sophie, however, was gazing at the floor with no visible sign of emotion.

"We might as well start looking about for anything else we can find," she finally said. "This appears to be an office. If there are documents, it seems logical we'd find them here."

There were many documents, and multiple ledgers. All of them seemed completely innocuous, however, the sort of thing that might be found in any warehouse. The smugglers appeared to be using some sort of coded system to record their transactions, as all the descriptions of goods were written in the form of cryptic initials and symbols with no apparent key.

"*One of* . . . is this an omicron? *One of omicron to RP on such-and-such a date, via H. Ten pounds sterling*," Sophie read from one of the books.

"At least the money part's clear enough," Dan quipped. He was searching the higher shelves along one wall but finding nothing. "And the dates."

"Yes, the accounting looks sound. But what does omicron stand for? And here's a theta, I think, and a phi."

Freddie looked over her friend's shoulder at the ledger. "We should bring it back with us anyway. The proper authorities might be able to make some use of it."

"So you do plan to go to the proper authorities at some juncture? I'm relieved to hear that."

"Of course I am. And if I bring evidence back to bring down a major opium smuggling operation, my father won't dare try to lock me up in a country house, or even cut me off without a penny as seems to be my other alternative."

"Darling," Sophie remonstrated, "it does seem a trifle serpent's-toothish of you to expect indefinite financial support *and* defy your father in this very public way. And he might very well still cut you off, for making a fool of him."

"If so, I'll deal with it later. Dan, grab those ledgers and the one on the shelf as well. We need to—oh." She stared at the wall opposite the desk. It was mostly covered with a large map of the channel and its coastlines. Pins dotted its surface, some with brightly colored heads and others with tiny flags stuck on. "I've seen this before."

"It's the channel," Dan said, as if she were slow.

"Yes, I'm aware of that. I mean I've seen this pattern before. The red pins . . ." Tracing an imaginary line from one of the flags to the east, she found another red pinhead, larger than the rest. "Atlantis Station. And the smaller ones are places where the seismograph has been attacked. What if Phineas has told—"

"He wouldn't," Sophie stated as firmly as she could in a whisper. "He wouldn't do that. They must have gathered the information from elsewhere. Were you saying earlier that we need to leave? Because I support that decision."

"I was going to say we needed to investigate the warehouse proper, and see if we can find any opium."

"Ah."

"If you'd feel safer here, you can stay while Dan and I go. Or Dan can stay too, and I'll go alone."

"Don't be ridiculous, Freddie." Sophie had her little pistol in her hand, ready to defend herself or her friends if necessary. "Lead the way."

"What we really could have used is a map of the warehouse," Freddie mused as she lifted her own weapon in readiness and opened the office's inner door and peeked into the warehouse. She expected darkness, but a line of dimly lit gas lanterns provided a chilly illumination over the broad expanse of the warehouse floor, which seemed to contain mostly unmarked crates, all the way to the broad, open rectangle of water at the building's far end. The submersible dock.

Gesturing with her free hand for the other two to follow, Freddie ventured forward into the vast space, stopping short between two piles of crates when she heard a clanking noise and a string of explicit curses from up ahead.

"This isn't sharp," the vulgarian said, "but it should do to fetch you out of the water. Let's see how long you survive in the open air, you poisonous, blinky bastard."

More clanking followed, then a wrenching metal-on-metal squeak and another loud curse.

A moment later a man walked through her narrow angle of view, carrying a long pole with a spike-barbed hook on the end. A fishing gaff. Freddie tiptoed forward until a sharp tap on her shoulder brought her up short and she nearly screamed. It was Dan, and when she turned with a furious query in her eyes, he gestured most emphatically that they should all return to the office.

She shook her head. There were three of them, and there

seemed to be only one man up ahead. Decent odds, and perhaps he would give up more information. She pressed forward to crouch behind a crate beside the dock itself. The man had disappeared, taking his wicked-looking gaff with him. When Freddie leaned forward, risking a quick peek to the left and right along the water, she saw no one.

Down in the water, a soft light glowed in a steady rhythm, mesmerizing.

What the hell is that?

But when she turned again to ask Dan if he knew, the big man's back was to her, his hands in the air. And Sophie, who'd been bringing up the rear . . . the man from the dock held her firmly around the neck with one arm, while his other hand pressed a revolver muzzle to her temple.

If Phineas hadn't already piloted much larger subs through the piers many times, they never would have managed to weave through the supports in the dark to get the *Gilded Lily* safely to Furneval's warehouse. Safety was, of course, a relative state in this context. Barnabas didn't care. Anything would be better than the literally hair-raising submersible ride through a pitch-black obstacle course.

"I'll surface as close to the dock as I can," Phineas told him. "Be ready to pop the hatch and jump out. If you can find a mooring rope, toss it over, but don't waste time with it. And for God's sake, no itchy trigger finger. I don't care if Furneval has a dozen men training guns on us from the side of the dock, I want you to keep your hand off your pistol until you're completely outside the vessel."

"Aye aye, captain."

"Now is not the time for sarcasm."

They broke the surface and Phineas spun the valve lock

and opened the hatch, looking about to get his bearings once he was atop the submersible. When he saw the tableau of players already there, he froze. "Oh, dammit all to hell."

"Just get out," Phineas reminded him.

"Yes, get out," said the man with the pistol to Sophie Wallingford's head. "Come join your friends. Your companion too."

Barnabas leaped awkwardly to the dock beside the hatch, his kick sending the sub bobbing away. A mooring rope lay coiled nearby, and he tossed the looped end into the hatch opening. Phineas, rising from the hatch, took the heavy hawser in the shoulder with a curse.

"Oh, you little bastard," hissed the gunman.

"Hello, Rollo," Phineas replied calmly, as he braced himself and pulled the sub and himself back toward the dockside. Once there, he jumped out nimbly and strode toward the group, with what Barnabas had to assume was more confidence than he actually felt.

"I'll save you for last," the villain declared, in a more conversational tone than before. "Too bad Edwin won't be here to help me. He'd have enjoyed what I'm going to do to your friends. It can be a memorial tribute of sorts, I suppose, for all of them."

"Believe what you will, but I am sorry for the loss of your men. I counted some of *them* as friends too. Not Edwin, I admit."

Freddie appeared unharmed, to Barnabas's vast relief. She had a weak little smile for him, which he attempted to return. Her presence there was a shock, as was Dan's, and he couldn't imagine what it meant in relation to the message the man had delivered him last night. His anger and melancholy vanished at that hint of a smile, melting away as shame heated his cheeks. He should never have believed ill of her.

Not his Freddie; she could never betray him like that, and he'd been a fool to even entertain the notion for a moment.

"I'm sorry," he murmured. He was glad to have seen her this one last time, if it was to be the end. It didn't feel like it ought to be the end, though. There were four of them there, ranged against Furneval. Surely they could do something to save Sophie and themselves, with the numbers so clearly on their side?

She just looked puzzled. "What for? None of this is *your* fault."

"Shut up, both of you," snapped the man with the gun, who Barnabas presumed was Rollo Furneval. He *looked* like a drug kingpin. A claret jacket, too bright for the current fashion, with flashy velvet trim and brass buttons. An ornate gilt poppy at his lapel, that looked familiar. The man wasn't tall but he was powerfully built, with dark hair mussed with sweat, and intelligent but shifty eyes. He looked like he might easily be a cold-blooded killer.

Sophie was pale, and her usually serene face now showed all her distress. Panic flared in her eyes, and where she clutched the arm that pinned her so close, Barnabas could see her knuckles were white as bone. She would leave a fine set of bruises on Furneval, at least. Dan and Freddie stood motionless, hands raised over their shoulders, and Barnabas quickly assumed the same pose. His pistol was still in his pocket, but it was useless to him at the moment.

"Right, then. The four of you are going into a cargo hold." Furneval nodded his head toward one wall of the warehouse, where Barnabas could see a line of doors. "Straight line, quick march. Or the lady gets it."

As the last words left his mouth, the earth shifted beneath their feet, the boards creaking ominously as a rumble began to build.

As they were thrown off balance, Furneval's grip on Sophie loosened, and she leaned forward, trying to break free.

Barnabas reached out a foot and touched Dan's boot, getting his attention. They shared a look, Barnabas thinking his hasty plan as hard as he could. *If we rush together, now while he's distracted, perhaps it will work.*

Dan blinked, then nodded. Barnabas glanced to his left to see Phineas watching him too. Three against one.

Barnabas folded down the fingers of one hand, counting down silently. On zero, they ran, closing the paces between them and Furneval in the second it took him to raise his gun and fire.

Not at Sophie, who had ducked under his arm and raced away, but at the closest of the three men. Dan howled in pain but kept running, diving straight into Furneval's midsection and flattening him to the dock. Freddie rushed past Barnabas and Phineas to kick the gun from Furneval's hand, stumbling as the floor pitched.

She ran to retrieve the weapon while the brothers dogpiled onto Dan and Furneval. Punches flew, bodies flailed, and eventually they wrestled Furneval into something like submission. Dan rolled away, his arms falling limp at his sides. His shirt and jacket were blood-soaked, but black powder marked the wound near his left shoulder.

"No!" Sophie shouted, running to his side. "Daniel, no!"

"Rollo Furneval," Phineas said, jerking Furneval to his feet and neatly twisting one of the man's arms behind his back to hold him. "I hereby arrest you in the name of—"

"Dear God in heaven!" Furneval shouted, eyes widening as he looked toward the water. "Run. *Run!*"

"I'm not falling for that one," Phineas snorted, jerking on the pinned arm. "Oldest trick in the—oh, *hell.*"

It might have been hell, at that. A watery hell, a maelstrom leading to the abyss, with man-thick tentacles rising from Satan's pit to drag sinners down to their doom.

The thing was pulsing in that same pattern . . . no, more than one thing, Barnabas realized with growing terror. He counted at least two heads and far more than the eight tentacles and two additional "arms" of one creature. And the appendages were busy, some of them, exploring out of the water.

A groaning metallic screech sounded from one side of the dock, and one of the tentacles raised something high in the air. In the dim light, Barnabas only made out a hazy rectangle, a darker frame with some translucent material in the center.

Water roiled over the edge of the boards, the product of either the flailing creatures or the still-trembling earth.

"He's right, we need to get out!" Freddie shouted. But another seismic jolt sent them reeling, and a pile of crates, stacked too high and precariously by Furneval's careless crew, chose that moment to topple. The top crate knocked the next row over as it tumbled down, the start of an oversized domino effect that left the warehouse floor between the group and the doors a nearly impassable landscape of upended containers. Some of the crates split as they fell, adding jagged splinters and stakes to the hazardous mix, as well as mounds of packets wrapped in burlap and oilcloth.

Sophie and Phineas pulled Dan clear of the danger zone, and then they all watched in horror as one of the larger tentacles, seeking restlessly along the dock, came within a few feet of their position. In desperation, Sophie seized one of the dark, greasy-looking bundles, which was at least as big as a small loaf and looked more solid in her hand. Barnabas thought she would fling it at the creature's limb like a projectile, but instead the clever woman bowled the packet into the path of the tentacle's next questing undulation.

The moment the cuttlefish's sensitive suckers contacted the thing, it wrapped its tentacle around it like a python and snatched it away . . . straight into the ready, gaping maw at the base of its appendages.

"My product!" Furneval bellowed, and sprang toward the dock's edge, ignoring the revolver Freddie still had aimed at him.

"Stop right there or I will shoot you, sir," she shouted at him. He slid to a halt on the slick, shaking boards, skidding around to face her. "And before you think to yourself, 'She's a girl, she doesn't have the nerve,' I feel I must tell you I look on that man you injured as a brother. Furthermore I have no intention of shooting to kill, and I shall feel no hesitation or guilt whatsoever about shooting to maim." She shifted her aim from his head to his leg. At point-blank range, there was no way to miss. Barnabas wanted to applaud.

It happened so quickly they had no time to react. Another massive tentacle, fast as a striking snake, encircled Furneval's waist and pulled him off his feet, dragging him inexorably over the edge. He grabbed at something, though, before the beast could pull him under. A mesh container of some sort, perhaps for shellfish or the like, had been fastened to the dockside and suspended in the water. Though being dragged over it must have cost him more injuries, Barnabas thought the odd cage might save the smuggler's life. While he hung over its lip, head and shoulders barely out of the churning water, Barnabas and Phineas had time to react, lunging toward him to help him struggle free of the monster's death grip.

Freddie had time to regroup as well. Furneval saw her pointing the revolver at him and screamed, but she shot true—straight into the meat of the tentacle, severing it from the creature.

"Good shot, sweetheart!" Barnabas shouted, grinning at her astonished expression. He and Phineas reached for Furneval's grateful outstretched hand when a change in the lighting registered with him. Instead of their steady blinking, the cephalopods had suddenly begun to shimmer in rippling waves along their length, mesmerizing.

All of them, including the two-foot-long specimen in the cage. Before they could reach Furneval, the small creature launched itself straight into his face, wrapping its tentacles around his head. His body twitched violently for a few seconds, then went limp, arms losing their hold on the cage. He sank back, the baby cuttlefish clinging to his face, and the swirling water covered him as though he'd never been there.

Barnabas registered, through his horror, the danger they were all in. More giant cuttlefish had risen to take the place of the injured beast and, he realized, the one that had swallowed the bundle of opium.

Freddie and Sophie, however, had already come up with a solution. They threw brick after brick of opium toward each tentacle as it approached their position, occupying and disabling the beasts, while Barnabas and Phineas cleared a navigable path through the wreckage of the warehouse.

"At least the earthquake has stopped," Freddie pointed out when he and his brother returned to show them all the way out.

"Small blessings."

Not nearly enough to balance out the greater misfortunes. Sophie had left the opium-tossing to Freddie and returned to Dan's side. Weeping, she pressed a fold of Dan's jacket against the hole in his chest in a vain effort to staunch the blood. The cloth was long since saturated, and Barnabas didn't have the heart to tell her that the hole in Dan's back, where the bullet had left his body, was thrice the size. Barnabas had glimpsed it in the melee and been momentarily astonished at the man's ability to keep fighting, before his attention was drawn to more pressing matters.

But even Dan's size and strength were no match for a bullet in the chest. Not the heart, perhaps, or he'd never have lasted as long as he had. But certainly his lung had been hit. Air bubbled ominously from the hole when Sophie took her blood-drenched hands away.

"Don't die. Please don't, Dan. I'm not worth this."

Phineas knelt beside her. "You are, but I know that hardly helps. I think it's time to say your good-byes." He put a comforting arm around her shoulders, but she shoved him away angrily.

"Don't touch me! You did this. If it weren't for you being such a juvenile fool in the first place, running off to cavort in opium dens and abandoning your post and—"

"But I . . . I was assigned to—"

"Daniel would never have been here, and this never would have happened."

Freddie flung another several thousand pounds sterling worth of opium into the water, but the cuttlefish seemed to have retreated once the quake stopped, either the seismic easing or the consumption of raw opium soothing their agitation. The small one too might have been sending a distress signal. Once it was free, perhaps the creatures saw no reason to stay.

When the water remained still for a few moments after the last packet had splashed down, she joined the group huddled around Daniel, taking one of his oversized hands into her two smaller ones and pressing it to her cheek.

Dan smiled in her direction, his strength waning fast but the shock evidently numbing him to some of the pain.

"Can't . . . feel . . ." he attempted, but lacked the wind to finish the thought.

"It was my fault," Freddie told him, leaning close to make sure he could hear. "You did the right thing, Dan; you were absolutely right to be worried. If I'd stayed where I ought to, this wouldn't have happened. You're a good man, and I'll make sure your mother knows. I'll see to it she knows you were a hero."

He blinked at her, then turned his head just far enough to see Sophie. He bestowed a final smile, sweet and boyish, on her.

"Lady . . ."

He used his last breath on the word. Barnabas didn't realize how loud his wet, sucking gasps had grown until they stopped, leaving only the plaintive sound of sobbing behind.

Kneeling by Freddie, Barnabas put his arm around her and pressed a kiss to her temple. She'd lost the cap at some point in her adventures that evening, and her ember-bright hair fell loose, tickling his nose.

"I love you," he whispered in the vicinity of her ear. "I love you."

She nodded, and replied in a voice choked by grief. "Yes. I love you too. Take me home, Barnabas."

Twenty-four

❦

He did take her home, though not as soon as Freddie would have liked. First they had to return to her father's home and face what Freddie was sure would be a storm of wrath like she'd never known.

Instead, when they trudged through the front door, heartsick and weary, Freddie was nearly bowled over by her mother.

In a stream of nearly incoherent French, Maman excoriated her father, wailing her chagrin over leaving Freddie alone and subject to the fickle lunacies of the English, and then several items about the state of her soul and the lackluster tone of her complexion that Freddie allowed herself to gloss over. She calmed her mother as patiently as she could, assuring her that she was safe, that England was hardly to blame for the state of her soul or skin and that they ought to be speaking English in deference to the others.

Sophie spoke beautiful French, of course, but she had no idea if the Smith-Grenvilles knew a word of it.

Then she attempted to make introductions, but as soon as she spoke Barnabas's name, her mother went off again.

Halfway through the fresh spate of outrage, her father stepped into the front hall, his aristocratic face lined with sorrow and relief.

"Oh, thank God, you're alive. Is that—the blood, is it yours? I'll send for the surgeon."

"Not mine," she hastened to assure him. "None of ours. It's . . . it was Daniel Pinkerton. He saved Sophie. Saved all of us, I suppose." But he was, very obviously, no longer among their numbers.

Murcheson turned white and swayed on his feet, grasping for the banister post to help support himself. His wife rushed to his other side, though whether to offer or receive comfort it wasn't clear.

"His mother. What will I say, how can I . . . I only wanted to keep you safe, Freddie. And keep the damn station open, though now that seems so unimportant."

"It's strangely beautiful," her mother said. "I had wondered all these years what the appeal could be. I'm glad I saw at last, even once."

"I sent for your mother as soon as I realized you were gone from your room. She'd just made it through the tunnel and up the lift on this side when the quake hit. In the nick of time."

"It's an uneasy place to be during an earthquake," Freddie agreed.

"How would you—never mind, it's better if I don't know. The station is gone, at any rate. Oh, it's still there, but we'll never get the funding to repair the damage it took during this big quake. And for all we knew it had to be coming, for all our scheming and secrecy, we weren't able to do much to prevent the damage. That failing will only increase the pressure to scrap Atlantis and the Glass Octopus."

"Even if the station and the submersible fleet had been instrumental in breaking up one of the largest illegal opium operations in the world?" Phineas stepped forward, nodding pleasantly at Mrs. Murcheson, then more soberly at her husband.

"Good God! Is that—but it can't be! You should have died from opium abuse long ago."

She thought that disingenuous at best and started to protest, but Phineas ignored her father's unconvincing interjection and continued.

"I can tell you everything, or rather Barnabas and I can. All the details you need to make the Agency out as the hero in all this. The two of us, along with the ladies. You'll get the credit, and we'll even return your submersible unharmed. Well, we'd have done that anyway. But the information won't be free, sir. I suspect you can guess what our various prices might be."

Freddie's heart thumped uncomfortably in her chest as her father looked from one of them to the other, assessing their collective and individual determination. They would never be sterner of heart than they were at this moment, though, with Dan's blood still staining their clothes and hands and his dying breath still fresh in their memories.

As if he sensed Murcheson might need convincing, Phineas began unwrapping the dark, dripping package he had carried with him from the warehouse. He let the contents roll from the cloth as it unfurled. The unsavory object landed with a wet smack on the polished marble floor, where it lay exuding the curiously enticing smell of very fresh salt fish.

"This was what killed your smuggler and his men. It's a fascinating story, and if any of these things survived, the story may be far from over. Do you want to hear the first part?"

Her father nudged the tentacle with his toe. Though the section was only the yard or so that had been wrapped around Furneval's body, then snagged against the water cage and been stuck there as the small squid attacked him, it was horrifying enough and hinted at the scale of the creature it had come from. Freddie's mother eyed it with a different kind of speculation. She adored seafood.

"Yes, Lieutenant Smith-Grenville. You have my attention."

FREDDIE HAD COUNTED her bath upon her last return home as the best in her life, despite the aftermath. This one was better, however. She didn't know if she could ever soak long enough to wash the feel of Dan's blood from herself, but she could enjoy the effort. She felt she'd more than earned a nice, hot, rose-scented bout of indulgence in one of Sophie's large, comfortable tubs with the hot water piped in.

She had declined to stay at her family home once the long debriefing ended, and returned with Sophie and the Smith-Grenvilles to Wallingford House to spend the night, propriety be damned. Her father had explained, he had cajoled and wheedled and nearly returned to threats before he remembered how ineffective that tactic had proven to be. What he hadn't done was the one thing that might have persuaded her to stay. He hadn't apologized.

Her mother knew, but to her credit, she didn't tip him off. When Freddie went to her room to gather a few things, her mother went with her.

"He won't say it, you know. He never does. And in this case I believe he doesn't regret what he did, only that you escaped. Stupid, to imagine you were still too frightened to attempt the drainpipe. He should have known. He thinks of you as a child yet, because you've never been away from him."

"How do you stand him?" She wasn't really attending to the answer, focused as she was on finding her hairbrush and fresh drawers and the like. Her mother took her time answering, though, giving the question more thought than Freddie had put into asking it.

"I still love him," she said at last. "I don't particularly want to, but I do. And he loves me, which I am vain enough to find endearing. He pursues what he does with passion and conviction, and if he too often believes the ends justify the means, well, at least it doesn't often affect me directly. But I always know. Sometimes I know more than I like, and then I choose to leave him for a time until I feel less involved with his other passions. It also gives him time to miss me."

"That's why you stayed in France?"

"I really do despise England," her mother reminded her. "You've grown very English yourself. And your young man, he's the image of the young British gentleman. But he is beautiful enough, I suppose. The grandchildren will be attractive."

She didn't feel especially English at the moment. In fact, she felt that the entire Commonwealth could go straight to the Devil, beginning with all of Whitehall and the entire senior command staff of the Royal Navy. Perhaps her father too, since he had left off his attempts to convince her and gone straight back to Whitehall to try to convince those same damnable people that he deserved to get his precious station back. She wondered if anything would change if he succeeded, if he would study and learn to work with the squid, or destroy them as an inconvenience? Either way, she was done trying to intervene there.

"I think you're getting ahead of yourself, Maman. Lord Smith-Grenville is a dear friend and I confess I'm fond of him. But he'll be returning to the Dominions with his brother soon, I expect. I have things to do here. There can't be any future in it."

Her mother just smiled and helped her pack, but Freddie had cause to recall her words later, when Sophie came knocking on the bathroom door.

"Freddie? It's me. May I come in for a moment?"

"Of course. It isn't locked."

Her friend entered the room looking fresh and dewy, clearly fresh from her own bath, wrapped in layers of frilled white linen. Her dark hair fell over her shoulder in a long plait, giving an impression of youthful innocence that Freddie hadn't seen in many years.

"I wouldn't have interrupted, but I'm too tired to stay up much longer and I wanted to talk before we went to bed."

"Talk away. I'm nearly done anyway. I'm knackered too."

Sophie frowned ever so slightly at the common turn of phrase, then shrugged it off. "I meant it when I invited you to stay. I wanted you to know that. And I suppose you still may for a time. I can keep a staff here in London, and I've no plans to sell the house."

"But?" Freddie urged with a sinking feeling. Not more change. Anything but more change.

"But . . . when the Smith-Grenvilles leave for New York, I'm going with them. I've decided. There's nothing for me here anymore, your own dear self excepted, and listening to them talk about the Dominions has made me long to see for myself. And to really do something useful. They've spoken of returning to California to help the remaining workers from Orm's ranch find their families or perhaps find new homes. I could help, I could . . . start again. In a new place, as a new person."

Freddie rather liked the person Sophie was already, but she knew what her friend meant.

"That does sound like heaven."

"Do you really think so? Oh, I hoped you would. Because Freddie—oh, I know I should let Barnabas be the one to say it, because I know he wants to, but I can't help it. I'm selfish and I'm asking you for myself, because I worry you'll say no to him just to be contrary. Will you come with us? Please say you will!"

BARNABAS FOUND HER the next day in Sophie's coach yard, packing her tools from the pony trap carefully into a small trunk. She was wearing a blue and white striped morning gown to do this, and the juxtaposition of the dainty dress and the heavy tools gladdened his heart for reasons he was at a loss to name.

"I missed you at breakfast." He tried not to pout as he said it but thought he was probably not too successful.

"I was still asleep."

"Sophie said she told you."

"I was glad she did. Glad it wasn't you who asked, I mean." She fitted a set of long pliers next to a spool of copper wire, jiggling the trunk's contents to settle them.

Barnabas's world shifted under his feet, for a moment more terrifying than any earthquake. "Well, I . . . don't know what to say, then."

Freddie looked up over her shoulder at him, then chuckled as she rose from where she'd been kneeling over the tools. "Silly."

"Am I?" He wasn't sure whether to be relieved or insulted, but a wind of hope blew over his heated, frazzled mind.

"Suppose you had asked me. It would have been tantamount to a proposal, wouldn't it? I would have been following you to your home, or off to California. Going for you as much as for myself."

"That would have been bad?"

"No. But it wouldn't have been the same decision to make. This way is better. I'm going on an adventure with a friend. With friends. It could lead to anything, but at least I would start off on the right foot."

He gazed at the trunk, pretending an interest in the tools so he wouldn't have to meet her eyes. "You . . . you are going, though? You told her yes?"

Freddie laid a hand on his arm, probably smudging his coat with tool grease. He didn't care.

"Silly," she said again, squeezing gently. "Of course I'm going. Don't they need tinkers in the Dominions as well as they do here?"

"The guild has too much power there. At least in New York. You'd have to become a makesmith to work as one there. I don't know about California."

"Barnabas, are you sulking?"

He wasn't. Well, maybe a little. "If I had asked, would you have said yes?"

"Had you planned to ask?"

"Yes." As soon as he'd mustered sufficient nerve.

"Then I probably would have said yes."

She sounded cagey, and that emboldened him to slip his arm around her waist and pull her closer. "Probably?"

After a moment of musing, she replied, "Most likely."

He caught her saucy mouth under his, savoring her taste and the freedom of kissing her where anyone might see them.

When he finally let her go, her eyes were closed, and a dreamy smile curved her kiss-reddened lips. "All right. I almost certainly would have said yes. Especially if you'd phrased the offer that eloquently." Opening her eyes, she lifted on her toes and awarded him another brief kiss before returning to her task. "But I'm still glad Sophie asked first."

"Do your parents know? Are they willing to fund your adventure?" He wasn't above offering to pay her way, though he knew without a doubt she would refuse that. Even Freddie had that much conventionality left in her.

"I've told them I'm going *with Sophie*. Another reason I'm glad she was the one who asked. For some reason they still think she's a respectable chaperone. Or perhaps it's just Father's guilt about Dan. In any case it's time I stopped looking for their permission or accepting their financial support. I'm an adult, and I have money of my own. I did sleep through breakfast, but after that I paid a visit to the jeweler who reset my diamonds. He knew their provenance, so he was surprised I wanted to sell them but was confident they were mine to sell. He gave me a decent price. I think he was too startled to haggle well. That, and he also took a very nice silver-backed hairbrush, though he was less generous about that. And then there's the money I'd saved from tinkering, of course. I've enough to pay for my passage and other expenses for quite some time, as long as I'm not too extravagant." She selected a claw hammer from the remaining tools she'd laid out and found a place for it in the nearly full trunk. "And there's always the chance I'll find some work to help pay my way. Small jobs, in and out. I'm good at avoiding guild attention."

Barnabas crouched beside her and anticipated her next selection, passing her the monkey wrench he'd fallen asleep with on that first mad midnight ride. It seemed a lifetime ago, looking back on all that had happened since. How amazing it was that they still had a lifetime before them.

"There's also the possibility you might . . . join forces with somebody from the Dominions. Do something official to pool your resources, something like that. Somebody you could have adventures with, if you didn't mind him being a little clumsy at times."

"Someone who would eventually become an earl and have to be tied down to an estate?"

He shrugged. "My father's healthy enough for now. And anyway, I've been rethinking what all that means. Considering how the Hardisons manage their estate and business together, I'm starting to realize one is only as bound by expectations and conventions as one chooses to be. I'll be an earl. That means responsibility, yes, but also the means to do what I damn well please. Including having a make-smith countess if I so choose."

"Supposing you met such a woman."

"Yes, just supposing." He nodded as somberly as he could manage.

Freddie giggled, breaking the pretense, and leaned over to press a quick kiss to his cheek, a moment of soft sweetness and the mingled fragrances of floral eau de cologne and engine grease. "We'll have plenty of time on the ship to decide on the particulars. As long as we begin with the adventures. Who knows, perhaps I'll tire of that after a time and be happy to settle down to something more conventional."

Barnabas laughed aloud, and she joined him.

"Phin assumed he and I could share a cabin on the trip, to save expenses," he mentioned, as if in passing, once they could speak again. "I told him I'd rather bunk alone, though."

She blushed a charming shade of pink, which Barnabas found all the more charming because he knew she was very far from a being a maiden or feeling shame. No, it was a flush of remembered heat, inappropriate to a sunlit coach yard where servants might saunter by at any moment. A pink that said she was thinking of all the things they might find to occupy their time in a ship's cabin together. He wondered if ship captains charged for their wedding-officiant services, and wished he'd thought to ask his friend Matthew, who'd had cause to resort to that service on his recent voyage.

"That was probably a wise decision," Freddie said softly, curling her hand around the wrench handle in a manner Barnabas found almost painfully suggestive. He wanted to kiss her again, to do a million lascivious things to her and have her do the same to him. But he could be patient, now that he knew they had a lifetime.

"Probably?"

She giggled again, a bright sound for a sunny day. "Likely."

"It's certainly, or nothing. I have my pride, Miss Murcheson."

When she turned the full force of her smile on him, it was almost too much to bear. "You can keep your pride, Lord Smith-Grenville. I know I already have your heart."

"And I have yours."

"Most certainly."

Her heart, and the rest of their lives. He couldn't imagine a better future than that.